# KING'S PROMISE

# KING'S PROMISE

*ESSENCE* BESTSELLING AUTHOR
ADRIANNE
BYRD

Recycling programs for this product may not exist in your area.

KING'S PROMISE

ISBN-13: 978-0-373-53447-0



www.kimanipress.com

**Printed in U.S.A.**

To Alice: Forever my inspiration

# ACKNOWLEDGMENT

To my family and friends, thanks for all the support and love that you've given me.
To my editor, Evette Porter, for helping me through one crazy year. To my wonderful fans and readers, thank you for allowing me to do what I do. It's always a pleasure to entertain you.
I wish you all the best of love.

The House of Kings series

Many of you have followed the Unforgettable series, which morphed into the Hinton Brothers series. Now I'm introducing you to the Hintons' playboy bachelor cousins—the Kings.

Eamon, Xavier and Jeremy, along with their infamous cousin Quentin Hinton, are business partners in a gentlemen's club franchise called The Dollhouse. One of their most popular and lucrative specialties is their bachelor party services. With clubs in Atlanta, Las Vegas and Los Angeles, the brothers are determined to make sure their clients' last night of bachelorhood is one they'll never forget. And the brothers are prepared for anything...except when love comes knocking on *their* door.

In *King's Promise,* love is the last thing on Xavier King's mind. In fact, he's renewed his vow to remain a player for life. But no matter how much he parties, it's getting harder to hide the feeling that there's something missing in his life. Enter Cheryl Shepherd, the sexy new bartender at the Atlanta club. But Cheryl has a few secrets of her own.

Next month, look for the final book in the House of Kings series, *King's Pleasure,* featuring Jeremy King. If you missed the first book in the series, look for *King's Passion*, featuring the eldest brother, Eamon, which was published in June 2011.

Remember, in love, never bet against a King....

Adrianne

# *Prologue*

Lying in a king-size dark oak paneled bed, Quentin Hinton huffed and growled among a set of tangled black silk sheets as orgasmic tremors shook him to the core. Eyes closed, he braced his chiseled body with his two muscular arms planted on opposite sides of tonight's passionate beauty.

"Mmm. That was wonderful, honey," the woman's angelic voice praised as she linked her slender arms around his sweat-slicked neck.

"You were wonderful," he said, returning the compliment before leaning over to the side and plopping down on the pile of fluffy pillows. Exhausted, Q glanced over at the digital clock next to the bed and puffed out his chest with a sense of pride, having calculated that he and this evening's *dessert* had been going at it for two solid hours straight. With that kind of performance, he estimated that his partner would be asleep in exactly four…three…two…

*"Zzzzzzz."*

Quentin smiled at the sound of soft snoring coming from

the woman lying on his left. He turned his head. Her hair was so mussed up that he could barely make out her face and was only fairly certain that her name was…

"Christina." Another woman's voice drifted into his head.

Quentin's neck whipped around to see Alyssa Hinton, or at least his imaginary version of her, sitting in the window seat of his bedroom, in the wedding dress she wore to marry his brother Sterling. "What are you doing here?" he hissed.

She shrugged. "You tell me. Since you're the one seeing things."

Quentin shook his head as he started to peel off the covers. "This is just going too far."

Alyssa quickly covered her eyes with her hand when he jumped out of bed. "Oh, my God! Hurry up and put something on."

Q frowned as he reached down and snatched his robe from the floor and pulled it on. "You're in *my* bedroom, remember?" He stopped and then looked over at the bed and then back at his sister-in-law. "Just how long have you been here, anyway?"

Alyssa peeked through her fingers and saw that Quentin was decent, so she lowered her hand. "I'd rather not answer that question."

Embarrassment heated Quentin's face—and he was *not* a man who easily got embarrassed. "You can't keep doing this!"

"Hmm?" The sheets ruffled behind him.

When he turned around, Christina lifted her head. "What did you say, baby?"

"Nothing," he lied to reassure her. "Go back to sleep."

Christina gave him a lazy smile. "What are you doing up? Come back to bed." She stretched out her arm to pat the empty space beside her for emphasis. "It's getting lonely over here."

"I'll be back in a minute. I'm just going to the bathroom."

"Mmm," she moaned, and then plopped her head back down onto the bed. "Hurry up. I'm missing you, big daddy."

"You got it." He waited a few seconds.

*"Zzzzzz."*

Quentin turned his angry gaze back toward Alyssa.

She just frowned. *"Big daddy?"*

"Drop it."

"Hmm?" Christina asked.

"Nothing," he hissed, and then stormed toward the bathroom. "I'm not going crazy. I'm not going crazy," he repeated under his breath.

"You might want to get a second opinion on that," Alyssa said, following behind him. "Like maybe go back and see that nice Dr. Turner you were talking to last month."

Quentin groaned. "I don't need a shrink. Thank you very much."

"And yet here I am," she volleyed back.

When they reached the bathroom door, Quentin stopped abruptly and looked back at her. "Do you mind? Can a guy get a little privacy?"

"Sorry." Alyssa folded her arms and leaned against the door frame. "A few minutes ago you were all too willing to show me *big daddy*."

Quentin slammed the door in her face, but he could still hear her laughing on the other side. "Women! Even the imaginary ones were impossible to live with." He shook his head as he relieved himself and even took a quick shower. By the time he had wiped away the steam from the mirror, he was reasonably sure that he'd pulled himself together.

That is, until Alyssa leaned over his right shoulder.

"Aaaaah!" He took his towel and covered the front of his chest like a damsel in distress.

Alyssa jumped and screamed, too.

*Knock. Knock.*

"Quentin? Are you all right in there?" Christina asked, twisting the doorknob.

Q finally clamped his mouth shut when he realized what the whole thing must have sounded like on the other side of the door. "Uh, yes! Never better."

There was a brief pause before Christina asked. "Why were you screaming?"

"What? Uh…"

Alyssa snickered and then immediately launched into a game of charades to help him out.

"I saw…someone? No. Something?"

Alyssa nodded.

"Like what?" Christina asked.

"I, uh…" He looked to Alyssa, who was running around the bathroom with her fingers in the shape of a V over her head."

"I don't know. It looks like a rabbit—no? A what? What the hell is that?" he whispered to Alyssa.

"A cockroach," she answered, offended that he didn't get it.

"A cockroach!" he thundered. "That looked nothing like—"

"You have roaches?" Christina asked, sounding disgusted.

"No!" he snapped at the door.

"You said—"

"Forget what I said." He glared back at Alyssa. "I, uh, just thought I saw a gray hair."

"Oh," Christina said dubiously from the other side of the door.

"A gray hair?" Alyssa challenged, frowning. "You'd freak out like that over a gray hair?"

"Maybe." Q rolled his eyes. "By the way, what happened to my privacy?"

Alyssa shrugged. "I waited until you had finished showering."

"I don't get this. How in the hell am I being haunted by someone who is still alive?" He headed toward the door.

"Maybe that's why you need to go back and see Dr. Turner."

"No! I'm not crazy!" Quentin snatched open the door.

Christina, clutching the top silk sheet to her chest, asked suspiciously, "Who are you talking to in there?"

"No one," he answered too quickly.

Christina peered over his shoulder and looked into the empty bathroom. "You know, uh, I really should be going. I, uh, have a very full day tomorrow." She turned and started grabbing her clothes.

"Wait. You don't have to leave," he said.

"Don't worry. I'll call you later," she said, moving like someone had struck a match to her behind. Less than two minutes later, she was dressed and racing out of the house with Q trying to catch up so that he could at least walk her to her car. But just as he reached the front door, it slammed in his face.

At the top of the stairs, Alyssa folded her arms. "That went well."

The next day Quentin stretched out his six-foot-two frame across the black leather chaise, staring up at the ceiling in Dr. Julianne Turner's downtown Atlanta office. Truth be told, he'd surprised himself by returning to the doctor's office for another round of therapy, especially since he didn't *really* believe that there was anything wrong with him.

"Oh, there's plenty wrong with you," said Alyssa, his hallucinated sister-in-law/fantasy-lost-love from across the room. She wore that damn white wedding gown again today. Their marriage was a scab that everyone had hoped would heal over time, but so far—no dice. He'd been the one who his li'l Alice had a crush on. It was he who had first fallen for the li'l minx when she'd grown up to become a beautiful fashion model. It was Sterling who had discouraged Quentin from pursuing a relationship with her—since according to his brother she was like their younger sister—only to have him turn around and marry Alyssa himself.

"I wish you'd put something else on," Q mumbled under his breath to his mirage.

"Like I have something to do with what I have on," Alyssa said, throwing up her hands. "I'm not really here!"

"What was that, Quentin?" Dr. Turner asked, sitting across from him in a straight-backed chair.

"What? Nothing." He shook his head at the doctor, who took great pains to hide her lush curves under large, unflattering clothes. The fact that she dressed so frumpy bothered him more than it should have. He didn't understand why beautiful women did things like that. Didn't they understand their power?

Alyssa smirked. "Are you really sitting there thinking about having sex with your psychiatrist?"

"Who said anything about having sex with my doctor?" Q snapped.

"Excuse me?" Dr. Turner said, looking up from her notepad.

"What? Nothing." He glared at Alyssa, who shrugged her shoulders.

All right, yes. Quentin knew that it wasn't exactly normal to be seeing and talking to someone who wasn't there. But as far as he could tell, it was just a coping mechanism until he could work through his conflicting emotions. So far, it was better than getting drunk and being pulverized in bar fights—which had actually been his first line of defense.

Dr. Turner started scribbling in her yellow notepad. "You think today you'll tell me who it is that you see and talk to?"

He hesitated as Alyssa raised her eyebrows. "I don't know what you're talking about," he lied. "I'm here because…I want to understand…"

"Love?" the doctor suggested.

Quentin bobbed his head while Alyssa shook hers.

"That's a tall order, Mr. Hinton," Dr. Turner said, crossing her long, chocolate-brown legs, which continued to distract him. A connoisseur of women, Quentin had spent his entire adult life enjoying learning all there was to know about women—sexually, that is, he proudly boasted. He loved nothing more than to lose himself in the curve of a woman's hip, the valleys between and around a pair of succulent breasts and, of course…other hidden treasures.

"Quentin?" Dr. Turner repeated, breaking his trance from her long limbs.

"I'm sorry. What?"

Alyssa huffed out a frustrated breath and plopped down in an empty chair across the room. "This is a complete waste of time. This isn't about love. To you this is about winning and losing."

Quentin frowned, but before he could ask Alyssa what the hell she meant by that, Dr. Turner cleared her throat. "I said that trying to understand love is a tall order. Many people spend their entire lives trying to figure it out, nurture it and even control it."

"I'll take *control* for two hundred, Alex," Alyssa said, mimicking a *Jeopardy!* contestant.

"Humph." A half smile curled Q's lips.

"I guess I'd be remiss if I didn't add those who try to run away from love," she said.

Once again, they had hit his category and the room fell silent.

"Have you given any more thought to calling your brother Sterling?"

*I think about it all the time.* "No."

"Do you think that you'll never be able to forgive him for the wrong you feel that he has done to you?" Dr. Turner asked.

Quentin held Alyssa's gaze from across the room. "I'm not sure."

"That's different from the flat *no* last week," the therapist gently reminded him.

He stopped and weighed his words carefully. "Trust… is still an issue." He shifted in his chair and ignored the way his beautiful mirage frowned at him. "No matter what has happened in my life, the constant power struggle between me and my father or the insane messes I found myself in, I always thought that I could trust my brothers. Sterling…Jonas. We're each different. Granted, they are megasuccessful and now happily married with children, and probably a dog and even a white-picket fence. I never questioned their loyalty or intentions. I believed that my brothers, more than anyone, always had my best interest at heart."

Q shook his head. "How do you learn to trust someone again after they've poured gasoline on that bridge and blown it up?"

"Perhaps by reaching out?" Dr. Turner suggested.

"So it's all on me?" The idea repulsed him. "I wasn't the one with the gasoline."

The statement hung in the air as Q struggled to swallow the huge boulder in his throat. He even blinked back a few tears. "It's not that I don't miss Sterling. I do. I just don't know how to go about forgiving him. But then when I think about my cousin Xavier—"

"Xavier King?"

Quentin nodded. "I told you about him and his brothers the last time."

"Yes, your coveted boys' club."

"I believe that *boys' club* is your terminology—not mine."

"But they were who you ran to as a substitute for your real brothers since Sterling and Jonas were no longer available bachelors for you to hang out with."

"I never said that my cousins were substitutes."

"Weren't they?"

Quentin shifted in the chaise at the provocative question. "No, not consciously."

Dr. Turner removed her black-rimmed glasses from her perky nose. "Do you mind if I disclose some observations that I've made about you?"

Quentin turned his tall frame onto his side to meet his doctor's soft, steady, brown-eyed gaze. "You mean that I actually get to hear a little of what you spend hours jotting down on your little yellow notepad?"

She smiled reflexively as she crossed her arms over her lap. "You're a creature of habit. You have a hard time adjusting to change. And when things don't turn out like you expect them to—as eventually happens—you seek out those things that will give you a sense of familiarity."

"Please." He gave her a dismissive shake of his head. "You don't know what you're talking about."

"No? When your father cut you off financially, didn't you rely on women to support you in a fashion that you were accustomed to instead of getting out there and making your own way?"

"Wait. I'm a successful businessman in my own right."

"Now, but not then. And when your brothers were no longer available to pal around with, you sought out the next best thing, which is a family of cousins whose dynamic was much like your own."

Alyssa waved her finger. "Ooooh. She really is good."

"You've said that before," Q reminded her.

"It's still true."

"I don't remember us discussing this before," Dr. Turner said.

"Sorry. Not you. I was talking to someone else," he said before thinking.

"I see."

He winced and waited for her to ask the obvious question again, but she surprised him and let the comment go. However, Dr. Turner's pen went back to scribbling. *Great. At this rate, I'll be in a mental hospital by the end of summer.*

"Xavier," Dr. Turner suddenly said. "You were about to tell me something about your cousin?"

Quentin allowed himself to relax a little. "Um, yeah. I was saying that my cousin Xavier had sort of a similar situation with trust when love came knocking on his door."

"Ah. Another player bites the dust?"

"Exactly." Quentin laughed, but continued to nod his head. "Of all the players I thought would ride this bachelorhood thing until the wheels fell off, it was him. I mean, I can tell you some stories that would make your hair stand on end."

"You two are best friends?"

"Absolutely," Q said, nodding, but then his smile slowly started to fade. "Of course, after his older brother Eamon married Victoria, I should have seen the handwriting on the wall."

"Oh? How so?"

"Bad things usually happen in pairs."

"I always heard they happened in threes," she corrected thoughtfully.

"That explains a lot," he grumbled with a roll of his eyes, and then stared back up at the ceiling. "Like I was saying, Xavier had to overcome some major trust issues. But then again, maybe all it takes is for the right woman to come along…."

# *The Loyal King*

# Chapter 1

"Welcome to The Dollhouse Atlanta," Xavier King exclaimed, sweeping his huge, muscular biceps toward the newly renovated club. The enormous white stone building looked more like a high-end shopping mall than a gentlemen's club smack dab in the middle of downtown Atlanta. "So what do you think?"

This latest renovation of the Atlanta club started off as a small-scale repair project, much of which resulted from the damage done by an old-fashioned bar fight involving a patron who had tried his best to permanently rearrange his cousin Q's face. But once Xavier got started, the project got bigger and bigger, to the point that the once modest-size club now rivaled the infamous Cheetah Lounge in square footage.

A little-known fact was that Atlanta was the strip-club capital of America. So Xavier took the attitude that The Dollhouse needed to go big or go home. He went *big*.

Really big.

Quentin Hinton, Xavier's best friend and cousin, stepped out of his black Mercedes and cocked his head so that he could get a better view of the exterior. "Hmm."

Climbing out of the backseat of the car, Xavier's younger brother Jeremy took one look at the place and declared, "I love it!"

Xavier's chest swelled with pride as his pearly white smile stretched from ear to ear. "I knew you would. C'mon inside. Let me show you what else I've done." He waved for them to follow him.

Once they entered through the glass doors, they walked across the black marble floors of the lobby.

"Niiiice," Quentin finally said, bobbing his head as he took in some of the erotic artwork hanging on the walls in gilded frames. "Took it old school, did you?"

"Just a little bit." Xavier winked and then turned. "Here is where the club's concierge/hostess will be," he said, pointing to a matte-gold podium. "This will also be where the limo service will check in or out when bringing in clients from Bachelors Adventures or patrons from any of the surrounding hotels." He waved them on to follow him through the lobby and through the club's main arched entryway.

There, both Quentin and Jeremy gave a low whistle of approval. The first thing that caught their eyes was the long U-shaped runway in the middle of the main floor with elevated seating along the side. The next thing that drew their attention was the two forty-five-foot-long bars surrounded by cushioned leather bar stools that flanked two lighted side-by-side dance stages. The rest of the seating on the main floor consisted of stationary counter-height tables with chairs.

"You're a genius," Q praised as a smile crept up his face. "If you tell me that you've added a loft upstairs, then you've just built my fantasy dream house."

Cocky as ever, Xavier raised his hand to his lips, blew on his nails and then buffed them on his chest. "Well, I don't like bragging. But—yes, I am a bit of a genius."

"And the head swells bigger," Jeremy joked with the appropriate eye roll.

They all laughed as the three continued to tour the redesigned club.

"See, the way I figure it, every evening the girls will descend the staircase leading to the main runway stage. That way, they can fill the room for a showcase revue and a two-for-one dance special. Off to the far right, we have a mini VIP area, which is where the customers can have a more private lap dance. And of course upstairs we have the main VIP room for private parties like Bachelors Adventures."

Xavier watched the two take it all in. Their opinions were important. Not only because they were family, they were business partners, as well. Until recently, there had been four owners. Quentin, the initial investor, and the three King brothers: Eamon, Xavier and Jeremy.

Eamon jumped ship after falling in love with billionaire heiress Victoria Gregory. It was a love that had almost fell apart after Xavier put his foot in his mouth by mentioning how much Victoria looked like Eamon's first love, Karen, who'd been killed by a drunk driver. It was definitely the wrong thing to say to a woman. The hardest part for Xavier was having to come clean to his older brother, and telling him what he had done. It was a good thing he had a strong bond with his brothers. Eamon never once blamed him for being dumped by Victoria and hightailing it back to New York. That was when Eamon made the decision that he wanted the rest of them to buy him out of the business.

Ever since then, guilt gnawed at Xavier. He couldn't shake the idea that somehow he was responsible for his brother tossing in the towel to become a full-time restaurateur…and husband. Turned out that chasing after Victoria was just the thing he needed to do in order to win her back. But the four musketeers were now down to three.

"Well. I gotta hand it to you, cuz. You outdid yourself on this one," Q said, patting him on the back. "This calls for a celebration."

Xavier's forehead wrinkled as he folded his arms. "Who are you kidding? Your getting out of bed is cause for celebration."

Quentin held up a finger. "This is true. But seeing as how this swanky new shindig is going to make us a whole lot more money, I'm going to take you two out for dinner."

Jeremy's brows hiked. "You paying?"

"No. I was just going to drive."

"Figures. You cheap bastard."

Feigning shock, Q pressed a hand over his heart. "I'm offended."

Jeremy rubbed his index finger and thumb together. "I've got the world's smallest violin playing for you right now."

Xavier shook his head while he listened to them carry on.

"Excuse me?" a soft voice floated from behind them.

The men spun around.

Xavier experienced a Mike Tyson punch to the gut when his eyes landed on a maple-brown sister with jaw-dropping Jessica Rabbit curves. How he managed to keep his tongue inside his mouth while his gaze roamed over her ripe cantaloupes that were posing as breasts and stretching the hell out of a black T-shirt with a decal that said Got Milk was a Sherlock Holmes mystery. Equally mystifying was how she managed to get her painted-on jeans over a red-beans-and-rice booty that at the right angle looked like an upside-down question mark.

All in all, those were just a few of the questions that he was more than happy to get to the bottom of.

"I'm sorry," she said, pushing up her designer shades and

flashing a smile that would make a Hollywood starlet green with envy. "I didn't mean to interrupt, but is this where I apply for the bartending position that was listed?"

Xavier was struck by the way her voice seemed a little older than she appeared, mainly because it had a sexy huskiness to it and a slight Caribbean lilt. His lips widened. It had been a while since he'd had an island girl.

Jeremy stepped forward first. "Actually—"

Xavier grabbed him by the arm and pulled him back. "Yes. This is the place, but I'm afraid the interviews are tomorrow from four to seven. Not today."

The woman looked down at the folded newspaper and read the classified ad again. When she saw that she did indeed have the wrong day her shoulders collapsed and she huffed out a frustrated breath. "Just great! I went through all that trouble to arrange a makeup lab test to come here today." She slapped her forehead with the newspaper and then turned around. "All right, thanks! I guess it's a sign that it just wasn't meant to be."

It was the sight of that thick butt walking away and possibly never returning that sprung Xavier into action. "Whoa! Wait," he called after her.

She stopped and turned back around. "Yes?"

Again, he felt that punch to the gut, and when he caught his breath he smiled. "Well, since you're already here, why don't you let me see that résumé?"

"Great!" She quickly reached into the bag dangling off of her shoulder and handed over a single piece of paper. "I really appreciate this. It's crazy trying to rearrange my schedule during the day—I'm in school. Med school, actually. Over at Emory, which is why working nights really fits my schedule."

Xavier bobbed his head while she rambled on nervously.

"Cheryl Shepherd," he read. "Twenty-seven… You're

clearly a med student like you said…but I don't see a lot of bartending experience."

"Well, I usually do a lot of small parties. Plus, I have an uncle who has a bar in Alabama. I used to help out there during the summers when I was in college." She tossed in. "I probably should've added that."

Xavier smiled, his gaze still caressing her curves. "Maybe we should give you a little audition behind the bar? See if you really know your stuff?"

"All right." She nodded her head. "I'm down with that."

He stepped back and extended his arm. "Right this way."

Cheryl looked in the direction of the bar and strolled ahead of him, giving him a bird's-eye view of all that her mama blessed her with.

Q leaned over and whispered in his ear, "Any chance we can talk her into putting all that into a thong?"

Jeremy shook his head. "I don't know if even the three of us together can handle all of that. Humph. Humph. Humph."

"Speak for yourself," Q said, moving Jeremy out of the way and straightening his shoulders. But before he could activate his pimp walk, Xavier cut his stride off by stepping in front of him and taking the lead behind Cheryl.

In her immediate wake, Xavier recognized the sweet raspberry nectar and magnolia scent of Givenchy's Hot Couture and his interest climbed a few more degrees. For some time now, it had been an abstraction of Xavier's to pair women's personalities with their choice of fragrance. What popped into his head as he followed her down the club's new staircase was…sophisticated, sensual and bewitching. Those were his favorite qualities—for now, anyway.

"Wow. This is nice," Cheryl praised, walking behind the bar and running her hand across the mahogany top. "Paid a lot of money for this baby."

"And you're going to be the first to try her out," Xavier said, settling onto one of the stools. There was so much to marvel about her curvy body that his gaze kept darting around, trying to decide what was his favorite part. It was a three-way tie between her face, breasts and butt.

Jeremy and Quentin caught up and flanked his sides.

"All right, boys," Cheryl said, flashing her Hollywood smile. "What will it be?"

"I'll have a Slow Comfortable Screw Up Against the Bedpost Mexican Doggy Style," Xavier ordered with a sly smirk. It was pretty much a frat-boy drink, but he wanted to see if this dime diva could handle a curveball.

Cheryl met his twinkling gaze and fired an imaginary gun at him. "You got it!" She immediate reached for the vodka, two different rums, Tequila Gold, Midori and gin, and threw in the appropriate mixers, and in less than a minute she set Xavier's drink on a cocktail napkin in front of him. "Enjoy your screw."

It took everything in Xavier's power not to lower himself into the gutter even more by responding to the pun. Instead, he reached for the drink and took a sip. "Mmm. This is a good screw." Okay, so he couldn't help himself.

"I'll have a Voodoo Sunrise," Jeremy said, seeing if he could stump the hopeful bartender. Her hands flew to the vodka, white rum, grenadine and orange juice, and a few seconds later, she sat his drink down.

"My turn. My turn," Q announced, and then clapped his hands and rubbed them together. "I have to make this one a good one to see if you got the right stuff. I mean…clearly you got the right stuff, I mean, damn. Look at you."

Xavier reached over and popped Quentin on the back of the head.

"Ow."

"Just order a damn drink." Xavier cut him a look that told him to knock it off.

"All right. Damn. There's no reason for all this black-on-black crime." He pumped his fist to his chest. "We're family."

Xavier rolled his eyes at his cousin's nonsense. Cheryl snickered. "Take your time."

Q turned and hit her with his dimpled smile, but before he could get his mack mojo going, Xavier elbowed him. It wasn't like him to cock-block this hard. But he instinctively felt the alpha-male impulse to mark his territory.

"I'll just have a Singapore Sling." Q looked over at Xavier. "If that's all right with you."

Cheryl hopped right to it, while Xavier and Q exchanged looks. No words were exchanged between the cousins, but their ESP battle went something like this….

*Xavier: Cuz, back the hell off. She's mine.*

*Quentin: I don't see any rings on her fingers. She's fair game.*

*Xavier: Family be damned, if you don't pump the brakes I'll take you out back and break your face.*

*Quentin: A'ight. A'ight. Stop the violence.*

"Your drink," Cheryl said, setting the third drink on the counter with a flourish and settling her hands on her hips.

Q picked up his glass, sipped, smacked his lips together while pretending to be in deep thought and then sipped again.

"Well?" Cheryl asked.

"Not bad. Not bad," Q said. "But I'm concerned about your presentation."

Xavier groaned and then propped an elbow on the bar so that he could massage the bridge of his nose.

"I'm sorry," Cheryl said. "I'm not sure I know what you mean."

"Entertainment." Q threw up his hands. "I know a little bit about being behind the bar and it's been my experience that people really like it if a bartender…you know, entertains a bit."

"Like hop on the bar and start dancing like *Coyote Ugly*."

Quentin tapped his nose. "Do you dance?"

"Uh, no. I'm not interested in being a dancer. I just want to tend bar."

"The job doesn't entail dancing." Xavier elbowed Q.

"What?" Q hissed. "Closed mouths don't get fed."

"Please ignore him," Xavier said.

Cheryl held her smile. "Aw. He seems harmless."

Quentin settled both his elbows on the bar and cradled his head in his hands. "I am completely harmless. Are you married?"

"Q," Xavier warned.

"No. I'm not," Cheryl answered.

"Boyfriend?" Quentin pressed.

"No boyfriend, unfortunately," she said. Her gaze cut over to Xavier.

He felt another gut punch and wondered how much longer it would take before he suffered a knockout.

"But if you're looking for more entertaining bartending..." She flipped the bottle of rum over her shoulder and then dipped her knees and caught the bottle with one hand behind her back. "I can do that, too."

"You're hired," Quentin said, grinning.

"Q!" Xavier snapped.

"What?"

Xavier jerked his head around toward his cousin, a look of annoyance plastered on his face. "You're a *silent* partner. That means *be quiet*."

"Touché." Q shifted in his seat and straightened an invisible tie. "I'm sorry, Ms. Shepherd. Apparently, I don't have the power to hire you. *But* I want you to know that I would hire you if I could."

"Me, too," Jeremy tossed in, draining his drink. "This is a really good Voodoo Sunrise."

Now three sets of eyes turned toward Xavier.

"You said that you're in school. How many hours are you looking for?"

"I'm looking for full-time work. Medical school isn't cheap," she joked.

"That's a lot of work," he noted.

"I can handle it," she said, thrusting her chin up. "You don't have to worry about me. I'm a hard worker."

Intelligence and determination glimmered in her maple-brown eyes as well as a hint of playful interest as she held Xavier's bold gaze. "You say that you used to work at your uncle's bar, but you know that working at a gentlemen's club is a completely different animal. Patrons are going to hit on you—some are rude, some are obnoxious. Do you think you can handle that?"

Cheryl cocked her head. "I didn't just get this body last night, Mr. King. Putting up with rude and obnoxious comments comes with the territory."

Xavier laughed. "Good answer."

Jeremy leaned over. "Now will you hire her?"

Xavier rolled his eyes. "Looks like if I don't hire you, your new fan club might revolt."

Cheryl flashed the two cousins an appreciative look. "A woman can never have too many fans. Thanks, guys." She winked at them and they literally slid their elbows out in front of them like she'd just melted their hearts. "So does that mean I have the job?"

"It's yours if you want it. Job starts Friday. Six o'clock sharp."

"Great! I'll be here!"

She finally tossed Xavier a wink and he nearly made a fool of himself, too, by gushing all over her. "Then we'll see you Friday."

# *Chapter 2*

*Lord have mercy.*

Cheryl had never seen three finer men in all her life. When she first walked in and they turned toward her, she honestly felt like she was the winner of some kind of man-fantasy lottery. But the one who was seriously buttering her toast was the one she could barely look at. And when she finally did toss him a wink, his smile turned predatory. How on earth was she going to manage working for this man without suffering through endless fantasies of ripping his clothes off and having her way with him?

Hell, even now she wasn't sure that she was walking a straight line toward the front door. It had a lot to do with knowing that there were three pairs of eyes following the sway of her hips and the jiggle of her ass. Of course, when she turned around at the glass door to give them a final wave, they all played it off and exchanged innocent smiles with her.

"Thanks again." She rushed out into the parking lot to her

old blue Ford Taurus, pretending that her heart wasn't racing a mile a minute. As she climbed behind the wheel, she saw the three of them walk out of the club, as well. They looked like *GQ* models, laughing and joking with one another.

Cheryl's gaze zoomed in on the tallest of the group, Xavier King, as she felt the muscles in her stomach quiver. When was the last time something like that had happened to her—junior high? She fumbled with the keys, trying to insert them into the ignition, while she took in his close-cropped hair, handsome chiseled features, smooth, milk-chocolate skin and a muscled body that was just screaming her name.

Even though he wore a bright white dress shirt and a pair of black jeans, Cheryl had no trouble picturing him stripped down to his birthday suit. How could she not? Broad chest, trim waist and powerful thighs—this was a man who hadn't let himself go since his days of earning money in the boxing ring. He was beyond fine, but the problem was that he knew it.

She had no problem imagining women tripping over their bottom lips trying to get his attention, and no doubt he had his pick. *Shoot, under the right circumstances...* "Shake it off, girl. Shake it off." Cheryl finally slipped the key into the ignition and started the car.

The men glanced in her direction and she exchanged a polite wave as she pulled out of the parking lot and headed out onto the street. No sooner had she taken a left onto the main road did her cell phone ring.

"Hello."

"Well, how did it go?" Johnnie asked.

"I got the job," Cheryl said, unable to stop herself from sounding cocky.

"It was the Got Milk T-shirt, wasn't it?"

"Are you insinuating that my body got me a job at a strip club instead of my amazing bartending skills?"

Johnnie laughed. "That's exactly what I'm saying."

Cheryl smiled. "Well…maybe it was more like a one-two punch."

"Uh-huh. You keep telling yourself that. How far are you from the station?"

Cheryl glanced down at the clock on the console. "Be there in ten." She disconnected the call. During the ten-minute drive, Cheryl had a hard time keeping her mind on the road and off Xavier King. How many hours did a man have to put in at the gym to get a body like that? Two hours a day—three?

She was sure that if she had a magnifying glass or a jeweler's loupe, she wouldn't have been able to find a single ounce of fat anywhere on his body. *And Lawd have mercy, that chest.* Not only was it wide, but he had just the right kind of muscles that didn't make him look like a steroid freak. They looked like the perfect place for a woman to lay her head down on every night.

Before Cheryl knew it, she was getting herself so hot and worked up that she had to turn on the air conditioner to try and cool off. By the time she reached the police station, she was reasonably composed, but she wouldn't have turned down a cold shower if the opportunity presented itself.

She parked, cut off the engine and reached over to the glove compartment to retrieve her badge and police-issue Glock before climbing out of the car. But the minute she walked into the precinct, she drew more than her fair share of stares from her male colleagues.

"Yo, Grier. I got some milk for you," Officer Daniel Banks hollered with his arms outstretched. "What's my prize?"

There was a ripple of laughter across the precinct floor.

Cheryl gave his ignorant ass the bird and kept it moving toward her department.

Her partner, Officer Johnnie Walsh, hung up the phone

on her desk and then glanced over at the ridiculously large clock on the wall. "Eight minutes. Not bad."

"I aim to please," Cheryl said, plopping down into the chair beside her partner's desk. "Have I missed anything?"

Johnnie leaned her five-foot-four frame back in her chair and exhaled a long breath. "Nothing that has anything to do with our case, if that's what you mean. But the mayor and the chief of police are in the lieutenant's office right now giving him a dressing-down over that botched armored-car robbery yesterday. Two cops down and the perpetrators getting away means the lieutenant isn't going to have much ass left to sit on for the rest of the year."

Cheryl glanced at the lieutenant's closed door and shook her head. "It couldn't happen to a nicer guy."

Johnnie laughed. "I take it that means you and the big man haven't kissed and made up yet?"

"*That* is never going to happen."

Johnnie shrugged and gave her the "I told you so" look a couple of seconds before it tumbled out her mouth. "I told you not to get involved in an office romance. Let alone with someone you work for."

Cheryl performed her customary head bob and eye roll. What else could she do? Johnnie had warned her repeatedly and she had ignored her repeatedly. Mainly because as far as Cheryl was concerned, her mother had been right: she had to learn to do things the hard way. It was one of the unfortunate side effects of never taking no for an answer, wanting to do things her way and having issues with authority figures. Combine all of those traits and it meant that Cheryl almost always stayed in trouble.

Johnnie's phone rang and she quickly picked it up.

Cheryl started to turn her head away from the door when it suddenly jerked open and the mayor and chief of police strode out like twin tornadoes ripping through the office. All eyes followed them until they were out of sight before looking back at Lieutenant Jason Mackey, who was last to exit his office.

To Cheryl's inquisitive eye, it looked like Jason Mackey's superiors had done more than just chew his butt off. They had beaten every ounce of confidence out of his usually cocky demeanor. "Aww," Cheryl said, low enough for Johnnie's ears only. "I almost feel sorry for him."

Johnnie placed a hand over the mouthpiece. "The keyword is *almost*."

Cheryl turned back around and flashed a smile. "Good ear."

Johnnie removed her hand and said into the line, "We're on our way." She hung up and climbed out of her seat. "Let's go."

Drawing in a deep breath, Cheryl pitched herself out of the chair and followed her partner into the department's smallest conference room. On a corkboard were photos and diagrams of how the police department believed Operation Striptease broke down. As Cheryl took her seat in one of the metal folding chairs, she stared at pictures of the suspected mules, Mario and Alejandro Gutierrez, hauling everything from marijuana, cocaine and heroine out of Mexico to the runners, Kendrick Hodges and Jermaine Wallace. From there, things tended to get a little tricky. Who was trafficking drugs and distributing them to the dancers and clientele at a number of strip clubs, lounges and gentlemen's clubs? More importantly, just how far up the chain did the illegal activity go? Cheryl had a little run-in with Hodges last year—picked him up on a breaking-and-entering charge. He was a mean son of a bitch who hated cops. She didn't look forward to crossing paths with him again.

In no time at all, Cheryl's gaze shot up to the top of the board where striking pictures of Xavier King and Quentin Hinton were posted. Each had a large question mark made with a wide, black Sharpie next to their faces. While other members of their team and even some from the Georgia Bureau of Investigation task force filtered into the room, Cheryl couldn't pull her gaze away from Xavier's handsome face.

Johnnie leaned over and whispered, "Between you and me, is Xavier King that fine in person?"

Immediately, the corners of Cheryl's lips curled. "Honey, his pictures don't nearly do him justice."

Johnnie leaned in so close that Cheryl felt like her partner was invading her personal space. "Ooooh. I know that look." Johnnie groaned, shaking her head. "I know that look."

"What?" Cheryl's brows knitted. "What look?"

"That bitch in heat look," Johnnie spat out. She had never been one to mince words. "You know, the one you always get two seconds before you land in hot water."

Cheryl nodded and began rolling her eyes again.

Johnnie's groan became louder before she hissed, "Get that silly-ass look off your face. Get your hormones in check and your mind on the J-O-B."

"Since when don't I do my job?" Cheryl asked, looking at her partner and friend.

Johnnie crossed her arms. "All I'm saying is that I've been gunning for that sergeant's badge and this case can make it happen. Don't screw it up."

"Again. When it comes to my job, I do my job."

"And when it comes to good-looking men, you lose your head," Johnnie reminded her. On cue, Lieutenant Mackey strolled his arrogant butt into the squad room and their eyes connected for a brief second before another officer captured his attention with a question.

Jason Mackey, six foot one with a smooth, dark-chocolate complexion, had first attracted Cheryl's attention five years ago when she joined the force, mainly because he knew how to wield his power and authority like no one she'd ever met before. Ignoring common sense and unsolicited advice from her partner, she gave in to their obvious physical attraction and proceeded to have a six-month affair that was totally against department policy.

Their first night together was great. The other five months and twenty-nine days was a complete nightmare. She suffered endless migraines and gut-wrenching regret. Mackey, however, was head over heels in love. Cheryl had to learn the hard way how bad and sticky it was to try to end an office romance—though Jason Mackey seemed hardly over it.

Slowly, she realized that Mackey was working his way around the room. She found herself feverishly praying for the meeting to hurry up and get started. But Cheryl wasn't that lucky.

"Officer Grier." Mackey's eyes roamed over her face before slowly following the contours of her curvy body. "Now, why am I not surprised that you didn't have a problem landing a job at The Dollhouse?"

She smiled. "Because you know that I'm good at whatever I put my mind to." *That didn't come out right.*

Mackey immediately hiked up a brow. "You know...now that you've mentioned it... You do have a point there."

From the corner of her eye, Cheryl saw Johnnie pretending to gag. However, when Mackey cast his gaze over at her partner, she had a straight face and quickly feigned an innocent smile. That alone was enough for him to continue to look at her suspiciously.

"So, uh, what was your impression of Mr. King and Mr. Hinton?" Mackey asked, returning his gaze to Cheryl. "Any red flags we should know of?"

"No. Actually, they seem like three normal—"

"Three?"

"Yeah. Uh, Xavier's younger brother was there, as well. Jeremy King. When I applied for the job, Xavier was with Quentin and Jeremy."

"Think the younger brother might have a hand in all of this?"

Cheryl started to shake her head.

"I mean, don't the other King brothers own The Dollhouse's other locations in Las Vegas and Los Angeles? What if they have a whole network set up?"

Mackey was getting that ambitious look in his eyes. No doubt expanding the scope of the investigation, as visions of a major drug bust danced like sugarplums in his head. The fame and the national recognition could land him something like head of Homeland Security.

When Cheryl glanced over at her partner to make sure that she got a good look at Mackey's daydreaming butt, she saw Johnnie had the same look in her eyes. "I don't know," Cheryl said. "They seemed like normal guys to me. My instincts tell me that they don't have anything to do with any of this," she said, gesturing toward the corkboard. Her comment was like a sharp pin in their fantasy career-making balloons. She'd swear on a stack of Bibles that she heard two thunderous pops—deflating their lofty ambitions—before they leveled disappointed frowns in her direction.

"But you could be wrong," Mackey said snidely. "It's been known to happen before."

Cheryl's eyes narrowed. "You asked me for my opinion and I gave it."

Mackey smiled when he sensed that he had hit a nerve. "And if you're wrong, you won't have any problems slapping the handcuffs on Mr. Big-Time Ex-Boxing Champion, will you?"

"Absolutely not. I am a police officer first and foremost, and if and when the time comes to slap the handcuffs on Xavier King, I'll do so without hesitation."

# Chapter 3

Across town, Xavier, Jeremy and Quentin were being seated at a private table at Ruth's Chris Steak House. Whenever they got together, the occasion usually called for something involving steak—or beer—but definitely a steak.

"Here you go, gentlemen. Your waiter's name is Sasha and she will be with you in a minute," their hostess said as she flirted and then added a wink.

All three men gave her their best player's smile before easing into the leather chairs around the table and opening their menus. Once she turned and walked away, they looked at one another and said in unison, "She wants me."

They immediately looked at one another skeptically. They knew that any one of them could easily turn heads when it came to the ladies. Xavier, a former heavyweight champion, stood a solid six foot four and was muscular with smooth chocolate skin and licorice eyes. His natural swagger was loaded with confidence that he'd earned in and out of the bedroom. Unlike his older brother Eamon,

Xavier didn't have a single monogamous gene in his body, and that was a good thing in his opinion. It didn't make him a jerk or anything. He truly believed that life was meant to be enjoyed to the fullest, and more than anything he enjoyed the pleasure of a woman's company, or two, but definitely no more than three. And he had it on good authority that they enjoyed him, too.

"A hundred bucks says that she was winking at me," Q said, easing back in his chair and puffing out his chest.

"In your dreams, grandpa," Jeremy countered. "The only thing that dime would give you is a senior citizen discount on your meal."

Xavier pressed his lips together, but a snicker still managed to escape.

"Senior—what?" Q's face colored with embarrassment. "I'll have you know that the forties are the new thirties, young blood."

"Sure. Sure." Jeremy bobbed his head, but crudely gestured with his hands in a way that implied Q was a whack job.

Quentin's indignation deepened, causing him to smack the table with his hand and up the ante. "A thousand bucks."

Both Xavier and his nearly look-alike brother straightened in their chairs now that there was some serious money on the table.

"What exactly is the bet?" Xavier asked.

"Simple. Whoever gets her number wins."

The King brothers rolled their eyes and waved him off.

"Please," Xavier said, reaching for his water. "That's child's play. Who's to say that she won't give her number to all three of us?"

Q conceded his point. "All right. Let's make it whoever can get her in bed. Sounds fair?"

The brothers looked at each other and shrugged.

"All right," Jeremy said. "Why not? I don't have any plans tonight. You in, bro?"

Xavier looked at his watch and remembered that he actually did have other plans after dinner and heaved a reluctant sigh. "Sorry. I'm going to have to leave this easy money on the table. But you two go for what you know. I'll be interested in seeing how this one pans out—old school versus new school." He pointed a finger at his brother. "Don't you let me down."

"Please." Jeremy leaned back in his chair so that his ego would have enough room at the table. "I got you covered like Allstate. Don't worry about me, be concerned about grandpa here. I don't think that he's going to accept the fact that his player's card expired—a loooong time ago."

If looks could kill, Jeremy would have been slowly disemboweled by his cousin.

"I see right now that it's time to smack you on the ass and send you back crying to your mama," Q said, smirking. "When it comes to women, all the real players know to call me the Professor."

"Oh? Is that right?" Jeremy laughed.

"That's right. Look it up in the dictionary. You'll see my picture in there."

While the two cousins argued and goaded each other as to who was the better player, neither of them noticed when the hostess waltzed back by the table, leading another party to their table, and very slyly slipped her number next to Xavier's silverware.

Xavier caught the slick move, picked up the scrap of paper, looked at it and then tucked it into his black jeans with a smirk. Old school, new school—there was nothing like just being the best school. "Will you two knuckleheads shut up and get back to telling me how much of a genius I am with all the new renovations?"

That stopped the argument long enough for them to flash him a get-over-yourself look.

"What? That is why we came here, isn't it? To celebrate my genius?"

"Frankly, I just tagged along for the free meal," Jeremy said.

"Free?" Q frowned. "The only thing free, cuz, was the ride over here. That fancy new renovation job is coming out of my pocket."

Xavier shrugged. "You're the one that wrecked the place."

"When I said I would pay for the damages, I was thinking a few tables and chairs. I didn't think that you'd go buck-wild and gut the place."

"Maybe next time you'll be a little more specific," Xavier said with absolutely no remorse.

"Does that mean you'll pay for renovations in the Los Angeles club?" Jeremy asked, since he managed that location.

"Hell to the no!" Quentin said, twisting his face. "What do you think I am—First National Bank?" Then, suddenly, he closed his eyes and groaned.

Xavier frowned. "What's up with you?"

Q shook his head. "I sounded like my father just now."

Xavier and Jeremy exchanged looks and busted out laughing.

Quentin and his father's contentious relationship had been gossip fodder for family members over the years. Roger Hinton, perhaps the most successful man in the family tree, built his fortune in commercial real estate and computer technology in the early eighties, and was one of only a handful of African-American billionaires. Brilliant in business, he'd raised two sons who were equally ambitious and nearly as successful in their own right. Then there was his third son, Quentin, who by all accounts until recently showed an almost violent allergic reaction to the very thought of holding a job.

After much back and forth, disinheritance, bribery and being swept back into the family's good graces, the one business that Q invested in—The Dollhouse—had made him rich in his own right. Brilliant or lucky? Most of the family decided it was luck. Xavier thought it had more to do with his own brilliance.

True, his older brother Eamon already owned The Dollhouse in Atlanta and he was content to keep it a small club while he fiddled with the idea of opening a restaurant until Xavier saw its true potential, and expanded the operation by capitalizing on a niche market—bachelor-party planning—and launched Bachelors Adventures. The concept was simple, and Xavier saw an opportunity to capitalize on an underserved market. Sure, any strip club could host a bachelor party. But not many catered to fantasy-driven bachelor parties, complete with themes and costumes—if that's what you wanted.

A bachelor party was a rite of passage. It was a big deal, and since it would be in poor taste to have a wake the night before a wedding, most men felt they deserved to party one last time like a rock star. There was no event too small or too big that Bachelors Adventures couldn't make happen. That simple business concept and the power of an influential word-of-mouth campaign is what really put The Dollhouse on the map, and not only made them serious contenders in their industry but solidified their reputation as *Kings*.

"Hello, gentlemen. My name is Sasha and I'll be your waitress for the evening. Are you ready for me to take your drink orders?"

They quickly put their conversation on pause and turned their attention to an extremely petite red-bone sporting short, natural hair in spiral twists. Her black-rimmed glasses gave her a studious look and her bright-white smile was warm and inviting.

"Three Heinekens," Xavier ordered for everyone.

Sasha quickly scribbled it down and then asked whether they were ready to order food. Once they'd selected their entrées, she took their menus and promised that everything would be ready in a few minutes. Of course, when she walked away, they gave her retreating figure another look.

"How about double or nothing," Quentin asked.

Xavier rolled his eyes. "I think you need to put your dick on a shorter leash."

Q's face twisted in horror. "Why in the hell would I want to do that? The happier he is, the happier I am."

Xavier's brows lifted. "Have you forgotten who you're talking to?"

Clearly, Q had because he immediately started shifting around in his chair.

Sasha proved to be good at her job and quickly returned with their beers, setting their bottles down in front of them. "Your food will be right up."

The men flashed her quick smiles as they reached for their beers and returned to their conversation.

"So what do you think of the spanking-new bartender you hired today?" Quentin asked, seemingly having tired of arguing with Jeremy.

Xavier leaned back in his chair and gave the question some serious thought. "She'll certainly make things interesting."

"I'll say," Q responded, reaching for his beer. "I don't think I've ever seen you cock-block so hard in my life."

"Please." Xavier gave a halfhearted laugh and rolled his eyes. "If anything, I was trying to prevent you guys from embarrassing yourselves and scaring the woman."

Neither his brother nor his cousin looked like they bought that load of crap.

Jeremy was the first to call him on it. "Please. You were throwing so much shade that I thought we were in the middle of a cave. But that's all right. I'm gonna let it go. But only because I'm heading back to Los Angeles tomorrow and you know how I feel about long-distance relationships."

Quentin laughed. "Yeah. The same way you feel about *all* relationships. You don't *do* them."

Jeremy bobbed his head along with the joke, mainly because it was true—for all of them. In their world, marriage was a dying institution. Who needed a piece of paper? Life was meant to be lived and enjoyed—the less drama, the better. And if there was one thing that all three men at the table agreed upon, it was that relationships ultimately involved a whole lot of drama.

"Frankly," Jeremy said. "Business has more than doubled at our L.A. club, so we might want to look into expanding some more."

"In a down economy?" Xavier asked.

Quentin laughed. "Our business is recession-proof."

Xavier conceded the point. "Maybe I'm not feeling it because I've been renovating for a hot minute. All I've been doing is writing checks."

"There's still revenue from Bachelors Adventures coming in," Q reminded him. "You've been on top of your game keeping those parties going at local hotels and other venues."

"True that." Xavier nodded. "I have this Lawrence of Arabia one coming up with this big-wig CEO out of New York. We're blowing up off word of mouth."

Q shrugged. "The old-fashioned way of doing business."

"We may have to look into expanding into New York, too," Jeremy interjected.

Q and Xavier frowned.

"What?" Jeremy shrugged. "If there's money to be made and our hustle is strong, what's the problem?"

"There is such a thing as growing too fast, you know?" Quentin warned.

"Just like there's such a thing as striking while the iron is still hot," Jeremy volleyed, unfazed.

Xavier smiled at the raw, unadulterated ambition gleaming in his brother's eyes. Jeremy made no bones about the fact that he was out to make his paper. Ambition was great. It would probably take his brother a long way. At least, Xavier hoped it would—unlike his own.

A wave of disappointment and regret started rolling inside him again, but he ignored it and plastered on another smile. Somehow, over the years, he'd become the brother that everyone brought their problems to without anyone ever really asking whether he had any of his own.

For the record, he had quite a few of them.

He suspected that most people thought that because he could take and land a hard punch, and that he could handle just about anything. For the most part, they were right. He knew how to duck and dodge most of life's problems. But the death of a dream…is something very few ever get over.

In 2002, he was on top of the world after becoming a national Golden Gloves champion with his eye toward the Olympics, the International Boxing Federation, the World Boxing Association *and* the World Boxing Council heavyweight titles. He wanted it all, like his heroes Muhammad Ali and Mike Tyson, who once had the world at their feet. He wasn't inspired so much because of the money and endorsements—though those were nice, too—but it was the recognition that came with being the best, being number one.

Then came the fight that changed everything…

"Hello." Quentin snapped his fingers in front of Xavier's face and brought him back from his ruminations. "There he is." Q smiled as their plates were being set on the table. "Still thinking about that hot bartender?"

Xavier rolled his eyes. "No."

"Riiiight." Quentin picked up his fork and knife and started cutting his steak. "The only time a man drifts off like that is because he's thinking about a woman."

Xavier laughed as he unrolled his linen napkin and started in on his baked potato. "Believe it or not, not all men spend their every waking moment thinking about women."

Jeremy and Quentin stopped eating and looked at him. "They don't?" they said in unison.

"Since when?" Jeremy added.

Xavier's laughter deepened. "You two aren't serious, are you?"

They looked at each other and then back at Xavier, their expressions unchanged.

"You both need psychiatric help," he said, and took the first bite of his steak. He immediately moaned as he savored the cut of meat.

"Well, since you're not interested in Ms. Got Milk, then you won't mind if I stick around and see what the deal is with her. Hell, I can give her a run for her money behind the bar." Quentin smirked.

Xavier's frown returned. "Weren't you just betting on who would get our hostess in bed a few minutes ago? Now you want to try to move in on my new bartender?"

"What? A man can't multitask?"

Xavier shook his head. "I hope that you're donating your brain to science because something is seriously wrong with you."

"What? Aren't you at least happy that I'm not drinking myself to death and getting into bar fights anymore?"

"Newsflash—you're not going to be able to screw Alyssa out of your system, either," Xavier schooled.

"Ouch. Harsh," Jeremy mumbled under his breath.

Q nodded. "I wasn't ready for that sucker punch."

"Sorry," Xavier said, and meant it. "That was uncalled for."

"No. But it's probably true, too," Quentin said.

Xavier's brows rose in surprise. "It was?"

Quentin shrugged as he pretended to think about it. "I said *probably.* I'll get back to you with my findings."

Xavier and Jeremy had to laugh. At the end of the day, Q was doing whatever he had or needed to do to get over his broken heart. The only thing was, Xavier questioned who really broke it—Alyssa or Q's older brother Sterling.

Xavier counted himself lucky for never having gone through anything remotely similar—since he'd never been in love.

And God willing, he never would be.

# *Chapter 4*

As her first day at The Dollhouse approached, Cheryl delved deeper and deeper into Xavier King's background, almost to the point of making it a miniobsession. Her eyes pored over his family's history like it was the latest Dennis Lehane bestseller. On paper, the King brothers' parents struggled to raise them on a city bus driver and substitute teacher's salary in a low-income section of Atlanta. There was no record of any of the brothers getting into any real trouble growing up—just a single missing person's report for Jeremy King when he was six years old. Apparently, the kid had run away from home after finding a box of puppies in the woods and had become upset when his father told him that they couldn't afford to keep them and would have to take them to the pound. Two days later, Jeremy's childhood friend broke down and confessed that Jeremy was living in their backyard in his tree house.

Cheryl smiled every time she read the old newspaper story. Not to mention, Jeremy was an adorable kid. But even looking at those old articles, her eyes would eventually drift to a frowning Xavier standing in the background. The other material Cheryl dug up on Xavier included spelling-bee championships, high school football accolades and scholarships. At nineteen, the football accolades turned to success in the boxing ring. Xavier won the national Golden Gloves heavyweight championship in '02 and '03 and even made the Olympic team in '04. But his career abruptly ended with a near-perfect 21-1 record without any real explanation as to why he left boxing.

He just stopped fighting.

As far as Cheryl could tell, Xavier just disappeared from the spotlight for two years and then reappeared as a gentlemen's club owner, where accusations and suspicions of drug trafficking continued to swirl.

Cheryl's gaze settled once again on the department's black-and-white photographs of the sexy club owners. And try as she might, she just didn't or couldn't see them as criminals. Maybe it was something about Xavier's dark soulful eyes. They struck her as being too honest…and playful. Now since she'd had the pleasure of being in the same room with the man, she would testify on a stack of Bibles that Xavier King did indeed dominate a room. The power of his gaze, the line of his shoulders and the unmistakable strength in his bulging arms… "Whew!" She reached for her cold bottled water and downed most of its twenty ounces, trying to put out the fire of her own making.

Something creaked and Cheryl's head whipped around to her bedroom door. There standing at the threshold, rubbing the sleep out of his eyes, was her six-year-old nephew, Thaddeus. A smile spread across her face again. "Heeey, li'l man. Whatcha doin' up?"

"There's a monster in my closet," he whined. His footed pajamas shuffled across the hardwood floor of her bedroom as he made his way over to her.

"A monster?" she responded with wide-eyed shock. She circled her arm around his tiny shoulders. "Are you sure?"

Thaddeus poked out his bottom lip and nodded.

"Oh, no. That just won't do."

"Will you come in my room and shoot it with your police gun?" he asked hopefully.

"How about I just go in there and check it out for myself?" she suggested. "I'm tough. I'm sure that I'll be able to handle that monster with my bare hands."

Her bravery made his eyes grow wider. "You sure? What if it hurts you?"

"Are you kidding me?" Cheryl curled her right arm. "Check out these muscles," she said, and waited for her nephew to give her Michelle Obama–like arms a good squeeze.

"Wow. You are strong," he said, awestruck.

"I sure am." She winked at him and stood. "Now let me at that monster hiding in that closet. We don't have time for none of this foolishness, do we?"

Thaddeus shook his head and then fell in line behind his aunt as she strolled out of her bedroom and headed into his room. "That monster is going to get it," he declared confidently.

"He sure is," Cheryl agreed. "Just let me at him."

They stormed into his Spider-Man–themed bedroom together. Cheryl flipped on the light switch and made a beeline to the closet. At the last second before touching the doorknob, Thaddeus gave her a quick last warning, "Be careful, Aunt Cheryl."

She tossed him a confident wink and then threw open the door.

Thaddeus gasped and covered his eyes. But when he didn't hear any hissing, growling or Lord knows what else his active imagination had anticipated, he slowly peeked through his small fingers.

"Huh." Cheryl settled her hands onto her hips and looked around. "There's no monster in here."

Frowning, Thaddeus raced over to the closet and mimicked his aunt's stance. "Where did he go?"

"I don't know." Cheryl pretended to be dumbfounded before suggesting, "Maybe he heard you going to get me and he got scared?"

Her nephew nodded at the explanation. "Yeah."

"Well, he better run. I was really going to put a hurting on him," Cheryl bragged as she dusted off her hands.

"Were you going to use karate on him?" He shifted his gaze from the monsterless closet and stared up at her.

"You know it." She tried to run her fingers through his thick blondish-brown hair, but as usual it was a bit tangled with its wayward curls. "When is your mother going to fix your hair?"

"She was supposed to do it tonight, but she fell asleep."

Cheryl shook her head. "All right. Back in the bed you go, li'l man. You have school in the morning."

Thaddeus poked out his bottom lip, but shuffled his way over to his twin-size bed where Cheryl peeled back the top sheet and waited for him. When he got close to the bed, he launched himself onto the mattress and laid his head on his cartoon-character pillow.

Cheryl couldn't resist tickling his side to elicit one of his hilarious, funny-sounding giggles. Once she got it, she leaned down and planted a wet kiss on his chubby cheek. "Good night, li'l man."

"Night, Auntie. When I grow up, I'm going to be a police officer just like you."

Cheryl's heart squeezed as tears quickly flooded her eyes. "And I'm sure that you'll make an excellent police officer." She stole another kiss and then tucked him into bed. "Sweet dreams," she said at the door before turning off the light switch.

Her smile was still stretched across her lips as she walked from her nephew's bedroom and headed toward the kitchen. There, her younger sister, Larissa, was slumped over her biology textbook and snoring softly into the pages.

Cheryl stopped at the entry to the kitchen and shook her head. She couldn't help but be sympathetic to her sister's hectic schedule. She worked full-time in a clothing store, while juggling being a single mom and going to college at night to become a nurse. It was a lot, and Cheryl was extremely proud of her sister. Because Larissa had her son so young, she could've continued her life making bad decisions. But when Thaddeus's father decided not to be a part of his biracial son's life—along with his well-to-do family—Larissa didn't fall apart. She picked herself up, dusted herself off and got busy trying to ensure a better life for her and her son. A lot of times that meant having to lean on family members, but everyone in the Grier family was more than willing to help as long as Larissa was committed to doing what was right.

Cheryl was no different.

Three years after Thaddeus was born, the Grier sisters were thrown a major curveball when their parents were killed in an electrical fire in their family home. The fire occurred in the middle of the night. Larissa managed to save herself and Thaddeus, and their mother did manage to get out, but she later died in the hospital. Their father never made it out of bed. The fire department report said that there had been some bad wiring in one of the upstairs bedrooms—the room where their father had installed a ceiling fan two days earlier.

After such a devastating blow, Cheryl and Larissa relied on each other more than ever. As a result, Larissa and Thaddeus moved into Cheryl's single-family ranch in the small Atlanta suburb of Marietta. It was a bit of a tight squeeze, but the sisters were doing all they could to make the living arrangement work.

Cheryl placed a gentle hand on Larissa's back and spoke just loud enough to break through her snoring. "Rissa, why don't you go to bed?"

"Hmm?" Larissa lifted her head, but didn't open her eyes.

"Go to bed," Cheryl said, using the opportunity to close her sister's schoolbooks.

"Can't," Larissa moaned. "I have a big test tomorrow and I'm not prepared." She sat up and stretched.

"You're not going to learn anything by drooling on your textbook. I don't think that's how it works."

"I knoooooow." She dropped her head into the palms of her hands for a second and almost immediately drifted off to sleep again.

Cheryl put her sister's book back on the table and chuckled when her sister jumped. "I'll put on some coffee for you."

"Thanks." Larissa grabbed her book again and opened it up. "I can't wait until this quarter is over with. It's really kicking my butt."

"Didn't it just start?" Cheryl asked as she shoveled Folgers grinds into the coffee filter.

"What's your point?"

"Hang in there. Next year this time, you'll be holding that degree."

"More like I'll be falling out and crying, and calling out for Jesus," Larissa corrected.

"Whatever. You just make sure that you get that degree, too." Cheryl hit the brew button and then turned back toward the table. "About Thaddeus's hair..."

Larissa groaned. "Oh. I'll take care of it this weekend. Drae recommended this great barbershop in Atlanta and I'll take him there."

"Do you want me to take him?"

Larissa's eyes widened with hope. "Will you have time? I

thought that you were starting some new super-duper secret case tomorrow?"

"I am. But I can take Thaddeus Saturday morning, if you want."

"If I want? Girl, if I had the energy I would jump up and kiss you. That means I can sleep late for once."

"Not a problem." Cheryl pulled out a chair and sat down while she waited for the coffee to finish brewing.

"I know that you probably can't wait for me and Thaddeus to finally move out and find our own place."

Cheryl frowned. "I never said that."

"Oh, please. You don't have to." Larissa eased back in her chair. "Any sane single woman would love to have her place back—child-free, so that you can do what single women do with the opposite sex."

"Give it a rest." Cheryl stood and went to the cabinet for two coffee mugs. "I like having you and my Energizer Bunny nephew around. We're a family."

"True. But I imagine that one day—maybe one day soon—you'd like to start your own family."

Cheryl glanced over her shoulder.

"Maybe with a certain lieutenant?"

"Oh, God, please. Just say you're kidding."

"What?" Larissa shrugged. "You know Jason still has the hots for you. He still calls—"

"What?"

"C'mon. Don't play coy. You know that man is like a puppy dog around you." Larissa laughed. "I don't know what you put on him, but it's clearly something that he can't shake or take a pill for."

Cheryl huffed out a long frustrated breath and poured their coffee. "I tell you what. I don't know what the hell I was thinking when I hooked up with that man. Maybe I bumped my head or something."

"You mean to tell me that you don't feel anything for him?"

"Zip....nada....nothing." She quickly added French-vanilla creamer and sugar to their mugs and headed back to the table. "You know it all happened so soon after Mom and Dad died and... Maybe I was just weak. He caught me at a vulnerable time. Insert standard cliché here."

"Sounds like it makes life real interesting around the department," said Larissa as she carefully picked up her coffee mug. "Was he at least good in bed?"

"Excuse you."

Larissa shrugged and refused to retract the question. "Hey, I can't remember the last time I even had sex. So you're going to have to forgive me for getting all up in your Kool-Aid. I have to get my jollies off some kind of way."

"You know...if you want to go out sometime, I can babysit Thaddeus."

"Ughh. The last thing I need in my life right now is the complications of a man." Larissa shook her head. "Maybe after I get at least one thing off my plate."

"So does that mean that you're going to take a rain check?"

"Is the offer good until next summer?"

"As a matter of fact it is."

"Then, yes, ma'am. I will." Larissa straightened up in her chair and flashed her sister a silly grin as she thought about a potential date she might have...a year from now. "Now all we have to do is find you a *new* man."

Instantly, Xavier's face popped into Cheryl's head, and less than a second later, her body was flush with a tingling warm sensation.

"Ooooh. Looks like you already have a new man in mind," Larissa said, easily reading her sister.

"What? No." Cheryl shook her head but the damage had

already been done. She popped out of her seat. "You want some cake?"

"Liar, liar, pants on fire!" Larissa wagged her finger. "Who is he? And where did you meet him?"

"It's no one. Stop it." Despite her protests, Cheryl couldn't look her sister in the eye. She made a living deceiving criminals when she went undercover, and yet she was unable to get a simple lie past her sister. So she did the next best thing, she sliced them both two huge pieces of lemon cake.

"Pathetic." Larissa laughed as she accepted her late-night snack. "Go ahead. Keep your secrets. Deny your *only* sister the pleasure of living vicariously through you."

"Oh, God. Someone please give Ms. Larissa Grier her hard-earned Academy Award."

"I'm still waiting for a name."

"Then you're going to be waiting for a long time," Cheryl said, still struggling to push Xavier's image out of her head.

Larissa's laserlike gaze studied Cheryl as she shoved the first bite of cake into her mouth. "Uh-huh. We'll see."

# Chapter 5

"Five…four…three…two…one. Welcome to The Dollhouse!" the staff yelled the moment the gentlemen's club's doors opened for business.

Given the amount of money that Xavier had spent on advertising for the grand reopening of the club, there was a large crowd on the other side of the door and they were as hyped as the staff was as they streamed inside. While the music pumped at an unbelievable decibel, the customers crowded around the tables near the main stages first and then around the bars.

Xavier experienced a wave of nervousness not unlike what he'd felt before a big fight. It was time to bring his A-game. This was a night to impress and he wanted nothing but happy customers.

Dressed to kill in a black double-breasted blazer, a classic white dress shirt and reflective aviators, Xavier made sure that when his guests saw him, they saw a well-groomed, stylish and confident man. *He* was the man of the hour and this was his playground.

At exactly 9:00 p.m., the Dolls descended the stairs of the main stage and strolled around for a parade revue and table dance. The crowd went wild at the sight of the first gorgeous beauties Xavier had lined up for them that evening. If he could, he probably would've broken his arm trying to pat himself on the back as he watched everyone's reaction.

"Two minutes in and I'd say that tonight's reopening is a raving success," Q said, standing to his right. "You might be a genius, after all."

"I'm glad that you finally recognize," Xavier said, swinging his arm around his cousin's neck and then strolling deeper into the jubilant crowd.

Immediately, guests started hailing the cousins to stop by their tables so that they could congratulate them on the renovations. Everyone from the governor to local celebrities wanted a few minutes of their time. Before long, the Dolls were sliding down their golden poles and his smiling waitresses and bartenders kept the drinks flowing.

No doubt about it, the reopening was a hit.

In all honesty, Cheryl didn't know what to expect her first night on the job. She had been in her fair share of nightclubs and she had indeed bartended in her uncle's sports bar back in the day. But the over-the-top numbers from The Dollhouse strippers, or rather *dancers,* had *her* blushing for the first couple of hours of her shift. How in the world the women were able to dance, slide and shimmy—forget the poles—in those incredibly high heels was clearly above her pay grade.

Between the music and the dancing her senses were on overload, and she struggled like hell to hear the drink orders that were being yelled at her from patrons and the waitresses. It was damn near one o'clock in the morning before she remembered that she was also supposed to be keeping an eye out for any suspicious activity.

*This is going to be much harder than I thought.*

"So how are you holding up?"

When Xavier's warm baritone wrapped around her ears, Cheryl's hand slipped on the bottle of vodka and she had to make a desperate second grab to hold it. Luckily, she caught it before it hit the floor.

"Nice catch," Xavier praised.

She turned to see him leaning in between two patrons who had been nursing the same beer for the past hour. "Thanks. And I'm doing okay…I think."

"I haven't heard any complaints. That's a good thing."

Cheryl appreciated the praise but was suddenly having a difficult time concentrating when he started smiling and looking at her like she was a T-bone steak. "Thanks."

A few more drinks were yelled out at her and she immediately got to work. However, she was very aware of her new boss's gaze following her every move. Butterflies flooded her belly and there was a visible tremor of her hands. Could he see it, too? After passing a pair of drinks to Lexus, Cheryl stole a glance to her left only to have her gaze crash into Xavier's again. Again, her fingers slipped on another bottle.

"I hope that I'm not making you nervous," he said, amusement clearly dancing in his voice as well as his eyes.

"I'm only trying to impress the boss."

"Then consider me *very* impressed."

That damn bottle slipped again, but this time hit the floor with a loud *crash.* Cheryl jumped back but caught the reflexive curse word before it flew out of her mouth. Embarrassed, she looked back up, but Xavier was gone.

*Cheryl, get it together.*

For the next two hours that is exactly what she did. By the time the doors closed at three in the morning, Cheryl felt as if she'd just completed a triathlon and she needed someone to wring her out and put her on a shelf away somewhere. The night flew by with the onslaught of customers. The club officially closed at 3:00 a.m., but at three-thirty there were still patrons lingering around at the tables and bar, taking their sweet time nursing their drinks.

One thing for sure, Cheryl was more than impressed with the tips she'd made for the evening. She wouldn't know the final tally until she went home and counted it all, but she made a mental note that bartending could be her second career if she ever decided to turn in her shield.

At 4:00 a.m., the last dregs started drifting toward the front door and Cheryl rushed to finish cleaning up her station so that she could get out of there. She wasn't the only one. The two remaining waitresses couldn't wait to plop down on the bar stools and pull off their high heels.

"Good Lawd, my dogs are barking up a storm," Lexus complained, rubbing her painted toes and sighing like she was starring in a Calgon commercial.

"I hear you," Cheryl said, flashing a smile and welcoming an opportunity to start bonding with the staff. If she was ever going to know the ins and outs of everything that went on in the club, she was going to need to connect with The Dollhouse grapevine.

Lexus pulled out her wad of cash and immediately started counting. "You're really good behind that bar," Lexus complimented. "You certainly held your own."

Cheryl laughed. "It was either that or give everyone a real show when I set my head on fire."

Lexus laughed, but clearly she was a master at multitasking because she had yet to stop counting her cash during their brief conversation. "Don't worry. You'll get used to it—and you might even start having a good time."

"Advice from a veteran?"

"After you get a week under your belt, you'll be considered

a veteran, too." Lexus finished counting and her smile grew wider. "Definitely a good night. You're now my official bartender. You were working rings around Randy on the third station bar. The waitresses over there spent half the night threatening to lynch him. Frankly, I'd be surprised if he comes back tomorrow."

Cheryl's chest expanded with pride.

As Cheryl waltzed from behind the bar, stuffing the night's booty into the side pockets of her black leather duffel bag, she opened her mouth to bid Lexus a good-night. From the corner of her eye, she caught sight of Xavier and Quentin talking and laughing together as they descended the main staircase.

Lexus looked up at Cheryl and then over to see what had captured her attention.

"Uh-oh."

Cheryl blinked and then jerked her head away. "Uh-oh, what?"

Lexus's smile turned into a smirk. "Which one has caught your eye?"

"What? Neither one," Cheryl quickly blurted out, and shook her head.

Lexus laughed. "Yeah, right. And I have a swamp for sale in the Louisiana bayou that you're just going to *love*."

"Please. They're not all that," Cheryl continued to lie, though she didn't know why she bothered. Her face was hot and once again she was having trouble meeting Lexus's gaze. What in the hell had happened to her lying skills?

"Look…what's your name again?"

"Cheryl…Shepherd." She reached out her hand. "Nice to meet you."

Lexus accepted her handshake but with a condescending smile. "Honey, the only way that you're going to convince me that you're not feeling Quentin or Xavier is if you're about to tell me that you're gay. And since there is nothing wrong with my gaydar, I'm going to go out on a limb and say that you're as straight as an arrow."

Cheryl finally met the woman's eyes and then, a second later, a smile eased across her lips. "All right, so they're cute. Big deal. I'm sure that there isn't a day or an hour that they don't have some woman throwing themselves at them."

"An hour?" Lexus glanced over her shoulder and sure enough there were now three women giggling and flirting shamelessly with the cousins. "Honey, if two minutes passes without some chick throwing themselves at them, then it means that there aren't any women within a three-mile radius. Believe that."

Lexus's words drifted over Cheryl while she continued to watch the three women she recognized as Dolls who had spent half the night sliding and gyrating on the club's golden poles. Cheryl self-consciously straightened her back and puffed out her chest. *They ain't all that!*

"It's Xavier, isn't it?"

Cheryl's head whipped back around and her face was scorching hot from having been busted. "I, uh—"

"Save it." Lexus waved off Cheryl's stuttering and shoved her wad of tips in her bra. "Trust me when I tell you that it's normal. There's isn't a woman who's worked with the Kings and Sir Quentin who hasn't at one time or another been in love with one of them or all of them. My ass included."

Cheryl hadn't meant to, but she gave the waitress a cursory glance and mentally compared their bodies.

"Hell, I'm not too sure that we all haven't slept with them at one time or another."

"What?"

Still laughing, Lexus pulled herself out of the chair. "C'mon. You can't be surprised. They're men…who own a gentlemen's club that is filled with naked girls. Surely you don't think they sleep alone."

Cheryl forced her lips to smile again. "Of course not. I'm not stupid."

Lexus shook her head. "Honey, sleeping with Xavier King may make you a lot of things, but *stupid* isn't one of them." With that, she winked and strolled off. "See you tomorrow night."

While the waitress's words slowly sunk in, Cheryl's gaze once again drifted back to the handsome cousins and their small clique of groupies. But this time Xavier looked up, smiled and winked at her.

More heat than she knew what to do with flooded her entire body and there had to be something wrong with her knees. At any second she was sure they were going to buckle and her ass would drop to the floor.

*Get it together.*

At last, Cheryl shook herself out of her stupor, gave Xavier a departing nod and then forced one leg in front of the other. But in order to leave the club, she had to walk in his direction. Turned out the closer she got, the weaker her knees became and the wider his smile stretched.

"Excuse me, ladies," she said, and waited for two of the girls to step aside so that she could pass.

During what took about two seconds tops, Cheryl could feel Xavier's gaze as though it was a feathery touch stroking the sides of her face. She even quivered and darted her eyes away.

"Good night, Cheryl," Xavier said.

There was something about the way he said *good night* that sounded familiar, though it was the first time he'd ever said it to her. How easy it was to imagine him saying, "Good night, Cheryl," every night for the rest of their lives before curling up together and going to sleep.

*What in the hell is wrong with me? Snap out of it!*

"Good night, Xavier," she responded softly, and maneuvered past him and his laughing clique. Cheryl didn't know why she thought that there would be some kind of relief once she passed him on the stairs. There wasn't.

None.

She knew he turned, not because she saw him, but because she could feel that feathery caress now floating down the back of her head and then lingering on her butt. All right. That knowledge did make her smile a bit. One thing for sure, none of the girls that she saw dancing tonight even came close to what the good Lord and her mama blessed her with.

"Excuse me, guys. I'll be right back," Xavier said.

Cheryl's eyes bulged while her brain screamed for her legs to move faster. And that was just what the hell they did. Then that magical baritone said, "Cheryl, wait up."

*Don't you dare stop!* She shoved open the glass front door and marched like a soldier headed off to war.

Xavier chuckled.

When she realized that the deep rumble sounded entirely too close, it was a nanosecond before his hand locked around her wrist. Cheryl gasped aloud as an electric charge surged through her body. Unfortunately for Xavier, it also activated her self-defense reflexes and before either of them could process what was happening, she'd turned and flipped his large frame over on the asphalt. Once reality settled in, Xavier was lying on his back on the pavement with Cheryl still holding his hand and her right foot planted squarely in the center of his chest.

He blinked. "I just wanted to see if you were interested in grabbing something at the Waffle House, but, uh, I can take a rain check."

Realizing what she had done, she released his hand and removed her foot from his chest. "I'm sooooo sorry. You just startled me." She dropped down and then tried to help him up.

Still dazed and confused, Xavier sat up and looked around. "How in the hell…?"

"I, uh, took some self-defense classes a while back." She waved off the question and gave him a nervous smile.

"You took classes or you taught classes?" He stood up. "I don't know whether to be embarrassed right now or impressed."

Cheryl smiled and stepped back. "Well, I did have the element of surprise on my side," she offered as a way for him to save face.

He nodded as he proceeded to dust himself off. "Good point. I'll add that to my version of events when I'm nursing my pride over a bottle of Jack Daniel's."

"Don't beat yourself up too bad. I've taken down men a lot bigger than you."

A singular brow arched in the center of Xavier's forehead. "Really? Care to tell me about it over waffles?"

"Uh, maybe another time," she said, clinging to the leather strap of her duffel bag and stepping backward toward her car. "I'm really beat and just want to fall into bed."

An effortless smile eased across his face, and though he didn't say the words, his eyes asked, *Want company?*

"See you tomorrow night," Cheryl said, continuing to walk backward to her car.

"Yeah." He started walking backward himself. "See you."

Cheryl bumped into the front of her car and then turned around so that she could go to the driver's side and climb in as soon as possible. After getting behind the wheel and starting the car, she was still a bundle of nerves. When she pulled out of the parking lot, Xavier, still standing at the front door of the club, lifted his hand to wave goodbye.

She smiled sheepishly and waved, then quickly jammed her foot on the accelerator and peeled off. Not until she was twenty minutes down the road did her heart rate return to normal and she felt like herself again.

"This case is definitely going to be a lot harder than I thought."

# *Chapter 6*

Xavier kept only a few secrets from his brothers—and Quentin, for that matter. And Cheryl Shepherd catching him off guard and flipping him on his ass was just going to have to go into his vault of secrets. Hell, he spent half the night playing and replaying his memory of the event. Sure, it had been a while since he'd climbed into the boxing ring. But damn, had his reflexes gotten that bad? When was the last time he struck out that badly?

*And what did she mean that she had flipped bigger men than him?* Was she some super vigilante that roamed the streets of Atlanta at night? As soon as that crackpot thought floated through his head, he shook it right out. But if he didn't come up with a better excuse soon, he was going to have a permanent scar on his fragile ego. By 9:00 a.m. he was crawling out of bed with laserlike determination to get to the gym.

The minute he waltzed through the doors of Ripped Gym, he felt as if he'd instantly been transported back in time. The bricks-and-mortar building was old school. No fancy elliptical anything crowded its floor. There were no televisions to distract you from focusing on your sole purpose, which was to train hard and work up a sweat. This morning the place was packed with guys pounding away at the heavy bags, jumping rope, lifting weights and punching the speed bags in a rapid-fire motion. Xavier's attention, however, zoomed in on the brothers sparring in the three boxing rings in the center of the spacious gym.

In the first ring, a mammoth of a man danced awkwardly on his feet while making wide swings at his opponent and forgetting to protect his chin. Unfortunately, his sparring partner, who was barely half the other man's size, danced gracefully on his feet, bobbing and weaving like a seasoned pro. In fact, Xavier got the distinct impression that he was just playing with the graceless giant the way David might have played with Goliath before he fired off that one good slingshot.

In the next second, that is exactly what happened. Big Man made a wide Texas swing, left his chin open and *boom!* goes the dynamite. Hell, there was plenty of time for anyone to yell, "Timber," when he pitched backward and fell to the canvas.

By the time he hit the mat, Xavier was shaking his head and *tsking* under his breath. He hadn't seen anything that sad, painful and funny in a long while.

"Ayo! It's the X-Man," old-timer Ricky Miller shouted from across the gym. "Please tell me that this is the miracle from God that I've been praying for."

Xavier frowned as his ex-trainer rushed over to him.

"Please say that you came to tell me that you're ready to get back into the ring again."

"Sorry, old man," Xavier said, shaking his head. "You know that I hung up my boxing gloves. I just came in for an old-fashioned workout."

Disappointment blanketed Ricky's face as he dropped his arms a few steps before he reached Xavier. "Damn. I should've known that it was just too good to be true."

Laughing, Xavier wrapped his arms around his old curmudgeon of a trainer and hugged him anyway. "I miss you, too."

"Humph. You sure have a funny way of showing it," he deadpanned.

Xavier bobbed his head while his arms swung back to his sides. "You're right. I've been meaning to stop by the old gym. But, uh, you know how it is. Life tends to keep tossing things at you."

It was a weak excuse at best and Ricky treated it as such by waving him off. "C'mon. You can't out bullshit a bullshitter. You ended your career, dumped me on my ass and then ran off with your brothers to run a titty bar. I can see how all of that could keep a man busy. In the spirit of keeping it real, if Viagra mixed better with my heart pills, I probably would've done the same thing a long time ago."

Xavier laughed heartily and then experienced a twinge of guilt about how abruptly he'd ended things between them. "I'm sorry, Ricky. You deserved better."

"Damn right I did." He sniffed and then settled his hands on his thin hips as he examined Xavier from head to toe. "Well, clearly you haven't gone the route of other ex-champs and turned into a big tub of lard. So what have you been doing to keep yourself in shape?"

Suddenly modest, Xavier shrugged. "I still get in a four-mile run most days, watch what I eat and do this whole muscle-confusion phenomenon that's sweeping the country."

"Oh, Jesus, Mary and Joseph." Ricky rolled his eyes. "DVDs? You're doing workout DVDs at home? What are you, a chick? Are you bopping around in leotards and leg warmers, too?"

"All right. Reel in the outrage, old man. Times have changed."

"You're telling me?" Ricky adjusted his woolen cap. "Yesterday I was buying diapers for my newborn daughter, now she buys them for me."

Xavier's lips hitched up.

"That's the sad part. The funny part is that I actually like them. They're very comfortable. You'll see in about fifty years."

"Great. I can't wait." Xavier laughed and gave his friend another pat on the back.

"So if you're doing your workouts like Suzy Homemaker, what are you doing here?"

Last night's embarrassment quickly flooded Xavier's mind. "Well, you know, I thought I could use a tune-up on the reflexes and all. Just because I'm not in the ring doesn't mean that I want to get caught slipping or anything."

"Uh-huh." Ricky frowned.

Xavier swore he could see the spokes and wheels slowly churning in Ricky's head as he tried to decipher his real meaning. "And, of course, there's the added benefit of seeing my old friend again."

"Don't blow smoke up my ass, I might like it." Ricky's gaze cut across the room to a young but well-chiseled brother pounding away on an old, heavy bag that had about as much duct tape holding it together as the original leather. "Another five minutes and then I want you in the ring with Dog Pound!" He looked around. "Is Dog Pound awake?"

The awkward Goliath that Xavier observed earlier sat hunched on a small stool in the corner of the gym, raising his right hand as he squirted water from his water bottle all over his head. "I'm all right, Unc. Lucky punch, that's all."

Xavier snickered under his breath. Luck had nothing to do with that knockout.

Ricky mumbled something, but it was clearly with disgust.

"Problem?"

"What else can there be when you're dealing with family?" Ricky shook his head. "My sister Vera out in Texas sent him to me hoping that a father figure would do him some good. Seems he got into a little trouble with some local gang members out there. Good kid even though he's not the brightest bulb on the marquee."

"Any potential?"

"If so, I haven't found it yet." Ricky shrugged. "What he lacks in natural talent, he makes up for with heart. When I first started bringing him here, he got knocked out at least ten times a day. I got him down to just three."

"Progress is progress."

"Yeah, at this rate he should be ready for his first fight in about fifty years."

"I think you're underestimating your skills."

"And you keep forgetting how *old* I am." Ricky shook his head. "I still love the sport, but…well. What was it you said…life keeps tossing things at you?"

Xavier nodded while his gaze drifted back to the man pounding the heavy bag. He was impressed by the young fighter's stance, form and extreme focus on the task at hand. "He yours?"

Ricky followed Xavier's gaze and then lit up. "That he is. Until someone pinches me and tells me that I'm dreaming."

"Great form," Xavier complimented.

Ricky turned back toward his former fighter. "Yeah, sometimes he reminds me of someone else I used to know."

Xavier picked up on the not so subtle hint and smiled. "Aww. You say the nicest things. Give me a hug."

Ricky tossed up his hands and started backing away. "Nah. Nah. You've reached your quota. Now get away from me."

Enjoying the fact that he was making Ricky uncomfortable, Xavier continued to try to wrap his arms around him. "C'mon, now. You know you missed me."

"Stop it. Stop it. Stop it." Ricky kept flapping his hands to try and shoo him away.

Finally, Xavier just gave up and threw his head back for a hearty laugh. That's when he saw her.

Cheryl strolled into the gym in a pair of formfitting, black capri-length sweats and a bright red crop top that left her well-defined, six-pack abs exposed. When she walked, she had a sexy swagger that caused men to trip over their jump ropes, nearly drop their weight bars, stop mid-pull-up and, for one unlucky brother, take a knockout blow across the jaw because he got distracted. The amazing thing was she was oblivious to it all.

"I knew it was a mistake to turn this place into a coed gym," Ricky grumbled.

Entranced, Xavier watched Cheryl until she disappeared into the locker room. Once she was out of view, he snapped out of it and shook the remaining fairy dust from his head. "How long has she been coming here?"

"Not long." Ricky laughed. "I guess that means that you really will be hanging around here again…at least until you sleep with her and get her out of your system."

Xavier frowned and then glanced back at his friend. "Oww. That's kind of harsh, don't you think?"

"What? Am I wrong?"

"Well…yeah." Xavier folded his arms across his chest. "I'm not an asshole or anything."

Instead of answering, Ricky laughed and walked off.

Frowning, Xavier followed. He felt like he needed to say something to defend himself. "I'll have you know that I'm on good terms with most of the women I've been involved with."

"Uh-huh."

"I'm not a dog," he insisted. "In fact, I'm what most women claim they want—honest."

Ricky tossed up his hands. "Hey, no judgment here. My'kael, Dog Pound, let's go." He clapped his hands, urging them to hustle.

"I'm serious," Xavier insisted. "I'm not like my cousin or anything. I don't just hit it and quit it. I like to remain friends with my ex-lovers."

"Uh-huh."

With their headgear in place, My'kael and Dog Pound climbed into the ring.

"I've never used women."

Ricky yelled, "Dog Pound, make sure that you keep your chin tucked and your elbows in. None of that sidewinding BS you learned watching that damn *Karate Kid* movie."

"Plus, I never crept out in the middle of the night, called a woman by the wrong name in bed or not call when I said I would," Xavier continued.

"Look, X-Man. I said no judgment. You don't have to explain your sexual habits to me. Hell, I had ten kids and six wives. All of which is why I'm nearly eighty years old and still having to work for a living. That, and the fact that my one golden goose kicked me to the curb without an explanation."

*That again.* "I can only apologize so many times."

"How about I let you know when you hit the right number?"

Cheryl exited the locker room and started stretching. Once again, Xavier fell into a trance. She had a sweet, girl-next-door face, but there was a definite edginess there, too. Was it around her eyes or the firm line of her jaw? He watched her while she leaned, dipped and stretched. He couldn't quite pinpoint exactly what gave her that extra edge. Eventually, his eyes roamed away from her face and journeyed down her long neck and straight shoulders. But she rocked his world when she picked up a jump rope and started bouncing up and down.

Parts of Xavier started moving…and expanding. Xavier jerked his gaze away and turned around. Did he have a cup in his bag? Should he rush to go put it on? "Why did you make this place coed?"

"Why else? Money. Bad economy."

Xavier nodded while he tried to mentally will his cock to go down by envisioning himself jumping into an icy pond. It usually worked, but for some damn reason, Cheryl was swimming in that damn pond in nothing but her birthday suit.

"Speaking of which," Ricky said. "You wouldn't happen to need some help down there at the club—some security or something like that? My nephew would make an excellent bouncer."

Xavier glanced back at Dog Pound, who was preparing himself for the coming sparring session by delivering a few punches to his own head.

"You'd be doing me a *big* favor," Ricky pressed.

*At least his size was intimidating.* Xavier looked back over at his former trainer and realized that perhaps he did owe the old man a few favors. "Sure. Just send him over to the club Monday and I'll stick him at the front door."

When Ricky smiled this time, Xavier swore he saw the weight of the world lift off his shoulders. He sensed something else was going on. "Is there anything else that I can help you with?"

Ricky's salt-and-pepper brows shot up. "You can tell me that you're going back into the ring."

Xavier laughed. "Other than that?"

"Then I'm good." He turned his attention back to his boxers in the ring. "All right, you two slackers, show me what you got!" Ricky slapped his hands together.

Xavier folded his arms and watched the sparring match

with an increasingly interested eye on Ricky's new protégé, My'kael. It only took a minute for him to realize that the kid really had something—something great.

Finally remembering that he only had a limited amount of time himself, Xavier went to start his own warm-up exercises. During his stretches and lunges, his gaze shifted back across the room to Cheryl. At the sight of her throwing punches at one of the speed bags, he instantly became hard again. The sweat that poured over her body looked more like glistening body oil to him. But what had him totally riveted was the fact that his sexy bartender's nipples apparently hardened when she worked up a good sweat because they were visible and hard as rocks.

Images of him nestling his head in between her lovely breasts and sucking on those big nipples made Xavier light-headed. Cheryl's sexiness was different from the type of women he and his brothers usually hired at the gentlemen's club. Sure, she was curvy in all the places that counted, but it was the strength in her arms, abs and thighs that was turning Xavier on in ways he'd never experienced before.

Xavier partnered up with another dude to toss the medicine ball back and forth; while he did so, Cheryl moved on to do some shadow boxing in front of the mirror. There he checked out her form and footwork. *She's pretty good.*

An hour later, he knew that he needed to head out, but he wanted to stick around to watch Cheryl finish her workout. For him it was like watching his own private lap dance. *I have issues.*

Panting, Xavier grabbed his towel out of his bag and wiped himself down. When he started to return the towel it was then that he realized just how hard he was, mainly because it was visible.

Cursing, he grabbed his bag and slid the strap over his shoulder, moving it in front of his body to hide his…

excitement. *Time to go.* A second later, he realized a problem. He would have to walk past Cheryl in order to leave.

*If it wasn't for bad luck, I'd have no luck at all.*

Maybe if he dropped his head and looked off to the left, he could pass her without being recognized.

"Xavier," Cheryl exclaimed, smiling and pulling her earplugs out of her ears. "What are you doing here?"

"Uh..." He held on to that leather bag as if his life depended on it. "Actually, I've been coming to this gym since I was a teenager."

"Really? I didn't know that."

He rocked his head. "Yep. It's like a second home to me."

An awkward silence followed the minor revelation about his life, and they stood there for half a minute bobbing their heads and smiling way too broadly at each other. It was probably a good time for Xavier to just go along his merry little way, but...he really didn't want to leave Cheryl's presence. But damn if he knew what to say next.

*This is worse than my first school dance.*

"Uh, last night," Cheryl started. "I just wanted to tell you that I'm really...really sorry about that. I assure you that I don't just go around body-slamming people on the pavement on the regular."

Two guys off to their right twisted their heads around upon overhearing her.

The hairs on the back of Xavier's neck stood up as new waves of embarrassment washed over him.

"What? Did I say something wrong?" Cheryl glanced around to see what had captured Xavier's attention. But the minute she turned, the eavesdroppers had turned back around, pretending to mind their own business.

"Nah. It's cool." He tried to laugh the situation off, but it sounded more like a misfired weapon. "Besides, it was probably like you said. You just..."

"Had the element of surprise," she filled in for him.

"Yeah. That's it." He continued to laugh, but this time a little too hard and a little too loud. "I mean, let's be real. It's not like you could ever do something like that again." His head rocked back a bit with the next rumble of laughter and it took him a moment to realize that he was the only one laughing.

"What? You don't think I could do it again?" she challenged with a sudden glint in her eye.

Xavier's laugh died down and the smile melted off his face. "No… Well. I mean…c'mon."

Cheryl cocked her head and folded her arms across her chest. "C'mon what? You think that just because I'm a woman that I can't take you?"

Heads started to turn in their direction. Xavier was being backed into a corner. "Well…there is that. Plus, I'm…*me.*"

A single brow rose in the center of her forehead. "Arrogant, aren't we?"

"No. No. It's just…" Xavier's bag shifted. "I don't know if you're aware of this but I'm a Golden Gloves champion."

"More like…*were,*" she corrected him. "You were a Golden Gloves champion."

"Ooooh," a few of the guys chimed in.

Both Xavier and Cheryl looked around to see that they had at least half the gym huddled in a semicircle, unabashedly listening to their conversation.

"Be that as it may, you're hardly a threat to me. And I'm not being sexist. It's just a fact." His bag shifted some more.

Cheryl shrugged with an amused smile. "You want to settle this in the ring?"

"Ooooh," the fellas chimed in again as smiles spread across all their faces.

"There's no 'oooh,'" Xavier said, frowning at the crowd. "There's no way I'm getting in the ring with a woman." He faced Cheryl again and saw her smile widening, probably because he was doing an excellent job of making a fool of himself. "Look. You're going to have to accept my apology. I don't mean any harm," he said, releasing his grip on his duffel bag, which allowed for it to swing back to his side.

Cheryl shifted her weight and lifted a finger, but before she could start wagging it or giving him a piece of her mind, her eyes dipped.

At her startled gasp, Xavier followed her gaze. He was as hard as an iron fist. At the sight of the unmistakable bulge in his crotch, he grabbed the leather duffel bag again and shoved it in front of his body.

But it was too late. She saw. "Oh."

Actually, she wasn't the only one. Dudes started snickering and turning away.

Wide-eyed, Cheryl glanced away, as well, but there was still a hint of amusement hugging her lips.

After the initial heat wave of embarrassment, Xavier gave up the ghost and started laughing himself. "I, uh, think I'll just leave you to your workout. I'm going to jog home and take a very *long* cold shower."

"Yeah," she snickered. "That sounds like a good idea."

Xavier turned around, still clutching his bag in front of him, and strolled off. He smiled as he passed the other members. "Yeah. Yeah. Chuckle it up." He rolled his eyes and made faces at the guys until he exited the building. But before the door slammed closed, he heard everyone explode with laughter.

*Strike two.*

# *Chapter 7*

*Two weeks later...*

"There's still nothing out of The Dollhouse?" a frustrated Lieutenant Mackey asked as he stopped his nervous pacing in front of Detective Grier.

Cheryl glanced to her side at her partner.

Johnnie sucked in a brief sigh and turned her head away.

"Sorry. Nothing yet," Cheryl confessed. Her feelings for her lieutenant aside, she hated delivering this bit of bad news. In the past few weeks, the crap Mackey was taking from the mayor and the chief of police had only increased with the number of police screw-ups that had been hitting the news lately. He needed some good press—and soon.

Mackey tossed up his hands. "Then maybe you're just not doing your job right?"

"Excuse you?" Cheryl's head snapped as she looked up his long frame. "I'm doing my job. Don't you worry about *that*. But if there's nothing going on, then there's nothing going on."

"Are you sure you're not distracted?"

Heat charged through every pore of Cheryl's body. Every eye in the conference room had settled on her at Mackey's vague accusation. "Distracted by what? Naked women?"

The other members of their team, detectives Dominic Gilliam and Lester Royo, laughed.

One side of Mackey's mouth inched upward. "I was referring to Xavier King. But now that you've brought it up, it's not like you wouldn't be the first to start pitching for the other team."

"Go to hell," Cheryl spat out, before she could filter her response through the politically correct mechanism in her brain.

Instead of getting angrier, she seemed to have tickled Mackey's funny bone. His laughter was quick and genuine. "Calm down, Detective Grier. It was just a question."

Eyes narrowed, Cheryl leaned back in her chair and unloaded a barrage of invisible AK-47 bullets at the center of Mackey's forehead.

He smiled and then turned his attention to Detective Royo. "Any chance your informant got this one wrong?"

Royo tossed up his hands. "We've talked to him several times and he's pretty adamant about his claims."

"They usually are when they're trying to negotiate for a shorter sentence," Cheryl tossed out.

Despite her snippiness, Mackey mulled her words over. "Look, I only have a limited amount of time and resources for this investigation. In order to justify it, you're going to have to bring me something. That's just the bottom line. My bosses only respond to results—something to let us know that we're even in the right ballpark. Got it?"

All the officers in the room nodded and rededicated themselves to the case before being dismissed. The moment

Cheryl climbed to her feet, but before she could make it out of the room, Mackey called out.

"Detective Grier, I need a word with you."

She stopped and turned around.

Johnnie pulled up by her side.

"*Just* Detective Grier," he clarified.

Johnnie glanced over at Cheryl with an apologetic look before turning and walking out of the room.

Pulling in a deep breath, Cheryl coaxed herself to remain calm, despite knowing that it might be next to impossible.

"Close the door," Mackey said, taking a seat in one of the now-empty chairs and crossing his arms.

Cheryl had to pull in another deep breath as she turned to do as she had been instructed and then stuffed her hands into the pockets of her jacket. "All right. What is this all about?"

"Well, right now, I'm trying to think of a reason why I shouldn't write you up for insubordination," he started. "Telling your superior officer to go to hell?"

Cheryl simmered and folded her arms while she upgraded her imaginary machine gun to a rocket launcher.

"Can you think of a reason why I shouldn't?"

"How about you just go ahead and do what you feel you need to do," she said as calmly as she could. But there was no way she could mask the venom in her voice.

Again, Mackey seemed to get his rocks off irritating her. "What if I said that there was something you could *do* to talk me out of writing you up and having it in your *permanent* record?"

"Are you stupid enough to actually believe that just because we slept together once you can't be slapped with a sexual harassment suit?"

"What are you talking about?" he asked, confused. "I'm talking about your outrageous behavior this morning. You know, where there were a few witnesses to."

"Uh-huh." She crammed her hands back into her pockets. "So you're going to write me up. Got it. Can I go now?"

Mackey laughed. "What is it with you? Do you hate me *that* much?"

"I plead the fifth."

"C'mon. This isn't a court of law. You can talk to me. Tell me how you feel."

"And just confess all my hopes and dreams while I'm at it?"

"If you like." He chuckled.

"Mackey…let it go. It's over. *We're* over. So you can just stop trying to bait me into arguments in front of the squad. You can stop with the endless harassment about writing me up over bullshit, too. We're through. Over. Finished. We're never getting back together. You got that?"

Mackey nodded. "I'll make sure I'll have that written and ready for you to sign tomorrow."

Cheryl rolled her eyes. "Whatever. May I go now?"

"Absolutely. We're through here."

"Exactly," she retorted. Turning, she jerked open the door and marched out. Clearly, Mackey was a mistake that she was going to regret for the rest of her life.

"What did he want?" Johnnie asked the moment she stormed back into the detectives' area.

"To get under my skin," she answered, blazing past her partner's desk.

Johnnie jumped up, grabbed her purse and raced after Cheryl. "I'd say by the way you stormed through here that he's done an excellent job of doing just that."

"And I'd say that you are right. Then again, you usually are." Cheryl pushed open the front doors to the precinct and continued her mad dash to her car.

"So where are you going now?" Johnnie asked, struggling to catch up.

"Over to federal. I want to talk to Royo's informant myself. Maybe there's something we're missing on this one."

"What? You know it's not a good idea to intercede with another cop's informant. You can jeopardize the trust between him and his snitch."

"I'm not interested in jeopardizing anyone's trust. I just want to get a sense of whether this guy is for real or not. Because, I gotta tell you, I feel like we're barking up the wrong tree. Mackey has the FBI involved and all his hopes are on making some big bust that makes national news, and all we really have is a bunch of hearsay from some guy who could be getting his rocks off by sending the police on some wild-goose chase."

"Damn." Johnnie stopped walking.

Reaching her car door, Cheryl glanced back at her partner. "What?"

"That man got you fiendin' that hard?"

"What the hell are you talking about?"

Johnnie settled her hands on her hips. "Don't front. Xavier King."

"Oh, please. Don't you start that BS with me, too." She shoved her key into the car door lock. "There's nothing going on between me and the damn owner." She snatched open the door. "But I'm so happy to see that everyone has soooo much faith in me."

Johnnie dislodged herself from the center of the police parking lot and waltzed over to the passenger side of Cheryl's car. "What now?"

"Let's talk over breakfast. I'm starved," she said, climbing inside.

Cheryl considered whether she wanted to debate the issue with Johnnie or not, but decided on starting the car and driving them to the nearest International House of Pancakes.

* * *

"So talk," Johnnie said after they settled into their booth and their waitress had walked away. "I was hoping that you could tell me what's going on."

She tossed up her hands. "Nothing! I just want to hurry this whole damn case up so that maybe I can get that asshole off my back…and you."

"And that's it?"

"You don't think that's enough?"

Johnnie shrugged and eased back in her chair. "Mackey rides everyone's last nerve. Why should you be any different?"

"C'mon. You heard him in that meeting. He damn near accused me of sleeping with Xavier King. Why? I'm hardly around the man. I pour drinks. I keep my eyes and ears open—and that's it. I haven't done anything that even hints that I should be put on such a short leash. Oh, other than lose my mind one time and sleep with him."

Johnnie snickered.

"And don't you start in with that 'I told you so' crap right now. I'm not in the mood."

She held up her hands in surrender. "I didn't say nothin'."

"I don't know where all this is suddenly coming from with Mackey. Our thing was years ago. I've had other boyfriends since then. I'm sure he's been with someone else since then, too. Why all of a sudden is he riding me about Xavier King?"

"Someone said my name?"

Cheryl jumped before her gaze shifted to Xavier's sudden appearance at her table. "Mr. King." She blinked—her mind a blank slate.

"That is my name." His smile widened before he shifted his attention to Johnnie. "Well, hello."

Johnnie's mouth fell open and she seemed incapable of speech.

"Um, this here's my, um, *best friend,* Johnnie…Smith."

"Hello. Xavier King, aka your friend's boss over at The Dollhouse." He offered Johnnie his hand.

Moving like she was in some kind of trance, Johnnie slipped her hand into Xavier's. "How do you do?" she asked dreamily.

"I'm doing great," Xavier said, amused.

Cheryl frowned and then leaned forward to wave a hand in front of her girl's face. "Hello?"

"Hmm?" Johnnie's eyes shifted to her partner.

Cheryl gave her a look that clearly said, *What in the hell is wrong with you?*

As if a light switch had been turned on, Johnnie straightened up in her chair. "Oh. Yeah. Um." She snatched her hand out of Xavier's while her entire face darkened with embarrassment.

"So," Xavier said, drawing in a deep breath while his gaze shifted back and forth between the two of them. "I certainly didn't mean to interrupt you. But when I heard my name mentioned, I wanted to make sure that you were telling your friend nothing but good things about me. At least, I hope."

*Did I say anything damaging?* "Actually, I was just… telling her how well things were working out for me at the club. The, uh, flexible hours are really helping me with my class schedule."

"Glad to hear it. I'm sure if you're half as good a doctor as you are a bartender, then you're probably going to discover the cure for cancer."

Cheryl forced a smile. For some reason it bothered her to be lying to this man. "So, what brings you here?" she asked, looking around.

"Breakfast," he answered simply, and then glanced at his watch. "I'm supposed to be meeting Quentin, but clearly mornings are still a challenge for him."

She laughed.

"Since I'm here, do you mind if I join you two?"

"No! Please do," Johnnie said, immediately scooting over on the bench so that he could sit down next to her.

Cheryl delivered a swift kick under the table.

"*Ow.* What was that for?"

Completely embarrassed, Cheryl slammed her eyes closed and then dropped her head into the palm of her hand. What happened to her calm, cool, collected partner?

Xavier chuckled. "It's no problem if you'd like to be left alone with your friend."

Just when Cheryl opened her mouth to respond, Quentin strolled up, wearing a pair of dark sunglasses and looking like he'd spent the night sleeping in the same clothes.

"Sorry I'm late, cuz. Wild night—wilder morning." He hitched up a half smile. "I even have the scars on my back to prove it."

Xavier rolled his eyes, but there was also an amused smirk hooking his lips.

Finally noticing the two women in the booth, Quentin snatched off his glasses and flashed his famous dimples. "Well, who do we have here for breakfast?"

Cheryl shook her head. *Did he ever turn off the charm?* "Hello, Quentin."

"Ah. It's the hot bartender and her *lovely* friend…?"

"Johnnie," her partner answered with her brows dipping in the center of her forehead as he made himself comfortable next to her.

Xavier grabbed his cousin by the arm. "Don't worry, we're leaving."

"What?" Quentin asked confused.

"Don't." Cheryl shook her head and added, "You don't have to go."

Quentin shrugged his arm out of his cousin's grip. "Yeah! See? We don't have to go."

"Are you sure?" Xavier asked.

"It's fine," Cheryl answered, forcing a smile and scooting over.

"All righty, then." Xavier made himself comfortable next to Cheryl and returned the smile.

Almost immediately, Cheryl's nerves started tingling because of his close proximity. If there was anything else that impressed her, it was the fact that Xavier didn't need some expensive cologne—subtle or otherwise—to seduce her. He smelled like fresh, clean Ivory soap.

They flashed each other smiles again before their waitress returned, poured the men coffee and took their orders.

"So....why are you two ladies up at this ungodly hour?" Q asked, turning his attention to his seatmate.

"It's 9:00 a.m.," Johnnie replied.

"Don't remind me," Q complained. "Seems like I'm related to a bunch of early birds. Between my cousin here and my brothers, who like to get up at the booty-crack of dawn, I'm really starting to think that I'm adopted."

"You'd like that," Xavier said.

"Only because it would explain *sooooo* much."

The men laughed.

"So how long have you two been best buds?" Xavier asked.

Cheryl and Johnnie glanced at each other to see who should answer or rather, invent a lie. Johnnie gave her the nod, so Cheryl put her spin on it. "We've, uh, been friends since, huh, high school, actually. Home room—freshman year...sat next to each other."

"Ah. I guess that means you got the 4-1-1 on some major secrets on Ms. Shepherd?" Xavier asked Johnnie.

"Nothing I can repeat and live to see another day," Johnnie volleyed back.

"I guess that means that I'll just have to figure out a way to get the information from the source."

"You can try, but you'll fail."

Xavier's eyes twinkled. "A challenge?"

"You can call it what you want," she said.

"Careful. You're talking to a man who loves challenges."

The way his eyes looked at her, it was a struggle to keep air in her lungs, never mind stop her heart from pounding out of her chest. Somehow she feigned a confidence she didn't really feel. "I'm sure I can handle anything you toss my way."

Across the table, Quentin chuckled. "Did that sound dirty to anybody other than me?" He glanced at Johnnie. "Are you as dirty as your friend?"

Johnnie flushed.

Cheryl could tell that his dangerous dimples were starting to work on her partner. *And after all the crap she gives me?*

Their breakfast arrived and Cheryl couldn't wait to dive in. If her mouth was full, then she wouldn't have to say much. And the faster she inhaled her meal, the faster they could leave. Liking that idea, she grabbed her fork and proceeded to start shoveling food as fast as she could, so fast that from the corner of her eye, she saw Xavier staring and leaning away from her.

"Damn." Q lifted his sunglasses up and stared, too. "You know, the food is already dead. It's not going anywhere."

This time Johnnie delivered a quick kick to Cheryl's shin and she blurted out an "Ow." Or something close to it with a mouthful of food.

"Forgive her," Johnnie said. "It's a bad habit of hers—imitating a pig when she's eating."

"It's okay," Xavier said, standing and picking up his plate. "I can take a hint. Q, let's go so we can leave these lovely ladies to eat their breakfast."

"Mghdph. Hqunl," Cheryl squeezed out through her stuffed mouth.

Xavier's brows crashed together. "Please. Don't talk with your mouth full." He started to walk off, but then snapped his fingers and stopped. "By the way, I've been meaning to ask whether you wanted to bartend at a private bachelor party this weekend. It's run through our Bachelors Adventures services. The gig pays a flat three thousand for the night."

"Mghdph. Zlee."

"What?"

Johnnie jumped in. "She said, 'You're kidding me.'"

Xavier's breathtaking smile returned. "The gig is yours if you want it."

Cheryl choked down a lump of pancakes. "I want it. Thanks."

"Not a problem." He glanced back over at Johnnie. "It was nice to meet you." With that he and Q strolled off to find a vacant booth.

The minute they were gone, Johnnie delivered another swift kick to Cheryl's shin.

"What the…?"

"What the hell is wrong with you?" She glanced around this time to make sure that no one was coming up behind her or listening. "How are you investigating someone you're pushing away?"

"Oh? Now I'm pushing him away. Thirty minutes ago you and Mackey were practically accusing me of *fucking* him."

"I don't recall using those words," she said defensively. "Though if you were, I can't say that I blame you—with either one of them. They're so damn hot I think my panties have melted off."

Cheryl smiled and shook her head.

"One thing for sure—" Johnnie picked up a strip of bacon. "He likes you."

"What? Please." Cheryl waved off the comment.

"No 'please' me. I have eyes. That man was looking at you like he'd finally found The One."

"Watch it. Your romantic side is showing."

"I'm just saying. It was as clear as the nose on your face. To tell you the truth, I'm jealous."

"Gee. Was that what all that drooling was about?"

Johnnie frowned. "I wasn't drooling."

"Are you kidding me? You damn near put Niagara Falls to shame. 'How do you do?'" Cheryl rolled her eyes. "Pathetic."

"Whatever. If he was looking at me like I was a T-bone steak dripping with A1 Sauce like he was doing you a few minutes ago, chile, please. We would've given everybody up in here a show they'd never forget."

"I thought I was the one with the man problem," Cheryl reminded her.

"Shoot. Your butt must be contagious, then."

They laughed, knowing that they were just joking. They took their jobs seriously and they would never do anything intentionally to jeopardize them.

"But seriously," Cheryl said, sobering and leaning over the table. "What about that bachelor party?" Johnnie met her gaze and Cheryl instantly knew that they were on the same wavelength. "What if the drugs are being trafficked through someone working through Bachelors Adventures and not necessarily the club itself?"

Cheryl started ticking off the benefits on her hand. "It's mobile. Affluent clientele. Likely a smaller crew. It's perfect."

"Well, who books the parties?" Johnnie asked.

"No clue." Her gaze skittered across the restaurant to the cousins' table. Xavier looked up and caught her eye. "For all I know it could be Xavier himself."

Johnnie glanced over her shoulder at the men, too, and then back at her partner. "What's your cop's instinct telling you this time?"

Cheryl's gaze shifted back to her partner. "The only thing my instincts tell me about Xavier King is *run.*"

# *Chapter 8*

The following Saturday night, The Dollhouse was approaching a first—having to turn customers away. The word of mouth about the club's new renovations and elaborate exotic-dance shows had spread around Atlanta like brushfire. So much so that Xavier spent most of the week hiring more dancers, waitresses *and* bouncers. Ricky had been right. Dog Pound certainly did come in handy. He might not have been much of a boxer, but he could definitely lift some heavy dudes and toss them out when they got out of line. Just last night, he'd hauled one drunken patron who had to have been at least four hundred pounds, bare minimum, and threw him out the back door as if he were a lightweight.

Xavier was excited about tonight's bachelor party. The price tag for this one came in just under mid six figures and was for a young rap artist, Mad Monez. Xavier had never heard of him, but when he saw the over-the-top production the artist wanted to pull off for the cameras of BET, the only thing he wanted to make sure of was that the check would clear. After that, he welcomed the publicity of hosting such an event. However, while he was getting ready in his office, there was only one thing on his mind.

"I'm telling you that the girl can't stand me," Xavier confessed. "Three times I've tried to hook up with this girl and three times I ended up with egg on my face."

"Wait a minute. Wait a minute. I need a second." Quentin held up his hand while he tried to catch his breath in between peals of laughter. In fact, he hadn't stopped laughing since Xavier had started this damn story, and judging by all the shaking and trembling that he was doing, he wasn't about to stop anytime soon.

"I don't know why I bother to tell you anything," Xavier huffed, waving his cousin off and then turning back toward the mirror in his private bathroom.

"I like to think that you tell me these things because you know how much I'm in desperate need of a good laugh," Quentin said after coming up for air.

"Whatever."

"You mean to tell me that Cheryl Shepherd, our extremely *fine* bartender, flipped your big ass over in the parking lot. Do I have that right?"

Xavier ground his teeth together in annoyance.

"Damn. Have you gone that damn soft since you got out of the ring?"

"Like you could've done better," Xavier charged. "The moment you hit the concrete you would've cracked like Humpty Dumpty."

"Look. I'm a lover, not a fighter. Beside, *I'm* not an ex–Golden Gloves champion. I'm not the one that's used to making a living out of breaking brothers' faces. And I certainly wouldn't have gotten busted with a full woody in front of a crowd at the gym. Haven't you ever heard of a cup?"

"You know, when you came to me with your girl problems, I don't remember laughing at you."

"That was different," Quentin protested.

"How?" Xavier tossed up his hands. "I'm trying to tell you that I really like this girl, but she keeps treating me like I have the cooties or something. I'm surprised that when I look in the mirror I don't have acne and orthodontic retainer wires on my teeth. I'm looking for some help here. I've never been turned down this many times and certainly not by the same girl. I'm out of my realm. I'm asking you for help."

"Why? I'm not a loser. Three at bats and three strikeouts? That kind of help is above my pay grade."

"Thanks. Good to know." He tried to hold back his irritation, but he was sure that his so-called best friend could read him like a book.

"I don't know," Q said, shrugging. "There are other fish in the sea. That's the lesson that I'm trying to learn."

"By sleeping with *all* the fish?"

"How do you know what you like unless you try it?"

Xavier shook his head as he turned and strolled out of the private bathroom and back into his office. "You're not hearing me. I'm not interested in other fish. I'm interested in Cheryl Shepherd."

"Are you only interested because she's someone that you can't have?" Quentin challenged.

"Hmm." Xavier pretended to consider the question. "You know, one could ask the same question about you and your obsession with Alyssa."

Quentin stiffened. "I'm not obsessed."

"Right."

"And we're not talking about me. We're talking about you. What's with you Kings? You're always trying to flip the script on me."

"Fine. Sorry." Xavier acquiesced. "You're right."

Quentin's expression barely changed with the apology.

"All right. So answer the question. Are you *really* attracted to her or are you intrigued by the challenge she poses?"

Xavier dropped into his chair and thought about it. "I don't know. I'm certainly attracted to her…and maybe there's something about the challenge she presents. At this point, it's about fifty-fifty. That's not totally insane, is it?"

"No. Insane is when you start talking to people who aren't there."

Xavier frowned. "Come again?"

Quentin shook his head. "Nothing. Forget about it."

Xavier stared at his cousin for a moment, but then let the odd comment go. "Look. I have to go." He glanced at his watch and then popped back out of the chair. "You gonna come with or are you going to hang here at the club tonight?"

"Are you kidding? I'ma come with. Nobody throws a party like these barely legal rap stars. How old would you say this dude is?"

"Twenty-two."

"And he's getting married?" Q shook his head. "I'll give it six months."

Xavier frowned. "You're such a romantic."

"I'm a realist. Besides, it's a celebrity marriage. They tend to think marriage is what you do before you start dating."

Xavier laughed as he grabbed his car keys. "Let's roll out."

Cheryl had no problems finding her way to the multimillion-dollar home in the Atlanta suburb of Alpharetta for Mad Monez's bachelor party. Once she was within a mile of his home, she could hear the music bumping. When she pulled up to the wrought-iron gate, a security guard frowned at her shaking and rattling Ford Taurus. *Of all the days for this car to start acting up.*

"Name?" the guard asked, waving his hand in front of her face to clear some of the smoke coming out of her tailpipe.

"Cheryl Shepherd. I'm with The Dollhouse crew."

He quickly flipped to another page and found her name on the list. "Go on in."

Embarrassed, Cheryl shook her head and drove in when the gate swung open. She just hoped that detectives Royo and Gilliam were going to be able to crash the party tonight so that she could have a few extra pairs of eyes covering this place. But as she drove through, she witnessed just how tight the security was so she had her doubts.

Once she parked, she picked up her cell and called her partner. "I'm in."

"All right. Be careful and keep your eyes and ears open."

"Any word on Royo and Gilliam?"

"They claim that they're still working on an invite."

"Cool. I'll check in with you later." She disconnected the call.

When Cheryl opened her car door, she was nearly blown away by the hard pounding beats pouring out of the speakers. There was a whole caravan of entertainment media: BET, MTV, *Entertainment Tonight*, *E!* and even a few people from the local media. This Mad Monez must be Mr. Big-Time, she surmised. Frankly, it had been a long time since she'd paid attention to who was hot and was not in the music industry. Truth be told, it all sounded the same to her.

But one thing's for sure, The Dollhouse as well as Bachelors Adventures was getting some major publicity from this party. Along with the scantily clad Dolls from the club, the place was packed with video vixens, gold-digging divas and highly suspect-looking hookers.

*This is definitely going to be an interesting night.*

She was more than prepared to suck up and do her damn job. But by the time she made it to the bar that she was going to be working at, there was already a cluster of brothers who looked like the usual entourage that surrounds celebrities. All of them were grinning and throwing out their best lines at whatever woman would stand still long enough to hear them.

One dude in particular stood out, mostly because he was the loudest. "Yeah, yeah. Me and Mad Monez, we go way the hell back. I mean, like diapers and playpens. You feel me?"

Judging by the way the girl he'd managed to corner was side-eyeing him, Cheryl guessed that she *wasn't* feeling him at all.

"You know. If you play your cards right, I might be able to hook you up with my man. Nah-what-I-mean? Of course, you know that means I have to sample whatever you're offering up first. You know, so I can see if you're a five-star chick like I think you are." He grabbed his crotch and laughed.

Both Cheryl and his *five-star* chick rolled their eyes.

"My girl Pumpkin said that you were just the tour-bus driver," the woman shot back.

"Yeah, so? My boy hooked me up with a job. Good looking out. You feel me?"

"She also said that you just met Mad Monez two weeks ago."

That had him stuck.

Cheryl snickered as she made drinks for the other guests rolling up to the bar. By the time she looked back down the bar at the busted bus driver, the five-star chick was tossing her drink straight into dude's face.

"Dismissed," she said, and sat the glass down.

"Would you like another?" Cheryl asked the girl.

"No. I'm through here." The chick walked off.

"A'ight. You had your chance," the bus driver said, grabbing a stack of napkins and wiping himself down. "You'll be back. Mad Monez is going to take one look at those buck knees and fling you back into the sea."

*And you'll still be holding up the bar.*

Unfortunately, Mr. Bus Driver turned his attention toward Cheryl. "Yo, shawty. I'll have a Seven and Seven."

*Shawty?* "Coming right up," she told him, and grabbed the bottle of Seagram's.

For some reason, he took her answer as an invitation to start tossing his weak mack game at her. "Whoa, shawty. How did you get all of that in those jeans?"

Cheryl smiled even though she wanted to hit him with a side-eye herself.

"You're thick as hell. How come you ain't one of these dancers trying to get paid?"

"I'm cool where I'm at. Thanks." She set his drink down in front of him and then moved on to the next brother that rolled up to the bar.

"Humph. Humph," the bus driver said, shaking his head. "I *know* I can get you on Mad Monez's next video. You'll be a star. For real."

Cheryl's eyes threatened to roll out the back of her head. "Really. I'm good."

"No. What you are is fine," he said, rolling his beady-eyed gaze over her body. "I'm telling you that the camera would love you."

Cheryl ignored him and again moved to make the next drink. But a couple of seconds later, Mr. Bus Driver yelled above the loud music, "You got a man?"

*This is going to be a long night.* "Yes! I have a man," she lied, hoping that would just shut him down.

Two more guests stepped up to the bar. They each had two women tucked under their arms. "Nuvos for the ladies," one of them ordered.

"Coming right up."

"Yo, shawty. Is your man here tonight?"

Cheryl's hands flew to grab the glasses and bottles and poured the round of drinks ready in less than ten seconds.

"Damn, girl. You got skills, don't you?"

Cheryl collected her tips and kept her smile elevated at the right angles. What she wanted to do more than anything was bust a bottle over dude's head if he didn't shut up soon.

"Yo, shawty. You didn't tell me where your man at. Is he here tonight? Because if he isn't, then what he doesn't know won't hurt him. Nah-what-I-mean?"

"Look. I'm working," she told him. "If you want another drink, then I can get that for you."

"What are you going to do after your shift?"

"I'm going home to my man," she said, folding her arms.

"Oh. Is that right?" Xavier's deep baritone floated from behind her.

Cheryl jumped and spun around.

"Well, that explains a lot," he said, smiling.

"Oh, hey...baby," Cheryl cooed.

Xavier's brows crashed together over his eyes while confusion shone in his eyes. "I just came over to make sure that you were all set up and..." He glanced over Cheryl's shoulder to the dude hugging the bar. "You all right?"

"Everything is great."

"Good. Good." He still stared at her as though if he tried hard enough he would be able to read her mind. "Well...Q and I are floating around. You can grab one of us if you need any help with anything."

"Cool. I'll keep that in mind."

"Yeah. Don't worry," the grinning man at the bar cheesed. "*I'll* take good care of her."

"Is he—?"

Cheryl kissed him. Without thinking or processing what she was doing through the rational part of her brain. The reaction of her body felt like a nuclear meltdown. From the moment her lips landed on his, reason and reality fled. All her life, she had heard and read in fairy tales about how there would be magic and fireworks exploding in one's head when they finally kissed The One. Who hadn't laughed at that?

So why was it happening now?

Heat—a scorching heat—blazed through her body, yet it didn't burn. If anything, it felt wonderful. Parts of her body that she had long forgotten about sighed in relief. Like a drowning victim finally breaking through icy waters for air.

It was supposed to be a brief kiss. But before she knew it, she was leaning into his hard, chiseled frame for support and ignoring her lungs that were begging for oxygen. It was either that or fall at his feet. She didn't even come to her senses when he wrapped his arm around her body and pressed her even closer.

Cheryl felt every inch of him, above his waist as well as below it. Quite simply, she was lost—lost in her head and her emotions, which felt an unbelievably heightened sense of awareness. Just the taste of him was sweet with a hint of spice. And the way his tongue boldly explored her open mouth made her nipples hard and her clit thrum with a growing need.

Was she wrong for fantasizing about him laying her on this bar and having his way with her? Hell, at that moment, she didn't even care if the camera captured it all for public viewing. It made no sense. And if it wasn't for Xavier pulling back a little to nibble on the lining of her lips, she would have never breathed in the oxygen needed to allow reality to seep through.

Cheryl's eyes fluttered open and the cogs in her brain started to churn once again. She pushed back against his chest and forced the muscles in her legs not to atrophy.

Staring at each other, they wore the same confused look. *What in the hell was that?*

"Damn, y'all. I thought you guys were just going to inhale each other," Mr. Bus Driver said before getting up and turning away from the bar. "Get a room before you get her pregnant in front of everybody."

"I'm, uh—" *Should she apologize for that kiss?*

Xavier was equally lost for words. "Yeah. That was, um, interesting."

Cheryl lifted an inquisitive brow. "Interesting?"

"Nice," he corrected, smiling. "It was very, very nice."

She felt the heat rise again and she took another step back, hoping that would help clear her head. It didn't really. *Pull yourself together.*

"Well." Xavier clapped his hands together and then looked around the bar. "I see that you pretty much got everything under control."

"Yes!" She seized on the opportunity to change the subject and retain some shred of dignity. "I'm good to go over here."

Xavier took a step backward. "But if you need anything…"

"Yeah…I'll holler for you." Cheryl winked and shot her hand like a gun.

"All right." He took another step. "Then I'll just leave you to it." He turned around and ran straight into Quentin. "Ooof!"

Q twisted his face. "I see what you mean. She *really* can't stand you." He delivered a hard slap across his back and shook his head. "I can't believe that you almost had me feeling sorry for you."

Xavier rolled his eyes. "C'mon, let's go."

Cheryl's head didn't clear until the men had left and then she just slapped her hand across her forehead and chastised herself. "Stupid. Stupid. Stupid." Before the inevitable internal questions came, she received a stream of new drink orders. That occupied her mind for a few minutes.

The later the hour, the wilder the party got. However, the highlight of the evening came close to midnight when Cheryl got her first glimpse of the man of the hour. By then her expectations were high solely based on the rapper's posse bragging about all the record sales Mad Monez had been breaking since he had come onto the scene. There was plenty of talk about him becoming the next R&B mogul who was going to be expanding his empire into fashion, fragrances, cars and jewelry. However, when Mad Monez strolled by the bar with one video vixen and one gold digger tucked under his arm, Cheryl had to do a double take at the four-foot-ten megastar.

She frowned and had almost managed to convince herself that she was probably looking at the dude's teenage nephew or something.

No.

That was him.

Keeping her smile, she fought her instincts not to ask for ID when he ordered a rum and Coke. "Coming right up," she said.

"Wow." Mad Monez tilted down his sunglasses just enough so that he could peek over the rim. "What's your name, mama?"

*Here we go again.* "Cheryl," she answered, smiling and setting the drink down.

"You know what? I think I'd like to change my order."

"Oh? What would you like?"

"You buck naked with a bottle of baby oil, lying across my bed."

"I don't think that your fiancée would care too much for that," she volleyed in a lame attempt to remind him that he was getting married in the morning.

"Hell, she can join us." He looked around the room. "We can ask her. She's around here somewhere."

"Your fiancée is at your bachelor party?"

"Hell, yeah. And she's going to be the star of the show."

*I see this marriage isn't going to last.*

Mad Monez turned his attention back to Cheryl. "So what do you say?"

"Thanks—but I got a man."

The young rapper pushed up his glasses. "I didn't ask you all that. And what does your man have to do with me?"

Cheryl laughed. These young guys were all the same.

Mad Monez folded his arms and leaned over the bar. "I'm serious, li'l mama. Like the great 50 Cent says, 'Have a baby by me and become a millionaire.'"

She continued to laugh. "Does that line really work?"

"Like clockwork. I have six babies and four baby mamas."

*And how old are you again?*

"I promise you," Mad Monez carried on. "If you know how to work all that good junk in your trunk, I'll buy you a house *tonight*."

"Tempting, but I think that I'm going to stick with my man." She winked. "Now can I get you something else…to drink?"

"Humph. Humph. Humph. And you're faithful, too? Ain't that just my luck?" He smiled and winked back at her before slapping a hundred-dollar bill on the bar counter. "Here you go, mama. You earned that. But if you change your mind…?"

"I'm flattered," she said, and then watched him stroll off. The women flanking his sides frowned at her like she'd lost her damn mind.

Shaking her head, she shoved the hundred-dollar bill into her tip jar and went back to sloshing out drinks and dodging pickup lines. In truth, that was pretty much what happened nightly at The Dollhouse, too.

When the Dolls started their late, late show a few minutes later, all eyes zoomed in on them. As usual the girl's choreography was tight and they looked amazing when they dipped it low, backed it up and clapped hands free.

Through it all, Mad Monez looked like he was in hog heaven, especially when Diamond took center stage and started performing. It wasn't until the end of the slow, seductive song, which had even Cheryl blushing, did she hear whispers about Diamond being the bride-to-be.

*Great. A rapper and a stripper. Who didn't see that coming?*

"Now, that's a lucky son of a bitch," one dude at the bar said in all seriousness.

"I heard that," the man's sidekick said. "Heard that she's going to be hitting the road with us, too."

"Aw. Damn," the first dude complained, shaking his head. "The beginning of the end. First thing wives do is ban the groupies from the tour buses."

Cheryl snickered and shook her head.

"Heeeey. Don't I know you?" a man at the other end of the bar asked.

Cheryl glanced up and then blood in her veins froze. "I don't think so."

Kendrick Hodges nodded. "You look familiar to me."

She shook her head, though she remembered arresting Kendrick for breaking and entering last summer clearly. "Not ringing any bells," she said. "Do you go to Emory University?"

Kendrick's face collapsed. "What?"

"I'm in school there," she told him.

"Nah. I don't go to no damn university," he said, waving her off, but his gaze kept sneaking back over at her. "But I swear that you could pass for this one chick's twin."

"Oh? They say everybody's got one."

Kendrick bobbed his head while his eyes feasted on her hind side. "It ain't like me to forget a…face." He snickered.

*Asshole.*

"Anyway, I'll have bourbon on the rocks."

"Coming right up." She grabbed a bottle and flipped it behind her back, more to convince him that she was nothing more than a simple bartender. However, when she sat his drink down, his hand snaked out and grabbed her by the wrist and held firm. "Ow. Let go."

His grip tightened. "I swear I know you."

"Like I said. Unless you go to Emory…or hang out at The Dollhouse, I don't know where I would've bumped into you." She tried to tug her hand away.

Kendrick held firm.

"Is everything all right over here?" Xavier asked, stepping behind the bar, watching Cheryl and Kendrick's stalemate.

She tugged.

Kendrick glanced over at Xavier and finally released her. "Everything is just peachy keen," he said, smiling.

Xavier cut a look over at Cheryl and waited for her answer.

"Like he said, everything is cool."

Xavier looked far from being convinced and he didn't look like he was in any hurry to leave, either. "So what's been going on with you, Kendrick?"

"Same ole. Same ole, man."

"You know, now that the club is back open there is always a spot for you."

Kendrick shook his head. "Nah. I've decided to go into business for myself. Sort of like you and your brothers."

A few drink orders came in and Cheryl went back to work while pretending not to listen to their conversation, though she suspected that Kendrick knew the truth.

"So what kind of business are you in?" Xavier asked.

"You know me. I'm a jack-of-all-trades."

"That I do."

"I'm even the one who hooked you up for *this* gig."

That clearly came as a surprise to Xavier. "Is that right? Well, thanks, man. I really appreciate that."

"Well, our differences aside, you and your brothers know how to throw one hell of a party." Kendrick glanced back over at Cheryl. "Not to mention that you seem to find all the beautiful women, too."

They shared a laugh.

Xavier leaned against the countertop. "And have you seen about your old man?"

"Can't say that I have," Kendrick said, dropping his gaze. "But I'm sure I'll make it over that way soon. You?"

"Actually, yeah. I've been hitting the gym again these past few weeks."

Kendrick's lips hitched upward. "Really? Thinking about getting back into the ring?"

"Nah. Those days are well behind me."

"Are you sure? You look like you're in tip-top shape to me."

"Well, looks can be deceiving," Xavier said with a note of sadness.

"You don't have to tell me twice." Kendrick's gaze crept back over to Cheryl, but she was making sure that she kept looking busy.

"I'm sure that disappointed the old man," he said, but flashed his first genuine smile. Clearly, he and his old man didn't get along that well.

"You should get over there. I'm sure that Ricky would love to see you."

"Ah." Kendrick glanced at his watch. "That sure didn't take long."

"What?"

"You and my old man." He shook his head. "Sometimes I think you forget that he's my father. Not yours."

"I know that," Xavier said defensively.

"Do you? You know, sometimes I wonder because all while I was growing up, all my old man could ever talk about was you. How much potential you had and how far you were going to go. How hard you trained." Kendrick shook his head. "Nah. He was more your dad than he ever was mine."

Xavier stared at him. "Sorry. I never knew that you felt like that."

Kendrick shrugged and then tried to put a smile back on his face. "It's all good. And it's in the past, too. Right?"

"Right." Xavier nodded, but his expression held lingering doubts. "He would still like to see you."

"Did he tell you that?"

Xavier paused and that brief silence said everything.

"Yeah. Well..." Kendrick picked up his drink and started to back away. "I'm sure that I'll make it out there sooner or later. I'll catch up with you." His gaze swung back over Cheryl and he caught her listening. "Later."

She just smiled and hoped that he bought her story.

Once Kendrick disappeared into the crowd, Xavier exhaled.

"Former employee?"

"Yeah. And the son of a good friend of mine. He got in a little trouble a while back. I just wish..." He drew in another deep breath and shook his head.

Cheryl frowned. "What?"

He continued to shake his head. "Have you ever had to just stand back and watch someone make all the wrong choices because...they just wouldn't listen?"

"More times than I can count," she answered honestly. "It's not easy."

Xavier glanced off to where Kendrick had disappeared. "No. It's not."

There was more there, lying just under the surface, Cheryl realized. But there was no way for her to get at it right now. Luckily, their awkward moment came to an end when she was hit with another rush of drink orders. So much, in fact, that Xavier had to pitch in. With his help the rush only lasted twenty minutes. When it was over, Xavier and Cheryl glanced over at each other and smiled...until the memory of the kiss bubbled to the surface. The same heat and ache surged through her and, like some addict, she started trembling with an overwhelming desire to be swept back into his arms like one of those women on the cover of a romance novel.

She didn't have to ask whether he was thinking the same thing. It was written clearly in his dark eyes, just as she was sure that it was written in hers. This time, she saved herself by turning away before she was too deep into his spell.

"Right," Xavier said. "I better go and check on some of the other girls."

She nodded and was relieved to see him go.

It was near four in the morning before Xavier gave most of The Dollhouse crew the okay to leave, while passing out their pay in white envelopes. The Dolls left hours ago, but the service crew lagged behind. It didn't mean that the bachelor party was over. It wasn't.

Mad Monez and his crew were now plugged in out on the deck and performing some of the new material that he'd been working on in the studio. The crowd had dwindled to half its size, but people were still dancing, drinking and blowing trees. Most of the media outlets were gone. But BET and MTV were hanging steady.

Cheryl hung out for a little while, listening to Mad Monez's hard lyrics. To her surprise, he was extremely talented. It was clear why and how Mad Monez made mad money. As for catching sight of any drugs being trafficked at the place, she didn't have a definite yes or no. But she was curious about the stream of people going up and down the stairs.

Now that she was off the clock, this was as good a time as any to go check things out. Armed with the convenient excuse of looking for a bathroom, she turned from the outside deck and threaded her way through the crowd and headed upstairs.

Kendrick turned and followed.

# *Chapter 9*

Xavier couldn't stop thinking about that kiss. How could he? He'd never felt or tasted anything like it before in his life—and he'd had his fair share of kisses in his time. Even now when he was trying to describe the feeling to himself, he couldn't find the appropriate words to capture it. *Maybe you just imagined the fireworks.*

Of course he imagined it. There were no real physical fireworks being shot off in his head. That was ridiculous. He wouldn't have a head right now. *What about that heat wave?* He rolled that around in his mind for a little while as Mad Monez jumped around, grabbed his crotch and even danced with his future ex-wife. In the end, the heat had to have been part of his imagination, too. Since when does something hot feel good? Usually, that would be just cause to go to a clinic for a shot or a pill.

But there was definitely something *there* there.

So much so that his need to do it again, the craving,

bordered on being an obsession. Partly because it felt good, but also to prove to himself that he hadn't imagined it.

*But you just said that you imagined it.*

He paused and then shook all of that out of his head because it was confusing him. But the memory of that kiss refused to budge. He decided that it was time for him to leave. He turned to leave the deck with the intention of finding Quentin and whatever situation he'd managed to get himself into and then roll out. As he maneuvered his way through the crowd, he caught a glimpse of Cheryl heading in the same direction. He played with the idea of luring her to a private corner somewhere so he could coax another kiss out of her, but his track record with her made him reconsider. In all likelihood, that one kiss was all he was ever going to have to remember her by.

"Nice party, man!"

Xavier turned in time to see megaproducer Tygger Johnson strolling over with his high five hanging. "Thanks, man." They slapped palms and shoulder-bumped each other in greeting.

"I'm going to recommend you to my whole crew, dog. You really know how to set things off."

"Thanks, Tygger. I appreciate that. Love your music, man." There was another shoulder-bump and they parted ways while still grinning.

"You're the man," a couple of brothers hollered out to him while cocking and shooting their finger guns at him.

Xavier smiled and nodded, feeling like the MVP of a championship game. A couple of hours later, the cleanup crew would arrive and put the entire house back in order. Given the sheer size of the place, it would likely be an all-day job. While he mused, he spotted Kendrick from the corner of his eyes, quietly but stealthily heading up the stairs. His hackles jumped, and yet he didn't understand why they were tingling.

He stopped, looked around and tried to figure out what was wrong or missing from this situation. When he came up empty, his anxiety only increased. Turning, he headed for the staircase. Who knows, maybe Quentin was upstairs. Now that he thought about it, there was a high probability since that's where the bedrooms were. And where there were beds and women—that is where one would find Quentin.

Resolute, Xavier climbed the staircase, his sixth sense going crazy.

There were so many rooms upstairs that Cheryl didn't know which one she should try first. First off, it was just as loud up there as it was outside. Mad Monez was really getting his money's worth out of his speakers. *Better hurry and make this quick.* The best way to tackle this path was just to start opening doors. The first four were dark, but far from empty.

Springs were squeaking, headboards were banging and the men and women were competing on who could moan and groan the loudest. Those rooms Cheryl backed out of as fast as she could. At one room, she was actually issued an invitation to join in.

"No, thank you," she replied sheepishly. "You guys seem to be doing well without me," she joked, and rushed back out of the room.

But then a door opened all the way in the back of the hallway and an extremely thin woman stumbled out. Her inability to walk a straight line had her constantly zigzagging back and forth, crashing into one wall after another.

*Bingo.*

Cheryl headed down the hallway, stopping briefly to ask the wobbly girl if she was all right.

"Giiiirrrl, this is a great party." She erupted into giggles and started rubbing her nose.

"Can I help you with anything?"

"No. No. I'm good." She grinned with her eyes closed. "Better than good."

Cheryl lowered her voice. "What's back there? Anything I can get a taste of?"

"Honey, when I tell you that they got the best—"

"Is there a problem?" a voice thundered behind Cheryl.

She jumped and spun to see Kendrick standing there, looking like something that just sprung up out of the depths of hell. Cheryl swore that her heart had stopped for a moment. And for a full second, her mind had drawn a blank. "We were just talking," she said coolly.

"Is that right? Friends, are you?"

"No."

The woman next to Cheryl eased over to Kendrick and slid her hands around his neck. "Calm down, baby. She's cool."

Kendrick closed his eyes as if he was trying to get a hold of his temper. "Alicia, go and wait for me downstairs."

"But—"

"I said go!"

Alicia jumped.

"All right. Fine." Alicia frowned. Her good mood shot to hell and back. She cut Cheryl a nasty look as if she'd been the one to have messed up her high and then stormed off.

Kendrick turned back toward Cheryl, his lips sloping unevenly.

Cheryl prepared herself for anything.

Xavier reached the top of the staircase when he was almost bowled over by a woman who had to be ten pounds shy of a hundred. When he thought he caught the glimpse of tears, he reached out and grabbed her as gently as he could. "Sweetheart, are you all right?"

Clearly, the woman was just seconds from cursing him out. But when she got a good look at him, she stopped and a smile ballooned across her face. "Ooh. What's your name, handsome?" She brushed her hair back and then leaned her toothpick frame up against his body.

Xavier smiled, but stepped back. "I was just checking to make sure that you're all right, angel. I don't like seeing women cry."

She grabbed a lock of hair and then twirled it around her finger. "I can't think of a single thing a girl would be crying about when you're around," she said, moving forward again.

"That's a good line," Xavier said, winking.

"I have a million of them," she said. "Why don't we go somewhere and I can whisper a few more of them in your ear?"

"Tempting. But I'm going to have to take a rain check."

"All right. Don't take too long trying to cash it in." She teased. "It might bounce later."

"I'll keep that in mind." He winked and then continued onto the top landing. The moment he turned down the main hallway, his gaze zoomed in on the back of a tall figure.

"I asked you what the hell you were doing up here," the man hissed angrily.

Xavier didn't know what the hell was going on, but his senses and warning bells were going crazy and his feet were propelling forward before he could process why.

"I'm not going to ask you again!" The man turned to slam the woman up against the wall, his hand wrapped tight around her neck.

Screw thinking, Xavier just reacted. No doubt he took Kendrick by surprise when he grabbed him by *his* neck, lifted him up with one hand and slammed him against the opposite wall. His head hit first, but it *and* his shoulders made a deep indentation in the wall.

"What in the hell is going on?" he barked.

Behind him, Cheryl wrangled out a rough cough.

"Are you okay?" he asked from over his shoulder.

"Y-yes. I'm fine." She coughed some more.

Xavier's hand squeezed Kendrick's neck tighter. "I asked you a question!"

Kendrick pushed and pulled at Xavier's hand to no avail and no release.

Cheryl rushed up behind Xavier and grabbed his hand. "Let him go. It's all right. I'm not hurt."

*But what would have happened if it took me a second or a minute longer?* He cursed himself for that minute or two he'd wasted with that girl on the staircase.

Kendrick started turning purple, but try as he might, Xavier was having a hard time getting his hands to unclench.

"Xavier, *please,*" Cheryl begged. "You're going to kill him." When his hand started to tremble, she reached up and grabbed his face and forced him to look at her. "Xavier…let him go."

Their eyes connected.

"Let him go."

Another long second ticked by before Xavier finally relaxed his fingers.

Kendrick's gasps for air sounded painful to the ear. When he was released, he collapsed onto the floor. His gasping sounded worse with each inhalation.

Xavier took a threatening step forward. "If I *ever* see you around Cheryl again—"

Cheryl blocked his path. "It's okay. Calm down."

Wheezing, Kendrick pulled himself up from the floor and gave Xavier and Cheryl a menacing glare before half running and half lumbering down the hallway.

Cheryl tried to get Xavier to focus on her, but he refused to look at her again until Kendrick was out of sight.

"Are you *really* all right?" he asked in a low flat voice.

"I'm fine," she said, frowning at him. "What about you?"

Ignoring her question and not wanting to take her at her

word, Xavier reached over and tilted her chin to the left so that he could examine her neck.

Cheryl jerked her head away and stepped back. "You could've killed him," she accused.

"He could've *killed* you," he responded.

"I can take care of myself."

"I thought so, too, but clearly your little kung fu wasn't working for you tonight. Or was there some Houdini move you were saving for when he was finished tossing you around like a rag doll?"

"Don't be glib."

"Maybe I'll stop when you give me a simple thank-you."

"Fine. Thank you! Are you happy now?" she snapped.

"As a matter of fact, I am!"

They glared at each other and then together realized the absurdity of it all. Slowly, smiles crept across their faces and they both blurted at the same time, "I'm sorry."

"Jinx," Cheryl said, and then laughed. "Seriously, thank you. He was a lot faster than I anticipated."

"You're welcome," he said, and then glanced at her neck again. "May I?"

She hesitated, but then finally turned up her chin.

Gently, he ran his finger along the silky column of her neck, relieved to see that there was no immediate bruising. However, the moment he started stroking her soft skin, he had no desire to stop. So when she turned her head to meet his gaze, he felt it again. The mysterious heat gave off the most intoxicating sensation. Then there was this magnet. What else could it be that was pulling him toward Cheryl with such a force he couldn't break away?

That is…if he wanted to.

As their mouths inched closer, he expected her to become defensive and block him once he invaded her personal space. But she didn't.

At the first brush of her lips, Xavier was filled with

such elation that he didn't understand why his heart didn't explode. But what started as a soft breezy kiss soon morphed into something hungry and ferocious. Before either of them knew it, they were clinging to each other and seemingly unable to get close enough to feed what they both knew it was time to satisfy.

Not wanting to take the risk of either of them coming to their senses, Xavier reached down and swept the beautiful bartender up into his arms and took a chance, kicking in one of the bedroom doors. As luck would have it, the bed was empty.

# *Chapter 10*

Passion seized Cheryl with such force that she surrendered without even trying to put up a fight. Vaguely, she was aware of being picked up, a door being kicked in and slammed closed. But as long as Xavier's soft lips didn't break from hers, she really didn't give a damn. She was too caught up in the very taste of this man. Such passion had to have been the original forbidden fruit that felled Eve in the Garden of Eden, and here he was now seducing her, taking her down a road that she knew, even in her lustful state, would be her ruin—her career and as a woman.

Gently, Xavier pressed her against a mattress that was soft and firm at the same time. He broke their kiss and she moaned with soft disappointment. But in the next second, his wonderful mouth began raining kisses down her neck, particularly where Kendrick had manhandled her. The soreness she hadn't admitted to vanished under the slight brush of his lips. Her next moan was one of pure pleasure.

While his lips worked their magic across her neck and

collarbone, Cheryl's mind was spinning with a kaleidoscope of colors until she was dizzy. Xavier's strong hands pulled her T-shirt from the waistband of her jeans and then slid it over her body.

"My God," he groaned.

Cheryl's eyes fluttered open, and as her reward, she saw his magnificent chest illuminated by the silvery moonlight. Muscular and lean, he was the quintessential female fantasy come to life. For insurance, she kept running her hands along every ripple and bulge just to verify that she wasn't dreaming. *When had he removed his shirt?*

"You're so beautiful," he whispered while his dark, twinkling gaze roamed over every inch of her body.

"So are you," she whispered back, reaching out a hand and touching his chest. Her lips curled up into a smile the moment her fingers glided over what felt like silk. It seemed inconceivable for something to be that hard and soft at the same time. But there was so much about this moment that wasn't making much sense to her. Tomorrow, she promised herself, she would figure it all out.

*Tomorrow.*

Xavier eased onto his side and took his time running his hands down the center of her body. His smile widened when her taunt muscles jumped and quivered at his slightest touch.

She liked the way he looked at her. There was something sweet and erotic about it. Like he was trying to etch every detail about her into his mind while fantasizing about what he'd like to do first with her. Hell, her head was cluttered with quite a few ideas of her own.

Xavier walked his fingers down her hard abs and then circled around the button of her jeans. As if she was watching some sex video, Cheryl's gaze focused on his fingers, waiting in rapt anticipation for him to unbutton them. She didn't even know that she had been holding her breath until he gave them a quick tug and the silver button of her jeans easily slipped out of the loop.

Even then Xavier took his time unzipping her jeans and sliding them down her hips. Thank God she'd worn silk instead of her usual cotton panties, and that they matched her black lace bra. No woman wanted to get caught up in a romantic situation wearing a pair of granny panties. That's a humiliation one could never recover from.

Xavier shifted his weight so that he could pull her jeans all the way down her legs, and then tossed them over his shoulder. Then he held her right foot and brushed a kiss against her painted toes.

A sliver of ecstasy rippled all the way up her legs and hit her throbbing G-spot like a bullet. That certainly had never happened before.

Xavier lifted her right leg high into the air and started raining more kisses along the back of her ankles and her calf. And when he made it to the small dimple on the back of her knee, the crotch of her panties was soaked through and through. Xavier lifted her left leg and repeated the same process. When he hit that second dimple, she was stunned that she was gasping from her first orgasm.

Hell, he hadn't even touched her pussy yet.

"You okay, baby?" he asked rather cockily. He knew what he was doing and he did it well. "How do you feel?"

Panting, Cheryl wished that she had the words to describe what she was feeling, but at that moment if he'd asked her her name, she wouldn't have been able to come up with an answer.

He lowered her legs but he remained planted between them. "You can't tell me how you feel, baby?" Those wonderful lips started traveling up her inner thighs while his fingers crept toward the thin lace on her hips.

Cheryl's breathing thinned and her nipples enlarged to three times their normal size. The honey churning out of her pussy was nothing compared to when Xavier's teeth latched onto the front of her panties and proceeded to pull them off.

At the sight of Cheryl's neatly groomed thatch of curls between her legs, Xavier's heartbeat shifted into overdrive while his cock finally burst out of the side of his black briefs. He wanted to take his time, but his second head was threatening to veto that notion.

In fact, it was more than willing and prepared to just dive right in and bask in the warm pool between her legs. Tempting, very tempting—but the desire to do this right won out. As luck would have it, the single hook to Cheryl's bra was nestled in the front and, with a simple pinch, it sprung open and her beautiful brown cantaloupes bounced free.

"Oh, God," he moaned, trying to capture this memory, as well. But he only had a few seconds before he tilted forward and stretched his mouth over a taut nipple.

Whatever sliver of reality Cheryl had managed to hold on to went up in a puff of smoke when Xavier sucked and spanked his tongue against her nipples. Of course it didn't help that she could also feel his iron rod pressing against her lower thigh while he slipped one finger in between the wet folds of her pussy.

The hell with oxygen—who needed it, anyway, she deliberated with herself. All that mattered in life was this feeling, this incredible sensation that was pulsing wickedly throughout her body. Did he have something special on the pads of his fingers? How did it know how and where to rotate on her clit? How did it know just when to speed up or slow down to maximize and intensify these sensations?

If ever there was a manual on how to operate or pleasure a woman's body, Cheryl was convinced that Xavier had memorized the damn thing. He was doing so much by doing very little so far. How in the world was she going to handle it when he finally joined their bodies together? Was she going to be literally climbing the ceiling? Could that cliché actually be true, too?

Before she could mentally answer herself, an amazing wave started rising. Once again, she was dizzy, but was unsure whether it was from her lack of oxygen or the amazing feeling swirling inside of her. But she knew what was coming. She even foolishly tried to prepare herself. But in the scheme of things, who can really prepare for a tsunami?

As soon as that first wave hit, Cheryl finally gasped for air and her body arched high off the bed. In the next second, she was sure that she was drowning inside as wave after wave hit her hard. While she was trying to survive the tidal waves, Xavier's mouth finished waxing her breasts and started its descent down the center of her body. Just when she realized that she was, in fact, going to survive the flood, everything spun back out of whack when Xavier's mouth found a new home and latched around her pulsing clit.

Thrashing her head back and forth across the pillow, tears of pleasure slowly leaked from the corners of her eyes. Her moans and sighs were lost in the sounds of the music still pumping from the party outside, which was a good thing because surely under normal circumstances someone would have stormed the room by now to make sure that she wasn't being possessed by a sexual demon of some kind.

She wasn't so sure that she wasn't possessed.

Xavier's tongue slapped, spanked and punished her clit like it owed him money or something. There was just no break from the onslaught of sensations and Cheryl was beginning to think that she had bitten off more than she could chew by climbing into bed with this man. What would happen if she just couldn't keep up? Could she wave a white flag—issue a rain check?

Another wave started to build. Cheryl thrashed and tried to pull away from Xavier's feeding frenzy, but his muscular arms slid underneath and then locked around her thighs, easily holding her in place. The wave rolled toward her. In a desperate bid to save herself, Cheryl reached between her legs and tried to pull his head away from her open legs, but it was like trying to move a mountain.

It wasn't happening.

Her moans and sighs heightened, transforming her normally alto voice into a soprano. Then *pow!* The vision behind her closed eyelids went completely white. There was no color at all—and it was so blinding and all-consuming that she wouldn't have been surprised to discover that she had actually died. Which, given all the ways one could leave the earth, she would've considered herself rather lucky.

A minute later things finally started to come back into focus and she couldn't remember a time when she'd felt more mellow and contented in all her life. When she could finally focus on the man that was lying in between her legs, his face wet with her dew, she sat up and pulled him into a soul-stirring kiss.

Xavier's breathing was as hard and choppy as the incredible woman's before him. The pleasure of sharing her sweet taste gave him a wild thrill, especially since she seemed to get off just as much as he did. While he stretched her back across the bed, he reached down with one hand and removed his briefs. His cock sprang straight up and slapped against the soft wet hairs guarding her sweet pussy. Now that he'd had a taste of her true essence, he knew that he was now and forever an addict.

The plan was to hike up her legs and ease into her, but Cheryl had other ideas and it was only gentlemanly of him to let her lead for a while.

Cheryl rolled Xavier over onto his back and started her own little payback plan. She tattooed a series of kisses across his strong jawline, his thick neck and, of course, the wide span of his chest. When she reached his chiseled six-pack, she had the delightful pleasure of watching his muscles quiver just as she had done for him. When she finally worked her way down to his thick shaft, which stood as hard and straight as a black obelisk, she didn't just try to inhale him.

No.

Instead, she convinced herself to take her time, teasing him by raining small kisses around his lower belly and down his strong thighs. She experienced a surge of power, listening to *his* breathing as it slowed—and she was sure that he thought his butt was being slick when he tried to nudge his cock toward her face. On the third time he tried, she cut him a small break and peppered just a few kisses along the side of his shaft, but then she moved her head to continue her own thing.

Xavier laughed. "Oooh. I'm going to pay you back for that," he promised.

Cheryl smiled, but acted like she didn't hear him. The next time she passed by, she gently blew air across the tip and watched him squirm.

"Oh, my God," he groaned. "You're driving me crazy."

"That's the point," she whispered.

He folded his arms behind his head. "Oh, is that right?"

She nodded and blew another breath of air, and since it was standing up between them, they both watched as his muscles contracted, making his cock jump up and down on its own. Cheryl laughed.

"You're evil," he said.

"Evil, huh?" She arched up a brow. "So what will you think if I do this?" She rolled out her tongue and flicked it across the top of his enlarged head.

Xavier's stomach muscles clenched while he sucked in a sharp breath, but before he could exhale, she did it again.

And then again.

Just when he was sure that he was about to go out of his mind and grab her so that he could end this insane torture,

Cheryl's full lips and mouth stretched wide open before lowering over his cock. When she sank her head down as far as she could go, Xavier nearly sat up straight at the tight fit at the back of her throat. In no time, she had set this incredibly slow pace of sucking him in and out of her mouth.

Xavier couldn't curl his hands and toes tight enough and it seemed like a total waste of time trying to steady his breathing. This was happening to a man who'd spent years training his body to do what he wanted it to do. Now, every cell in his body had declared mutiny and he was in real danger of shooting off waaaay too soon.

"That's enough," he decided, grabbing her by the shoulders and lifting her up.

"But I wasn't finished," she complained, giggling.

"Oh, yes, you were," he said, pressing her onto her back and claiming the top position. "You think your ass is slick, don't you?" He parted her legs.

"I'm sure that I don't know what you're talking about."

"Uh-huh. We'll just see about that." He pulled her legs up, completely lifting her lower body off the bed so that he could hook her knees over his shoulders as he leaned over. He dispensed a little mercy when he first pressed his cock at the apex of her pussy. He didn't just thrust in with one good stroke, but instead eased his way through her warm silky walls so that her body could slowly adjust to his size. Turned out that it might have been mercy for her, but it was pure torture for him. So much so that his chest felt like it was seconds from collapsing—the way the body compresses when suddenly plunged to the depths of the ocean.

Apparently, Cheryl worked out more than just the muscles that were visible to the naked eye.

"How do *you* feel?" she asked as she squeezed her vaginal muscles tight around his shaft.

Xavier's mouth slid open, but no words—at least, no intelligible words—fell from his lips.

"You can't tell me how you feel, baby?" she asked, squeezing him tighter, which threatened to give him the orgasm that he was trying his best to delay.

*Oh, no. I can't go out like this.* Xavier dropped his head and tried to muster up enough stamina to hang in there.

"I can't hear you, X-Man." She relaxed a bit so that he could slide in farther. But before he was all the way in, she tightened up again.

He hissed out the Lord's name and resumed panting like a man who'd just completed a marathon. There were no if's, and's or but's about it, Cheryl was running this show and she was certainly about to teach him a thing or two.

Cheryl watched his forehead become slick with sweat while she tightened and released him at her leisure. She knew that he was fighting not to come too soon and, if she wanted, she could make him lose that fight.

That was *if* she wanted.

"Kiss me," she said, and then waited for his lips to find hers. Only when she could taste him did she relax her muscles enough for him to take temporary control. She had no complaints when he filled her up completely or about the rhythm he set sliding in and out of her body. However, she did underestimate her own body's reaction to his. Once again, she had lost control of her breathing *and* her thinking and in no time had torn her lips away from his so that she could beg him to make her come.

That was a mistake.

It was his payback time and he refused to let her come until *he* was ready for her to come. "Flip over," he ordered, pulling out and stroking himself while he waited.

Cheryl scrambled as fast as she could, but received a quick slap on the butt when she apparently took too long.

He chuckled at the way her bottom bounced, so he smacked the other cheek so that he could watch as it jiggled again. "You're going to have to move much faster than that, baby. Get on your knees."

Smiling, she hesitated a second, just so that he would warm her butt with another stinging smack. Cheryl didn't even want to admit how much she loved that. Of course it was only second to how much she loved feeling him sinking into her from the back. From then on, they were making the bed jump and bounce hard against the wall.

Whenever she got cocky and started to control the rhythm, Xavier delivered another hard smack against her upturned cheeks. In no time at all her ass was on fire and the headboard was making some major dents in the wall. Pound for pound, Cheryl and Xavier were each other's match. She didn't know how many orgasms she'd had; she lost count. All Xavier knew was that he'd never met anyone like Cheryl before. He'd certainly never been with anyone who made him feel what he was feeling now.

By the time he collapsed onto the bed, he was a sweaty mess and was in some serious need of vitamins and Gatorade. They were only going to close their eyes for a moment. After all, they were in someone else's home. But exhaustion snuck up on both of them and the minutes turned into hours.

# *Chapter 11*

Cheryl's eyes sprang open.

Since she didn't recognize the lamp on the nightstand or even the nightstand itself, she concluded that the wild night of sweaty sex with Xavier King hadn't been a dream. At that moment she would have liked for it to have been a dream, because it would have meant that she hadn't compromised her undercover investigation, or what little morality and ethics she had left. She glanced down at the muscular arm draped around her waist and sighed with disappointment in herself.

This was *waaaaay* worse than sleeping with her lieutenant. But as images of last night started floating back to her, the assessment seemed a bit harsh. Still, it was a bad decision. *Now I just have to hope that no one ever finds out.* With it being so far from Christmas, Cheryl wasn't about to hold her breath on that one.

As slowly and quietly as she could, Cheryl lifted Xavier's

arm up and rolled from underneath him and then climbed out of bed.

"My clothes, my clothes. Where are my clothes?" she mumbled under her breath while she frantically searched around the room. There was one shoe under the bed, her jeans flung behind a vanity and…was that her panties circulating on the ceiling fan?

*Good Lord, Cheryl!*

For a brief moment, she debated whether to climb up on the bed and try to retrieve them. She'd rather not, but there was just something about leaving a pair of her good panties rotating on the blades of a ceiling fan in some celebrity's house that screamed "ho" to her. Cheryl cursed under her breath as she once again tried to be as quiet as she possibly could. She climbed back onto the bed and reached up to snatch her panties down from the fan blade. While she was up there, she caught a glimpse of something out of the corner of her eye.

*Is that my bra?*

She squinted as she looked at the top of the oak armoire, and sure enough, there it was dangling from the side. "How on earth did that get over there?" Realizing that she had spoken too loudly, Cheryl slapped her hand over her mouth and glanced at the bed.

Xavier moaned and shifted.

Cheryl held her breath, but her heart started to sink when she watched as Xavier's hand searched the empty space where she was supposed to be. *Please go back to sleep. Please go back to sleep.*

Xavier's head popped up off the pillow.

*If it wasn't for bad luck, I'd have no luck at all.*

He looked around, confusion contorting his face. Then he turned and spotted her standing on the bed nude, with her panties clutched in her hands.

"Good morning. Don't you look—" his eyes roamed over her body "—breathtaking."

*You don't look bad your damn self.* Cheryl flashed him an awkward smile. "Morning."

When she didn't follow up with an explanation of what she was doing, he asked. "Trying out a new position or…is this just something you do first thing in the morning?"

"I…"

The bedroom door bolted open and Quentin and a gold-digging diva from last night's party stumbled inside.

"C'mon on, baby. We…" The couple's eyes widened at the sight in front of them.

Cheryl silently screamed and dived back into the bed and tossed the sheets over her head so fast that she looked like a blur to everyone. She cringed when she heard Q's shotgun laughter.

"Well, all right, X-Man."

"Back it up, Q," Xavier said. "I'll holler at you later."

"What? You don't need me to referee or anything?" Quentin chuckled, backing out of the room. "'Cause it looked like, at any second, your girl is about to take your head off."

"Out!"

Quentin tossed up his hands. "All right. All right. I'm going, you lucky dog."

Cheryl slapped a hand across her face and was sure that she was just going to die of humiliation. But it wasn't over just yet.

"Bye, Cheryl," Q called out to her.

"Bye," she said flatly from underneath the covers.

"Okay, now will you get out," Xavier said, irritation evident in his voice.

Still chuckling, Quentin said, "I'm out."

Finally, Cheryl heard the door close and she quickly tossed the covers off of her head and scrambled back out of the bed. "I can't believe this."

Xavier sat up. "Wait. It's okay. He's gone now."

Cheryl stormed over to the armoire and snatched her bra down and started getting dressed.

"What are you doing?"

"What does it look like I'm doing?" She jammed her legs through her panties and jerked them up.

"Yeah, but why? You don't have to leave just yet."

"What the hell are you talking about? This isn't even your place. Or is this just something that you're used to doing after these wild bachelor parties? You and your horny cousin!"

"What?" Xavier bounced out of the bed just as she was snapping on her bra. "You think that I do this all the time?"

She stopped and jammed her hands on her hips. "Don't you? Or are you going to tell me that you've never slept with women who attend these things. A stripper, a groupie or a bartender? Ever?"

Xavier's mouth fell open, but he couldn't get a denial past his lips.

"Yeah. I thought so." She marched around him and grabbed her jeans.

"Wait. So I'm the bad guy now?"

"I didn't say that," she snapped, trying her best not to start ogling him. He was *naked,* after all. "Look. I'm just as much at fault for what happened last night—if not more so." She grabbed her shirt. "To tell you the truth, I just want to forget that the whole thing even happened."

At that, Xavier reached out and grabbed her by the arm. "What the hell do you mean?"

"Just what I said." Cheryl jerked her arm free. "Last night was a mistake. Surely you realize that. You're my boss."

"Okay." He folded his arms. "But we're also two mature adults, who, in my *humble* opinion, had experienced something…extraordinary last night."

"Uh-huh." She pulled her shirt down over her head. "It

was more like we were two people at a celebrity bachelor party who got horny and decided to fuck each other because we weren't thinking clearly."

Xavier's expression twisted. "Maybe I should be asking you how often *you* have done something like this."

"Why? Would it mean something more just because I'm a woman? It's all right for men to sleep around, but not women?"

"Whoa. Whoa. Where is all of this coming from?"

"It's coming from a place of regret. And I regret *everything* about last night. Not because I didn't enjoy it, but because it was wrong." She resumed her search around the room. "Now, where is my other shoe?"

"Damn. Do you always sharpen that tongue first thing in the morning?"

Cheryl sucked in a breath and tried to rein in her anger. "Look. I'm not mad at you. I'm mad at myself. I know better than this. Sleeping with a colleague…let alone your boss, is never a good idea. Nothing good can come out of it. So, for me, can't we just pretend like last night didn't happen?"

Xavier looked at her like he'd never met her before. "I'm not sure that I can do that—or if I even want to."

"Great. Just great!" Cheryl tossed up her hands and then threw out her best card. "Then maybe I should just look for another job." *Or more like, get myself pulled from the case.*

"Whoa. Whoa," he said again, grabbing her arm. "Are you serious?"

"Why wouldn't I be serious?"

He cocked his head. "This has happened to you before, hasn't it?"

She tried to pull her arm away, but he wasn't having it this time.

"You had a relationship with a coworker…or a boss before?"

"That's none of your business," she snapped, and finally managed to jerk her arm free from his grasp.

"It may be none of my business, but it's completely relevant to this situation. Just because you were burned once doesn't mean that it's going to happen again."

"Yeah, right. Next you're going to tell me that you're the settling-down type."

Xavier nearly choked on air.

Cheryl smirked. "I thought so." She dropped to her knees and then looked under the bed. "There it is." She reached and dragged out her shoe.

"Cheryl, I don't want you to quit," Xavier said quietly as she jammed her foot into her shoe.

"Great. I don't want to quit. I like my job."

"But I don't want to stop seeing you, either."

"I'm sure that you'll see me around the club," she said, combing her hair with her hand.

"You know what I mean."

"Well…" She tossed up her hands. "We can't always get what we want."

"Stop pushing me away," he thundered. "We both enjoyed last night. It was…nice."

She laughed. "Nice?"

"Pleasurable…enjoyable…earth-shattering…take your pick."

"I'll take nice. Thanks." She flashed him a sarcastic smile and started for the door, but once again, Xavier grabbed her by the arm.

"Why are you being such a…"

Cheryl's brows lifted while she waited for him to finish the sentence.

"I just don't understand what happened," he corrected. "Last night—"

"Last night was last night," she said. "Look around. It's morning."

He released her arm and then just stared at her. Either he was still confused or no one had ever talked to him like this before—or it was a combination of both. Yeah. He was used to being the one who gave the "let's be friends" speech.

"Look. I'm sure that there are plenty of women who'd love to have—or continue to have—sex with you. I'm just not one of them."

"I see." His jaw clenched. "So all that moaning and groaning and scratching up my back was just my imagination? Is that what you're telling me?"

She sighed.

"Or maybe you have a split personality." He nodded as if he liked that answer best. "Is that it? Because, if so, I'd really like to talk to that Cheryl right now. She was a lot more fun."

"Exactly," she praised in a hallelujah voice. "Fun. That's all it was. Just fun. I don't see what the big deal is that we can't just put it behind us. It's over. I enjoyed the carnival ride, now it's time to go home."

"Why do you insist on demeaning what happened last night?"

"Why are you insisting that it was more than it was?" Realizing that she was going to have to be more brutal, she took a deep breath and then met his confused gaze head-on. "All right. You want to know what I felt last night?"

"That would be a nice place to start." Xavier folded his arms and looked like he was bracing himself for anything.

"I felt like I was with a man who definitely knew his way around a woman's body. I was with a man who takes extremely good care of his body and knows how to work the tools the Man up above has blessed him with. Did I come last night? More times than I can count and harder than with anyone I've ever been with before."

Xavier's expression started to soften with the barrage of compliments.

"Does that satisfy your ego?" she asked calmly.

Just like that, his eyes narrowed again. "It's not about my ego."

She laughed. "It's always about a man's ego. I wasn't born yesterday."

"Then clearly you don't know me as well as you think you do," he said. "Have I slept with a lot of women? I'm not going to lie. I've had more than my fair share. But I'd like to think that I've always been respectful. I've always been kind. And I've never lied or pretended that my relationships were something that they weren't. Out of all the words that can be used to describe me, the one that means the most to me is *honest*. I'm an honest man, Cheryl. What you see is what you get." He stepped closer to her. "And if I tell you that I felt something between us last night, it's because I did. And if I'm standing here looking you in the eye and telling you that I *still* feel something for you, it's because I do."

Cheryl swallowed hard at the intense scrutiny of his stare.

"Now if this whole tough-girl act is just some routine that you need to go through in order to protect yourself from me, baby girl, it's not necessary. I'm not going to hurt you. But if you honestly believe that you need to cut this off, then I'm going to let you do what you need to do, because I'm not trying to hurt you. I'm feeling you. I want to get to know you. That's all." He let the words hang in the air while their eyes remained locked.

Cheryl definitely felt as if the ball had been snatched out of her court.

He stepped back. "So what's it going to be?"

She eyed the door and then swung her gaze back to him. Why did this feel like a *Sophie's Choice* moment? Her eyes swung back and forth a few more times before she reached deep down to summon the strength to walk to the door. As she passed by Xavier, she caught the look of disappointment in his face. By the time she reached for the doorknob, it felt as if her eyes were swimming in pools of acid. Pulling the door open, she half hoped that he would stop her. She bargained with her conscience that if he did, then she would stop and just give in to the emotions sloshing around inside her.

He didn't say anything.

She walked out the door and refused to look back.

*The Bigger They Are...the Harder They Fall*

# *Chapter 12*

"Xavier King sounds like a real stand-up guy," Dr. Turner said, swiveling around in her chair. "He doesn't mince words. Says what he means and means what he says."

Quentin's lips curled upward. "Careful. It almost sounds like you want to ask how it is that we're best friends."

"I would never ask something like that," she said.

"No?" He glanced over his shoulder to see that she had removed her glasses, but held the tip of the temple bar between her teeth. That helped draw his attention to the beautiful shade of red lipstick she wore today. "Are you sure?"

She looked up and smiled. "I'm sure."

Their eyes locked for a moment, until a pair of fingers snapped in front of his face. Q jumped before his gaze shot over to Alyssa shaking her head.

"I swear some things never change with you."

"Do you ever stop butting your nose into other people's business?" he asked, annoyed.

Dr. Turner frowned. "You came to me, Mr. Hinton. Remember?"

"Not—oh, never mind." He waved his comment off. What was the point?

"Okay." Dr. Turner slid her glasses back on. "In the beginning you said that Xavier had his own issues with trust. But just now it sounded as if he has no problem putting himself out there. By his own declaration, he's an honest broker when it comes to relationships."

"And he is—in relationships, and in business. Now, that doesn't mean that he doesn't have his fair share of secrets. But there's always an argument as to whether omission is the same as lying. One thing's for sure, a lie is a lie. And our sexy bartender was spinning a whole lot of lies around The Dollhouse…and to herself."

"Do you like Cheryl Shepherd?"

"I like anyone with a shape like hers. Hell, I thought that was the only reason my man Xavier couldn't let things go with hcr. I mean, he was miserable…."

# *Chapter 13*

*Two weeks later...*

"I just don't understand women," Xavier complained to Ricky as he unleashed a steady barrage of punches to the speed bag. "I mean, all you ever hear about from them is how hard it is to find a good man. But when one is standing in front of them, jumping and waving and screaming, 'Hey, here I am,' what happens?"

"You get punched in the gut," Ricky said flatly.

"You get punched in the gut!" Xavier answered without acknowledging Ricky's response. "And what's worse is now every evening she's working at the club, she talks to everyone *but* me. It's like I don't even exist except when it comes to signing her checks. How insane is that?"

"Completely insane," Ricky droned.

"Completely insane!"

Ricky rolled his eyes. "Look, Xavier. I get the whole brokenhearted, kicked-in-the-gut blues thing. Believe me,

I do. But you're going to have to at least change up the material a little bit, because you're starting to sound like a broken record."

One punch missed the speed bag and threw Xavier's rhythm off. "What are you talking about? I don't have a broken heart. How can I? I was only with the girl one time. That's hardly enough to call it a broken heart."

"I stand corrected." Ricky sighed. "You're just whining about how this Cheryl lady just hit it and quit it."

"No. That's not it," Xavier said indignantly.

"No? You're not just sitting by the phone or waiting for her to flash you that look that says she wants another round with the big X-Man in the bedroom? Surely if you could just get her in between the sheets one more time, you could really get her to fall in love with you."

Xavier missed another punch and turned to his ex-trainer. "No. That's not it, either."

"You could've fooled me," he mumbled under his breath, and then glanced down at his watch. "Now where in the hell is this kid at?"

"I just want some answers," Xavier complained. "And I don't think that what she told me was the truth. I swear I can see it in her eyes—the few times I can get her to look at me."

Ricky frowned as he looked over at him. "See, this is why men should stay away from those damn girly workout DVDs. Men should only discuss their feelings over meat or alcohol. All this wishy-washy, mushy stuff is just too much. Have you ever thought maybe *she's* just not that into you?"

"You got jokes."

Ricky laughed. "A whole bag of them."

The door to the gym swung open and My'kael rushed inside and flashed Ricky an apologetic smile. "Sorry. Got here as fast as I could. My baby Tiana has been running a fever and I had to try and get an advance on my paycheck down at Oscar's."

"I understand. I understand. Go and get changed," Ricky said, glancing at his watch again.

"Thanks, Coach." My'kael turned and gave Xavier a quick nod.

Xavier smiled back and then watched as the young boxer raced off to the locker room.

"Aw…I don't know," Ricky said, shaking his head sadly. "He might have potential, but he might have too much baggage dragging him down."

"He said that his little girl is sick," Xavier said, shrugging. "Surely you're not that heartless to cut him off because of that."

"According to him, his little girl is always sick. And that restaurant he's talking about, Oscar's? He got fired from that place about a month back. I know because one of my many legions of nephews sweeps the floor there."

Xavier frowned. "Why would he lie about where he works?"

"Why do people lie in general?"

"Because they're trying to hide the truth?"

"That—or they lie just because they can."

Xavier's frown turned into a half smile. "So which do you think it is with My'kael?"

"In his case, I'd say you're right. Times are tough, and the young men around here may not be so concerned about how they make their money."

Xavier let that sink in as he glanced back toward the locker room. He felt a strong sense of disappointment, even though he hardly knew the young man. But he did see what Ricky saw in him—a diamond in the rough. "Do you want me to talk to him?"

"Humph. No offense, Xavier—but you didn't exactly hang in there yourself. You could've gone all the way."

"Then maybe that's what I should tell him."

Ricky considered Xavier's offer. "You'd do that for me?"

"Of course I would." He winked. "What are friends for?" Xavier reached over for his towel and quickly swiped the sweat from his face. "I'll be right back."

Ricky smiled and slapped him on the back as he passed by. "Thanks, X-Man. I really appreciate it."

"Don't mention it. That's what friends are for." He strolled across the gym toward the locker room and quickly found My'kael lacing up his boxing shoes. When he looked up, there was an awkward exchange of stiff smiles. "What's up, man?"

My'kael shrugged.

*Not much of a talker.*

"Getting ready to put in a good workout?"

"Why? Are you writing a book?"

Xavier lifted a brow. "A bit defensive, aren't you?"

"Nah. I just don't like a whole lot of questions." He shifted his feet. "Especially from brothers I don't know. You feel me?"

"A'ight," Xavier said, nodding. "Then I guess there's no other way to come at you than to give it to you straight. My man Ricky out there is worried about you. Should he be?"

My'kael swore under his breath. "So what? He sent you in here to talk to me?"

"No. I offered," Xavier said, trying to remain cool. He never cared for the whole brother-with-a-chip-on-his-shoulder routine, anyway. "So why don't you just cut the BS and tell me whether you're taking this whole boxing thing seriously or if you're just wasting an old man's time?"

"Please. I don't believe in wasting time. I wouldn't be here if I didn't want to be."

"So what's with all the excuses?"

My'kael finished lacing his boot and stood. If he was trying to be intimidating, it didn't work. Xavier was taller, stronger and more ripped than he was. There was a quick calculation in the young man's eye and clearly he came to the same conclusion. "Man, why the hell do you care?"

"Because I happen to care about Ricky. He's a good man. And when I first walked into this place, boasting about how I was going to dominate the world of boxing, he was the first one who didn't laugh. He took one look at me. Told me to show him what I had and then just…poured everything he had into me. And in return, I tried my best to make both of our dreams come true."

My'kael nodded his head. "So why didn't you go all the way?"

Their eyes met for a long time and Xavier warred with himself as to whether he should tell the young man something that he'd never even confessed to his own family. But at the last moment, he realized that he really wasn't ready to do that just yet. "Because I gave up. Because I stopped trying."

There was a ripple of disappointment on My'kael's face like he'd sensed that Xavier was holding out on him. "Still, everything worked out for you, right? I know about you. You're making mad loot down there at that big strip club downtown. You gotta be pulling at least seven figures. So it's all good, right?"

"Not quite," Xavier said, lowering his voice and his gaze. "Eventually, everybody learns that money doesn't buy happiness."

"But it pays the bills, right?"

He nodded. "It does. But bills never go away. Dreams… unfilled. They'll chase after you until the day you die, especially when you give up on them. Even the ones you give up on for the right reasons. Giving them up for the wrong ones…well, that's just a hell of your own making."

My'kael's gaze fell. "It ain't easy being out here chasing a dream and not getting paid, man. I sound like a fool standing in front of my old lady and little girl and can't pay the bills."

"You need a job—just say the word."

"Man, I ain't looking for no handout."

"Who said anything about a handout? You work for me you need to be prepared to work. Do a good job, you make good money. But if you work for me, then I expect you to work hard at the club *and* in this gym. You got potential, man. And now that you got me in your face, I'm not going to just stand back and watch you waste it. You feel me?"

A slow smile hooked the corners of My'kael's lips and then at last he started nodding. "A'ight, then. When do I start?"

"Tonight. Be at the club by seven." He held out his hand and the two brothers shook on it.

"You slept with him, didn't you?" Johnnie asked, following Cheryl to her desk.

"What? What are you talking about?" Cheryl dropped down into her chair and turned toward her computer to look up a few names to see if there were any hits.

"See. You can't even look at me," Johnnie said. "When and where? That's all I want to know."

"Don't you have some work to do?" Cheryl snapped at her partner.

"When and where?"

"I made *one* mistake and now you think that I'm some morally corrupt cop? I'm offended."

"*You* are riddled with guilt. I said nothing about being morally corrupt. I just happen to know that if I wrote down a checklist of all the things that you like in a man, Xavier King would match up perfectly. Handsome, athletic, successful, smooth, cool—come on. You'd have to be Superwoman not fall for that brother. And now that this investigation is going on longer than we thought, we're talking about the laws of attraction and a numbers game."

"I'm not sleeping with him."

Johnnie cocked her head. "No. You're working at this desk. I'm saying that you have slept with him and you're playing this verbal rope-a-dope game with me instead of just answering the question."

Cheryl sucked in a deep breath and then glanced around the office to make sure that no one was listening to them before confessing. "So what if I did? Big deal. It just happened. I didn't plan it. It…it just happened."

"Oooh. I knew it." Johnnie snapped her fingers. "You lucky heifer." She rolled her eyes. "How was he? I know he was good. He was good, wasn't he? Tell the truth and shame the devil."

Cheryl dropped her head into the palm of her hand. "God. Why in the hell did I just tell you that? I'm never going to live it down now."

"What you're going to do is give me a blow-by-blow rendition of exactly how it went down. How many times it went down. And please, please tell me that there was some baby oil being slathered on that man's gorgeous body."

"What the hell? Aren't you getting any these days?"

"On a dry spell, two months, sixteen days—" She glanced at her watch. "And ten hours and…seventeen—no—make that eighteen minutes."

Cheryl snickered.

"Throw a girl a bone?"

Cheryl grabbed her purse. "C'mon. Let's go grab a cup of coffee."

"Now we're talking."

Cheryl shook her head as she walked around her desk, but when she lifted her head, she just barely stopped in time before she smacked into Lieutenant Mackey's chest.

"Good. I caught you," Mackey said, folding his arms across his chest. "You got a minute?"

"I, uh—" Cheryl glanced over at Johnnie, but couldn't think of an excuse fast enough.

"I need to see you in my office," he said, shuffling past her.

Cheryl groaned and briefly pinched the bridge of her nose.

"That wasn't a request, Detective Grier," Mackey shouted without breaking stride.

"I swear I can't stand that man," Cheryl hissed under her breath.

"We'll put that coffee on pause," Johnnie said. "You better get in there before he huffs and puffs and then blows the damn department down."

Cheryl returned her purse to the bottom of her desk drawer and then headed toward Mackey's office. She couldn't imagine what the hell he wanted, but she hoped like hell that it wouldn't take long.

"Close the door," he ordered as he dropped into his chair behind his desk.

*Not a good sign.* She closed the door and then faced him while folding her arms across her chest. "All right. What is it now?"

"Where is your report on Mad Monez's bachelor party? It's been two weeks."

Cheryl felt a kick to her gut. "I turned in a summary to the team. I haven't had time to do a full report, but I will get to it this week."

Mackey nodded as he leaned back in his chair. "Good… because I've already received Gilliam and Royo's. I just want to make sure that everyone's jibes, that's all."

That one was a kick and a karate chop. "Gilliam and Royo made it to the party?"

Mackey's smile was razor thin, an amazing feat since he

had full lips. "I guess they'll take it as a compliment that you weren't able to make them out. It must mean they blended in rather well."

She nodded and then tried to recall as many faces as she could from that night. But when it came to Mad Monez's bachelor party, there was just one part that stuck out in her mind. Did Royo and Gilliam know what happened between her and Xavier that night?

Cheryl met and held Mackey's stare for what felt like an eternity.

"Well, like I said, I look forward to reading your report."

*He knows.*

She nodded as her stomach twisted into knots. "Is that all?"

"Not quite." He sat up. "I'm pulling you off this case."

"What? Why?"

"Because you haven't been able to produce anything yet—nothing. This department can't continue to just pour taxpayer money into this without results. I'm thinking either we have bad information or you're in the wrong spot. Maybe you should've applied to be a dancer, like I first suggested. More than likely, you'd be closer to the action."

"If there is any action," she retaliated.

"Oh, there's action. Those kinds of clubs aren't run by Boy Scouts, you know."

"Careful. You might paint everyone with that broad brushstroke."

"I'm right. You're just too close to Xavier King to see it for yourself."

"What is that supposed to mean?"

He shrugged. "Just what I said." His gaze hardened. "You're too close."

"Why are you really pulling me off this case?" she said, taking a risk.

"I just told you."

"No. You're insinuating that I can't do my job."

He laughed. "Forgive me. I certainly didn't mean to *insinuate* that."

She relaxed.

"I *know* more than anyone that you go the extra mile to do your job." Mackey stood up from his chair and walked around his desk. "You're not above breaking the rules. That's one of the things that I like about you, Detective Grier. When you want something, you go right out there and you get it." He stopped in front of her and then surprised her when he brushed his hand against the side of her face. "Don't you?"

Cheryl flinched away from him. "Damn, Jason. Don't you ever quit?"

"Not when the stakes are this high." He smiled.

Her stomach churned with disgust. "Fine! If you pull me off the case, then I'm putting in for a transfer," she told him. "This has to stop."

"Did you tell Xavier to stop?"

In Cheryl's mind her hand whipped across his face. But somehow, some way, she managed to restrain herself. "Are we finished here?"

Mackey's lips sloped into an uneven smile.

"Tell you what, you have one week with Mr. Lover Boy to prove to me that you can really do your job. If not, you're off the case. Understand?"

Cheryl nodded.

"Good." He flashed another smile before calmly turning and walking back over to his desk. "And you can just forget about putting in for a transfer. You're not going anywhere. Not as long as I'm here. You made your bed. Now, you're just going to have to lie in it." He turned toward his computer while giving her a dismissive wave. "You can go now."

Cheryl pivoted on her heels and stormed out. *What in the hell have I gotten myself into?*

# *Chapter 14*

Another Friday night and The Dollhouse was packed. It helped that there were so many conventions going on in Atlanta. The Dollhouse Dolls were working hard. And as a result, money was raining left, right and center. With everyone seeming to be in such a great mood, the only two people who were acting like someone had shot their dog were Cheryl and Xavier. It was so obvious that a couple of the Dolls and waitresses started speculating and approached Cheryl to ask whether there was something going on between her and Xavier.

How was it that she was able to keep her cover as a cop, but was unable to hide her emotions toward Xavier from even the bouncers at the door? "There's nothing going on," she insisted to Lexus during their brief fifteen-minute break.

"Uh-huh. You keep telling yourself that." Lexus laughed. "Maybe, just maybe, you'll be able to convince yourself that it's the truth. But you ain't foolin' nobody with the BS."

*Maybe it is better if Mackey pulls me from this job.*

"What?" Lexus laughed. "Why should you be any different from anyone else around here? We've all fallen for that man at one time or another—and why not? He's a great guy. Certainly not the type you would normally think would run a strip club—him or his brothers."

"I'm sure that he's glad that you're giving him such a ringing endorsement."

"Does hiding behind sarcasm help?"

Cheryl glanced over at Lexus as she snubbed out her cigarette.

"I didn't think so." Lexus turned and strolled from the break room table near the time clock.

Cheryl lingered for a few more minutes while she pulled herself together, but when she finally turned to head back out to her station, she spotted Xavier and Quentin talking in low, hushed tones near the dancers' dressing rooms. It was no big deal, really, except that she was curious about the large, thick envelope that exchanged hands.

*It could be anything,* she reasoned. Yet, she couldn't pull her gaze from the envelope Quentin stuffed into the inside of his jacket. In the next second, a stream of dancers rushed toward the dressing room. As usual, a few of the ladies took the opportunity to flirt openly with the cousins.

Quentin was only too happy to join in.

Xavier just smiled good-naturedly, cracked a joke and then started to stroll off. But then he caught sight of her from the corner of his eye and his long stride slowed. In only a couple of seconds, so much was transmitted between them with just a simple look. Cheryl quickly turned away without as much as a smile before she headed back to the bar.

At her station, she immediately threw herself into work, which included doing a great deal of smiling and flirting of her own. At some point, she had the unmistakable feeling of being watched. But because of the large crowd, it was

damn near impossible to pin down just who those pair of eyes belonged to.

In the end, because she couldn't keep her mind or body from focusing on Xavier, she broke three bottles and messed up a string of drink orders. For her, the night couldn't end soon enough. But it stretched on, making her feel like a prisoner serving a life sentence.

The doors closed at three, but the last customers didn't filter out the door until damn near five in the morning. By then, Cheryl was so tired that she was convinced she was going to fall flat on her face before she could make it to her car.

"You go to Ripped Gym, don't you?"

Cheryl glanced up to see the club's mammoth bouncer, Dog Pound, smiling down at her. "Sure do." She squinted. "You look familiar."

"I should. My uncle owns the place. I'm down there four or five times a week. Getting in my workouts, you know how it is."

She bobbed her head. "Actually, I do."

"I've seen you down there—always causing a stir with the fellas. Are you thinking about getting into women's boxing? Heaven knows you're in shape."

Her brows shot up.

Dog Pound shrugged. "I ain't gonna lie. I've been checking you out. You got nice form—hand-eye coordination. You should think about it. I could even put in a good word with my uncle. He's one of the best, you know."

"Wow. That certainly sounds…interesting." She finished wiping down her station and then grabbed her duffel bag.

"Don't tell me that you've never thought about it," Dog Pound needled her as he followed her back toward the time clock. "Surely someone has said something to you before now."

"Maybe once," she admitted. "But really, I just like the

boxing-workout thing because I enjoy the endorphin high I get from it."

"I hear you on that," Dog Pound said, selecting his time card and punching out. Then, he apparently ran out of things to talk about, but he lingered around her awhile and mustered up some more courage. "So, um. Are you seeing anyone?"

"Uhh…" Cheryl drew a blank. Clearly, the gentle giant had a minor crush on her, but she wanted to let him down easy.

"I mean, I was just thinking that we could…I don't know. Go out for a movie or something sometime."

"Aw. That's sounds really nice, but, um, you know, between working here and going to school, I really don't have a whole lot of time for a social life." She winced a bit, picking up speed as she walked toward the door. "I'm sorry, but I'm really flattered that you asked."

"Yeah. Sure." He shrugged while his gaze zoomed all around.

"How about a rain check?" she offered, since she felt bad for giving him the brush-off.

"No. That's okay. I understand. You don't want to go out with me." He shrugged again. "It's no big deal. I just thought I'd ask." They exited out the side door of the club.

"I didn't say that—"

"Look. I'll catch up with you later." He stopsped and then started to hang a right toward his car.

Cheryl stopped and tried to think of something that would restore the man's pride, but all that happened was her standing there with her mouth hanging open.

"I'll see you around," he said, dropping his head and hurrying toward his car.

*Great. That went well.*

She watched him as he jogged the last few feet to his black SUV. From there, he wasted no time hopping in and starting the vehicle. The way he peeled out of the parking lot, you would have thought that the white flag had been dropped in a drag race. Cheryl closed her eyes and huffed out a long breath. This was definitely not her night. However, when she opened her eyes, she noticed a plastic bag lying on the blacktop in the direction that Dog Pound had just gone.

After glancing around, she rushed to pick it up. It was a small Ziploc bag, but inside were ten smaller packets of white powder. Once it was in her hand, she knew that she didn't need to taste it to know exactly what it was. She looked in the direction Dog Pound had gone and tried to convince herself that she was mistaken, that the bag of cocaine hadn't fallen from his jacket. After all, she didn't exactly *see* it fall, but the idea of the clubs' bouncers being the gateway for drug trafficking made sense.

*Wait. Even if this belonged to him, it doesn't mean that he's dealing.* That was true, she realized. But for the first time since she'd started this investigation, there was a bleep on her radar.

"Girl, that man comes in here every night promising to leave his wife for me," Jada boasted to the group of girls following behind her as they streamed out of the club.

Cheryl shoved the packet into her jeans pocket before flashing an awkward smile. "Night, ladies."

The dancers glanced in her direction and smiled back. A couple of them looked at her oddly, but nevertheless kept their Doll train moving toward their cars.

"See you ladies tomorrow night," she said, and then walked toward her own car. The minute she hopped in behind the wheel, she pulled out her keys and her cell phone.

"Hello."

"Johnnie, it's me. I think I may finally have something." Cheryl inserted her key in the ignition. "There's a guy working the door, who goes by the name Dog Pound. His uncle runs Ripped Gym. Offhand, I don't know his real name. Can you check him out?" She could hear Johnnie scrambling around on the other end of the line.

"I'll check into it the minute I get to the office. You really think you got something? Mackey is threatening to shut this down on Monday."

"I know. Just run the information and get back to me."

"You got it."

Cheryl disconnected the call and turned her key. Nothing happened. "No. No. No. Not tonight," she moaned, and then tried to start the car again. All she heard was one click and then dead air. "Great! Just great!" She jerked open her door and climbed out of the car. Within seconds, she had the hood up and was staring blankly at the battery. She didn't know why, because the one thing that wasn't part of her law-enforcement expertise was anything having to do with cars. She knew how to put gas in and when to have the oil changed.

"Is there a problem?"

Cheryl jumped and spun around. There was a mix of dread and relief when she saw Xavier standing behind her. "I, uh… It won't start."

He nodded and then moved to stand next to her. "Let's have a look. Can you try and turn it over for me?"

Cheryl struggled to ignore her body going haywire with him standing so close. For weeks she had been able to avoid this very thing from happening by staying away from him as much as possible. So she jumped at the chance to run, or rather hide, behind the wheel to try turning the ignition once again.

Click.

"Are your lights on?" Xavier yelled from under the hood.

Cheryl glanced around the dashboard. "No."

"It's your battery. Let me see if I can give you a jump."

She sighed with relief. "You need some cables? I think I

have some in the trunk," she yelled, and then hopped back out of the car.

"Sure. If you don't have any, I do," he called out before heading toward his SUV.

Cheryl searched around her trunk, but came up empty. "Now I know I have some cables back here somewhere," she mumbled under her breath. She had damn near leaned her entire body into the trunk before she remembered her sister asking to borrow her jumper cables about two months back. "Damn. She didn't put them back," she realized.

She heard Xavier pull his vehicle up in front of her car. Cheryl climbed back onto her feet and slammed the trunk down. "Sorry. It looks like my sister didn't return the cables."

"I didn't know you had a sister," Xavier said, but then added, "I guess there's a lot I don't know about you."

There was a brief, awkward silence. "Don't worry. I have some jumper cables." He strolled to the back of his SUV and within a couple of seconds came back armed with cables and then propped up his own hood. He quickly attached the appropriate positive and negative cables to the corresponding battery nodes.

"Should I try to start it again?" she asked.

"Let's give it a minute," he said, standing to the side of the car and folding his muscular arms.

Cheryl mimicked his pose and tried to keep her eyes on the open hood. However, she was finding it difficult to do. Despite her better judgment, her gaze kept glancing over at him and his incredible body. *Nineteen days*. That's how long it had been since she'd felt those heavenly arms wrapped around her body. *Nineteen days.* That's how long it had been since his pillow-soft lips had traveled down the length of her body. *Nineteen days.* That's how long it had been since he'd eased his way in between her legs, joining their bodies together.

She inhaled a deep breath and then started waving her

hand like a fan in the middle of church service. "It's hot out here," she mumbled.

Xavier glanced up frowning. "It's forty-eight degrees."

"I know. Ridiculous, right?" she said, ignoring his response.

He cocked his head and then just shook it as if deciding to let it go. "Go ahead, try to turn it over."

Cheryl jumped back behind the wheel. "Nothing."

"Did your lights even come on?"

She glanced around again and felt her heart sink. "No."

Xavier walked back up to the car and wiggled a couple of cables around, but the results were the same. "I'm sorry, sweetheart, but this battery is a goner." He started removing the cables. "If you want, I can give you a lift to your place. Your car should be safe here for the rest of the night."

"Um..." She glanced around as if she was going to find an excuse lying around somewhere.

"Are you kidding?" he asked, irritated. "You don't even trust me to drive you home?"

"I didn't say that," she answered defensively. "I was just... looking to grab my stuff. I'm not afraid of you driving me home."

Clearly, she wasn't convincing because he just rolled his eyes and slammed his hood down. "Well, come on if you're coming," he said.

Everything from the tightness of his voice and the tension in his shoulders told her that he was beyond pissed off. Maybe that meant that she didn't have to worry about the short ride. Still, the last thing she needed was for him to know where she lived.

Xavier opened his car door and hopped inside. Given the look on his face, she guessed that she had about two seconds to get out of her car or he was going to leave her right there in the parking lot.

"I'm coming. I'm coming." She grabbed her bag and then

raced to get into the passenger seat of his Escalade. But the moment she slammed the door behind her, she felt as if she'd climbed into a small cage—a comfortable, warm cage—but a cage nonetheless.

# *Chapter 15*

"So, where to?" Xavier asked, shifting his SUV in Reverse and steering away from her dead-battery car to exit the parking lot.

She had two seconds to make up her mind about where to have him drop her off. She knew that if she told him some lodge motel or something like that, it would only stir up more questions that she didn't have the answers to. So she took one look at him and just decided to go with the truth and gave him her address in Marietta.

If Xavier had any complaints about driving so far out, he kept them to himself and just hit the highway. For the first ten minutes, they rode in complete silence. Cheryl pretended that every building they passed was completely and utterly fascinating to her. But the silence just grew louder and louder.

"So…is this the way it's going to be between us?" Xavier finally asked.

"What do you mean?" She cringed at her own question.

"Okay. Never mind. I see how you want to play this." He sighed and shook his head.

A few more minutes elapsed before Cheryl caved. "It was just a mistake. I don't see why you can't understand that."

"If memory serves me correctly, there were two people in bed that night. It seems that both parties should have equal say as to what should and shouldn't happen moving forward."

"There's no point in our moving forward," she reasoned. "There's no chance of a relationship ever working out between the two of us."

"So you're a bartender as well as a psychic?" He released a sarcastic chuckle. "Damn. I wish you'd put that part in your résumé. It might've come in handy."

"You're upset."

"Did your ESP tell you that?"

She cut her gaze over at him. "Why can't you just let it go? What is it with you men? Do women give you as much trouble when you give the 'let's be friends' speech?"

"Oh, now I'm just like all the other men you've had in your life. Great."

"*All the other men?* What makes you think there were a lot?"

"Hey, I'm just using your own words. Do you hear me sitting here comparing you to anyone else? I was talking about you and me. Period! I'm just saying that I don't like how you handle your business. It's not always about you, you know."

"So now I'm selfish?"

"You're definitely something. I'll give you that."

"For your information, you're no picnic, either," she tossed back at him. "You want to give me grief, but you're no angel. How am I supposed to take a man who runs a strip club and has a bevy of women who smile and bat their eyes every time he comes around? I'm supposed to trust you in a serious relationship? Hell, you've never even been in one in your entire life."

"How in the hell would you know? You don't know anything about me."

"Oh, I know about you," she said, and then turned her head away from him before she was stupid enough or too emotional to blurt out about the background check and police report on him and his entire family.

"Let me guess," Xavier ranted. "You've been listening to gossip around the club. Is that it? I know how women love to gossip when they get together."

"And men don't? You don't tell Quentin or your brothers everything? You guys don't get together and compare notes about who slept with whom, and how good or bad someone was in bed? Please, men gossip more than women. That's a fact!"

"I don't know how many times I've told you that I'm not like other men. So please quit with all the comparisons. It's getting old."

"Got it, Mr. Boy Scout! You're Mr. Perfect, Mr. Honesty—whatever!"

Xavier glanced over at her, his face contorted in anger. "What the hell is with you? Why are you so bitter?"

"I'm not bitter!"

"No. You're a bowl of sunshine, tossing smiles and rose petals to everyone you see." He rolled his eyes. "You have to be the most difficult and frustrating person I've ever met."

"Aha! Now who's doing the comparing?"

"Trust me. The only comparing I'm doing is the short list of crazy people I've met over the years. And let me tell you, sweetheart, you're shooting to the top with a bullet."

Cheryl huffed and folded her arms. "Then count yourself lucky that I've spared you the headache of getting involved with me."

"Believe me. I'm counting."

As fast as the argument started, it ended just as abruptly and that damn silence started ringing in her ears. They flew past a couple of more exits before Cheryl said, "Get off here."

Xavier did as she asked without saying another word.

Cheryl snuck another look to her left and saw how hard his jaw was clenched. Then it surprised her just how much it bothered her that he was so angry. "I'm sorry." She turned back and glanced out the window as he cut his gaze over at her.

Those simple words were like a needle puncturing an inflated balloon. She even swore she heard a loud *pop!*

"I'm sorry, too," he said.

It should have ended there, but Cheryl started wondering about which part he was sorry about. Sleeping with her or because there was no future together. *What in the hell is wrong with you? You broke up with him.*

"Turn at the next right," she said softly, and then had to clear her throat because it suddenly felt as if her larynx was closing. But when she coughed, tears sprang to her eyes and wrecked her whole program by trickling down her face. Once that started, it was damn near impossible to try to shut them off.

"Hey, hey, hey. What are those for?" Xavier asked, clearly stunned at the sudden turn of events.

"Nothing," she choked out, but her performance would definitely qualify for a Razzie Award for Worst Actress. "It's the third house on the left," she squeaked out, wiping at her tears as fast as she could.

Xavier sped up so that he could whip into the driveway.

There was a brief rush of relief when she saw that her sister's car wasn't in the driveway. "Thanks. I really appreciate your driving me home," she managed to say before shoving the car door open and then running toward her front door. Not until she began scrambling for her keys did she realize that she'd left them in her car.

"Damn it!" She slapped a hand across her forehead and couldn't see how the night—or early morning—could get any worse.

Xavier shut off his vehicle. "Is there a problem?"

She turned to him with her bottom lip trembling. "I left my house keys in the car—and now I can't get in!" And the waterworks started again. She covered both hands over her face while her entire body shook with heart-wrenching sobs.

"Whoa. It's okay." He rushed over to her and pulled her into his arms.

Instantly, his body heat enveloped her and calmed her like a strong sedative. She clung to him and wished fervently that they could remain like this for—hell, she didn't know for how long—as long as it took to ease the guilt that had been eating away at her for the past nineteen days.

She never knew how much strength it took to push something you wanted away. It drained almost everything from her—her heart, her love, her sanity. If she didn't get pulled off this case, she needed to march into Mackey's office and just hand in her badge. Never in her life could she have ever dreamed of screwing up this badly, and frankly, being pushed past the point of even caring.

"It's all right," he whispered again, and then planted a kiss on top of her head. "I'm sure that we can figure something out to get you inside."

Cheryl sniffed but then burrowed her head deeper in the firm muscles of Xavier's chest. *Lord. Why does he feel so much like home?* The notion that you could feel like that with someone was foreign to her, but there was simply no other way for her to put it. She would cling to him forever if she could. She could lose herself in just his strength.

Xavier pressed a kiss to the top of her head as more tears streamed from her eyes and soaked his shirt.

"C'mon." He leaned back so that he could get a good look at her. "It's going to be all right." He smiled with an openness and honesty that completely melted her heart.

Cheryl sniffed again and then reluctantly pulled back so that she could dry her eyes. But once again Xavier surprised her by sweeping the pads of his thumbs under her eyes to help erase the tracks of her tears. After a minute, she felt a little better and tried to flash a smile up at him. "I guess this should clench the title for me on your crazy list, huh?"

"No. Believe it or not, you have a ways to go if you're going to bypass my cousin. Trust me."

She laughed while she continued to try and pull herself together. "Good to know."

At seeing her smile, Xavier's mood lightened. "All right, then, let's see about getting you in here." He winked. "Do you happen to have a spare key around? Maybe under a potted plant or mat?"

Cheryl wanted to hit herself in the head again. "Yes. Just a minute." She strolled around to the back of the house and reached for the magnetic holder tucked under the lawn mower. When she returned to the front door, she held up the key. "Looks like I was freaking out for nothing."

Xavier smiled. "Is it wrong for me to say that I kind of enjoyed you freaking out? It's the closest I've been able to get to you in weeks."

"Yeah. I'm…really sorry about that," she said, and meant it. "It's just a lot of…things I have going on right now. I shouldn't have overreacted like I did. I could've handled it better."

"Yeah…you could've."

"You're not going to let me off the hook easily, are you?"

"Not by a long shot." This time when he laughed, his eyes twinkled. This was a lot better than the tension that had been festering between them.

But with nothing else to say, Cheryl turned toward the

front door and slipped her spare key into the lock. Even then she was slow to turn it.

"Is there something else wrong?" Xavier asked, moving up behind her until his chest pressed against her back.

She closed her eyes while the marrow in her knees weakened. "I was just thinking..."

Xavier pressed a kiss to the back of her head. "About what?"

"About...inviting you inside."

His arms slid around her waist and his hands dipped low to squeeze her pussy through the seat of her jeans while he pressed another kiss to the back of her head. "Would you like for me to come inside?"

Cheryl exhaled shakily. "Oh, God, yes."

"Then I would *love* to come inside."

# Chapter 16

Cheryl was certain that she came the moment he squeezed her crotch outside the front door. After that she was in a mad rush to get this man into the house and into her bed as fast as possible. They stumbled into the house, tugging and pulling at each other's clothes as if their bodies were experiencing three-alarm fires, and the only way to put out the fire was to join their bodies before they both went up in flames.

They were going at it so hard it was a wonder that they even remembered to kick the front door closed. After that, Xavier pinned her to the wall in the foyer where he ripped her shirt and bra from her body in just a few seconds. She relieved him of his shirt just a second later. However, when it came to removing their jeans, it got a little tricky, and before either of them knew it, they had collapsed to the floor while they kissed and squirmed their way out of the remainder of their clothes.

Neither of them was interested in foreplay. Tender kisses and caresses would come later. At least, that was the understanding they came to after the simmering looks that passed between them.

Xavier locked his lips around her mouth while she wrapped her legs tightly around his waist, so that she clung to him like a layer of skin. He completely lifted her body off the floor. From that position, he had no trouble entering her tight pussy, which greeted his thick cock with a firm squeeze.

Almost all the air in Xavier's lungs oozed out of his chest in one long, steady stream. Judging by the way Cheryl's mouth popped off of his, she experienced the same phenomenon. He loved watching as wave after wave of euphoria washed over her beautiful face and the glow that accompanied it.

*I can spend my entire life making love to this woman.*

The moment that thought drifted through his head, he recognized the truth. No one had, and he imagined no one ever could, make him feel exactly what he was feeling right now. What was happening between them was more than just sex, whether she wanted to recognize it or not. He'd had his fair share of sex, but this was something else entirely. This was more powerful than anything he'd experienced before, just as it was sweeter than anything he'd ever known.

*Is this what love feels like?*

The question stunned him, but it was one that he suddenly felt he needed an answer to. If it was, he suddenly felt cheated for never having known that something that felt this good even existed. He suddenly understood, profoundly, the pain that his cousin and his older brother Eamon had gone through when something this powerful had been snatched from them.

*What if in the morning she pushes me away again? What will I do? How could I possibly handle it?*

Xavier slammed his eyes closed and tried to push the thought as far out of his mind as he possibly could. All that mattered at the moment was for him to try and make her feel what he was feeling. He hoped that it would be his salvation in their relationship. "Where's your room, baby?"

"F-first room on the right," she answered, panting and then bringing his lips back toward hers so that she could have another taste of him.

Xavier didn't bother trying to stand. Instead, with her clinging to his waist and neck, he simply crawled while she continued bouncing her thick, juicy body on his hard cock. This was surely how they did things in the animal kingdom. No need to disconnect or disengage. Judging by the way she was panting and trembling, she was more than just enjoying the ride.

Then he felt that tremble he was waiting for, the one that let him know that Cheryl was on the verge of her first orgasm. Then he felt it again. On the floor by the foot of the bed, Xavier stopped and unwound her hands from his neck so that he could plant her upper body against the floor and watch her face when he started hammering his hips into hers.

"Look at me," he ordered.

Cheryl's eyes fluttered open just as his strokes started picking up speed. He didn't have to ask her how it felt or whether he was tearing up her G-spot. He knew, because it was written all over her face; it danced in her eyes. There was only one thing that he wanted her to know.

"I miss having you like this," he panted. He took her wrists in one hand and then pinned them high above her head while he substituted fast strokes for deeper ones. "I love the way you feel. Do you know that?"

She thrashed her head from side to side.

In no mood to give her any mercy, he wanted to show her that he knew how to work her body. With his one free hand, he slipped two fingers under the base of her clit while he continued to stroke as deep as he could.

Cheryl gasped as she arched her body. But that just gave him better access to all the goodies that he was having fun playing with. With her orgasm rocketing through her body at a clip she wasn't prepared for, a hoarse cry rang out from her throat at a pitch she had never been able to hit before. Her mind soared so high that she thought she was having an out-of-body experience.

When she finally came down, Xavier's sexy-as-sin grin greeted her. There were no words to express how it felt to get that one big explosion out of the way. One thing for sure, *thank you* certainly didn't seem like enough. But she surely could try to repay the favor.

Smiling, Cheryl unwrapped her legs from Xavier's waist and eased him out, momentarily disconnecting their bodies. "Let's try out the bed," she suggested.

To prove that she didn't have to ask twice, Xavier jumped up from the floor and then offered his hand to help her up. But once she climbed onto her feet, she gave him a hard shove so that he would fall back onto the bed, his glazed cock standing as tall and as high as a flagpole.

Meanwhile, a sly smile inched up the side of his face and his gaze tracked her with a combination of adoration, lust and love. That last emotion surprised her, yet it pleased her, as well. Wasn't that the same emotion that she was wrestling with every time she thought about him? For weeks now, she'd thought that she was going insane. Love didn't just spring up organically like that. Did it?

She searched her memory for the few times she had discussed love with her mother before she passed. And the only thing she could remember her ever saying was, *It just happens.* Like there was no rhyme or reason to it. At least, it wasn't something that could ever truly be explained even after all these thousands of years of men and women cohabitating the earth.

*It just happens.* Cheryl climbed up on the bed and crawled

slowly up his cock, glazed with her body's juices. Her mouth watered while she ran her tongue down its pulsing head. It might just be her imagination, but he even tasted like chocolate. She didn't stop at the base of his cock. She kept going until she'd tea-bagged him, taking each of his smooth balls into her mouth and sucking them until he started to hiss and moan.

Smiling, she worked her way back to the head and immediately gave him a couple of jawbreakers. Xavier jumped and sucked in a breath.

"Damn, baby," he panted, and reached for her.

She allowed him to stroke her head while she continued to set a good rhythm. Soon Xavier swept Cheryl's hair back away from her face so that he could watch her. Within minutes, pre-cum started to drip from the tip of his dick, and she vacuumed it up with as much gusto as if she'd had Hoover stamped on the bottom of her ass.

Clearly, this was her superhero's kryptonite, because his strong muscular legs started trembling. His hands no longer tried to just brush her hair, but to hold her still so that she focused at an angle he found particularly enjoyable. The muscles tightened in his stomach as they started to quiver, and then his knees came up so that they were propped up on either side of her head.

"Ooooh, damn, baby," he muttered as his hips thrashed so that they rose off the bed while he stroked his way to the back of her throat. A few times she gagged a bit, but she held firm as he called out to his Lord and Savior.

Just when Cheryl thought that he was about to blast off, he pulled back. His dick sprung from her lips with a *pop* and then swung like a pendulum in front of her face.

"Not yet," he said, smiling and grabbing her. "Pick your poison, sweetheart."

She blinked up at him.

"It makes no difference to me what position. I'm going

to tear it up, anyway." He stroked his hard cock while he waited impatiently.

Remembering how good it felt to take him doggy-style, Cheryl quickly scrambled to get on her knees. But this time, she gave it an added twist by dropping her shoulders to the bed instead of her arms. This way, she could play with her clit while he hit her from the back.

Xavier saddled up behind Cheryl, leaned down and planted a big kiss on her right ass cheek. "Are you ready, sweetheart?"

"Mmm-hmm." She wiggled her rump back at him in anticipation, only for him to slap both cheeks just the way she liked it.

"You didn't think I forgot, did you?"

"You better not have." She wiggled again.

He laughed and sent two more stinging blows to her upturned cheeks. Just when the sting started to fade, Xavier eased into her wet pussy inch by glorious inch.

Cheryl reached down to her clit to feel her own honey start to drip into her hand. When he was just halfway in, her mouth started to sag and her eyes started to roll to the back of her head.

"A'ight, baby. I got you." Xavier slapped her ass again. After a while, she felt like he had worked his way to the back of her throat. "How you doing, baby?" he asked, chuckling.

"Ooooh." That was all she could manage to get out.

"You like that?" As she stroked him, his hips smacked her butt.

"I'm not going to lie, baby. You got a man caught up," he panted.

She liked it when he praised her, and liked it even more when he kept her ass feeling like it was on fire.

*Smack! Smack!*

More honey dripped down between her legs and she twirled her finger faster and faster, while she had her own talk with God. Mentally, Cheryl started climbing the walls, struggling to catch her breath, absolutely loving the magic Xavier was working in between her legs.

*Where in the hell has this man been all my life?*

In no time at all, their bodies start smacking, squishing and making all kinds of funky noises. And since her bed wasn't as strong as the one Mad Monez kept in his crib, there was a high risk of their breaking the bed.

"Oh, God. Oh, God." Cheryl recognized that familiar sensation building between her legs and she was helpless to do anything about it. No. That's not right. She didn't *want* to do anything about it. She wanted that pleasure train to hit her full force. And when it did, she yelled out while her body's juices overflowed into her hand.

As tremor after tremor shook Cheryl's body, Xavier got caught up in her aftershocks. While her vaginal walls contracted rapidly he tried to hang on to what little bit of sanity he had. But it didn't seem to be working. Fearful that he was going to come before he was ready, he pulled out of her trembling hot spot and rested his glistening cock between the soft pillows of her ass.

Hot and sweaty, Xavier waited a few seconds to catch his breath. Still, he was bewitched by the sight of his cock rubbing her honey glaze over her backside. It looked so good to him that, for a few minutes, he started smacking her butt with his cock so that he could watch the small waves ripple around him.

When he'd had enough fun, he told Cheryl, "Stay just like that for me, baby." He took a couple of steps backward on his knees, laid down on his back and wiggled his way in between her legs. Once he hooked his arms around her waist, he forced her knees to spread out farther so that the honeycomb he was seeking would slide down to his open mouth.

At the first taste of her sweetness, his cock found a few

more inches to stretch out. He twirled his tongue around her clit, slid back to the entrance of her pussy and then quickly tongued her clit again.

"Ooooh," Cheryl moaned as her firm thighs quivered and quaked.

A few times, Xavier would just hold his tongue still and encourage her to rock and gyrate on her own. That had her hissing and moaning, too. At this point, she was like a drug to him. He couldn't get enough and didn't care if he overdosed. He reached up and pulled her open brown lips even wider. Her glistening pussy looked like a plump strawberry and he wasted no time trying to eat as much of it as he could.

When her legs really got going, Xavier released her lips so that he could go back to smacking her ass again.

*Smack! Smack!*

Cheryl gasped and grabbed her bedsheets in her clenched fists. The warmth of his mouth, the slippery slickness of his tongue and those stinging slaps against her ass had her mind so far gone that she didn't know what to do. But that final sweet release remained just beyond her reach. That is, until she got her hips involved and started humping his face.

She tensed and started to lift her body up for a break, but Xavier locked his arms around her waist and held her close. With no other choice, Cheryl worked her hips like an electric mixer, drilling and grinding, and when the next orgasm hit, she was screaming so loud it wouldn't have surprised her if someone in the neighborhood had called 9-1-1.

Now that she was sopping wet and he'd almost drowned, Xavier released her hips and rolled her over. He could've waited until she caught her breath, but he was fiending to get back inside her warmth.

He didn't take her by climbing into the missionary position, but instead laid down on his side, pulled her close and lifted her leg high into the air. Even then he held out a few seconds to tease his cock around her moisture-slick flesh, his mushroom-capped head hitting the back of her clit just right.

Cheryl rocked back against him, growing impatient for him to enter her completely. "Baby."

"Hmm?" Xavier was determined to hold out until he heard the magic words.

"Baby, *please.*"

He chuckled. "All you had to do was ask." He reached down in between their bodies and redirected his cock so that he could glide into her with one long, deep stroke. Unbelievably, she came instantly.

"Did you just come, baby?" he asked.

Cheryl continued to gasp to catch her breath.

"Do you think that means I'm done with you?" He moved his hips and kept her leg stretched high into the air. She shook so bad that she could hardly speak, but that didn't garner her any mercy from him. Not with her quivering vaginal walls feeling as good as they did.

"You better catch your breath, sweetheart. You got nineteen days to make up for, baby." He turned his head so that he could nibble on her earlobe. "After tonight I don't want to hear nothing about us not being together. You hear me?"

*Stroke. Stroke.*

"Understand?"

Cheryl still couldn't speak, but tears started to leak from her eyes.

"Am I hurting you, baby?" he asked tenderly. "You want me to stop?"

When she didn't answer, his hips stopped rocking. But suddenly, she found her voice.

"No. No… Please, don't stop."

"So you do like that, huh?"

*Stroke. Stroke.*

She didn't like it. Cheryl loved it. She was like putty in his hands and he knew it. Why should she fight it anymore? What was she getting other than a lot of frustrated nights with her body craving him and her mind obsessed with memories? If she gave in to him, she could have him in her bed every night—and every morning.

*Until he got bored and moved on to the next chick,* a voice reminded her.

*But he said that he's not like that. He's different.*

*And you believe that?* The voice laughed.

*Yes,* she argued back. She did believe it. Cheryl didn't know why, but she did believe him when he said that he was honest. Mainly because other than hearing how all the women at The Dollhouse had a crush on him, no one had a bad thing to say about him.

So maybe…after her case…there could be something?

The rest of Cheryl's reasoning flew out of the window when she felt that familiar pressure building inside of her. Xavier knew what was happening, too, and slid his hands down the inside of her legs so that his fingers could massage her clit while his strokes went even deeper.

"Look at you," Xavier said, wiping her sweat-slicked face as her sighs continued to climb the musical scale. "After tonight, I don't want to hear nothing about us not being together. You understand me?" he said, quickening his pace. "If you want to come, you better say something," he threatened.

"I—I hear you," she panted.

"We understand each other?"

"Y-yes."

"You're going to start being nice to me?"

*Stroke... Stroke...*

"Oh…God… *Yes!*"

With those words, Xavier flipped her onto her back, hiked her legs up and started drilling her deeper into the mattress. One…two…three orgasms exploded one after the other. When it came to the last one, Cheryl wasn't sure what happened. One second she was screaming and in the next she was fast asleep.

# Chapter 17

Xavier slept like a log. A lot of it had to do with the fact that he had Cheryl tucked under his arm. He didn't understand why, but she was like a soothing balm to his soul. To be honest, at this point, he didn't care why he felt the things that he felt. All that mattered was that he felt them. And he couldn't remember feeling happier and more contented in all his life.

That night was a turning point. He was convinced of that much. All he had to wish for now was that it would be for the better. Though he was still half-asleep, he pulled Cheryl's pliant body closer and then snuggled his face deeper into the nape of her neck and just inhaled. His calm deepened as his mind settled between reality and fantasy. In all honesty, it was the perfect place to be to just mellow out and chill.

Being a creature of habit, he usually climbed out of bed at nine o'clock to get in his workout. When his internal clock went off, his eyes fluttered open. As he focused, he was confused by a cute six-year-old staring him in the face.

"Who are you?" the little boy asked.

Xavier felt he should be asking him the same thing. But given that the boy was probably in *his* house, he decided it was best to answer. "Um, Xavier."

The kid's large soulful eyes blinked back at him. "Why are you in bed with my aunt Cheryl?"

"Huh…" As much as Xavier liked to be honest, he suspected that this was not one of those times. "We, uh, decided to have a sleepover." He glanced down at the bed and was beyond relieved to see that at some time during their early-morning sex-a-thon, one of them had the good sense to pull the covers up over them.

However, if he thought that he had satisfied the little forty-eight-inch-high private investigator, he was sadly mistaken.

"Why did she invite you over for a sleepover? Was she scared?"

"I, uh…" He tried to nudge Cheryl awake. He needed a little help with this situation.

"Because Aunt Cheryl is never scared," the kid continued. "She knows how to do karate and she carries a big ole gun."

*She does?* Xavier frowned and looked down at the woman curled up next to him.

It just so happened that she chose that moment to moan and stretch as she started to wake up.

"Good morning, Aunt Cheryl."

Cheryl's eyes popped opened. "Thaddeus!"

*Thaddeus? Interesting name.*

She clutched the sheet to her chest and then glanced back over her shoulder to see Xavier lying next to her.

"Good morning," he said.

Cheryl gasped and then flipped back around to face the wide, curious gaze of her nephew.

"Thaddeus!" a woman called from out in the hallway. "Where are you?"

"I'm in Aunt Cheryl's room," Thaddeus shouted, oblivious to the fact that maybe her aunt didn't want him or anyone else coming into her bedroom.

"Thaddeus," Cheryl hissed.

"What?" he asked, confused by his aunt's sudden distress.

Xavier chuckled just as the bedroom door flew open.

"How many times have I told you about coming in here and— *Ohmigod!*" The woman at the door jumped and her eyes bulged so wide that it was a wonder they didn't just pop out of her head.

"Good morning," Xavier said, thinking he should put on his best face and be friendly to everyone during this impromptu family reunion.

Unfortunately, Cheryl thought that it was best to jack the covers over her head and groan from sheer embarrassment.

"Thaddeus," the woman snapped, and then waved the kid over. "Come out of here and leave your aunt alone! Do you see that…she has company?"

"Mama, Aunt Cheryl had a sleepover."

"Come here, *now!*"

Thaddeus frowned, clearly confused as to why his mother was irritated at him. He shuffled his feet as he walked slowly toward the door. "I just brought her clothes in that she left in the hallway."

*"Hurry up!"* His mother continued to look mortified until he was within arm's reach. She quickly grabbed his hand and tried to rush him out.

Xavier watched, feeling bad for the little fella.

When Thaddeus glanced back over at the bed, Xavier exchanged a sympathetic frown with him. A second later, the door slammed shut.

"I'm going to hell," Cheryl groaned.

The comment seemed so out of left field to Xavier that he had to laugh. "I don't think it's that serious." He chuckled.

"I can't believe he caught you in here," she moaned. "I thought they were still in Alabama for her friend's wedding."

Xavier pulled up the top sheet to see Cheryl lying with her hands covering her face. "It's all right. He just thinks that we had a sleepover. No big deal."

"No big deal?" Cheryl snatched her hands from over her face and hissed at him. "He's a young impressionable kid. God only knows what he thinks of me now." She bolted from under the covers like a rocket, hardly giving him any time to enjoy the view before she was covering up in this big, fluffy robe. "I have to go out there and say something to my sister. Lord knows I don't know what I'm going to say."

"I take it that this must be your sister's place," he said, sensing that maybe he was responsible for getting her into some kind of trouble. "Is there anything I can do?" Xavier asked. "Maybe I can talk to your sister and explain…"

Cheryl turned and settled her hands on her hips. "You want to go and talk to my sister and explain…our relationship to her?"

"Sure," he said with a shrug. "I don't mind. It's the least I can do."

"All right," she said with a smile creeping across her face. "Why don't you explain to me first what you think our relationship is?"

"All right." Xavier sat up against the headboard. "First…I guess that despite my being your boss down at The Dollhouse, I believe that we are equals in entering this personal and mutually…*exclusive* relationship."

Cheryl's brows comically leaped to the center of her forehead. "Exclusive?"

He met her gaze and nodded. "A first for me, I have to admit. But then again, I've never met anyone quite like you."

"What? You have a penchant for crazy women?"

Xavier smirked. "Who knew?"

She laughed, but then leaned back against a wall so that she could study his face. "You're serious."

His smile stretched wider. "I'm dead serious."

Even then, she had a hard time getting that to compute in her head. "*You,* Xavier King, want to be in a monogamous relationship with *me?*"

"Problem?"

She opened her mouth, but no words fell out. It certainly wasn't because the idea didn't appeal to her. It did, more than she really cared to admit, but there were legitimate reasons why they couldn't be together. Like, he didn't know who she really was. Like, everything between them—other than the mind-blowing sex—was a lie. How was Mr. Honesty going to deal with that when the chips fell? And eventually they would fall. That was the problem with lies. They always surfaced.

"It's just that…all this is happening pretty fast."

Xavier shook his head, but his smile remained in place. "I'm not letting you get rid of me this time," he said. "Not without you giving me a fair shot or a legitimate reason why you want to bail."

*Oh. I have a legitimate reason, all right.*

"C'mon." He cocked his head and leveled his best puppy-dog stare at her. "Is the idea of being my *girlfriend* that repulsive?"

She hesitated only so that she could tease him.

"Oh." He slapped both hands over his heart as if he'd been shot through it. "You wound me with your callous silence."

"I think that someone may have missed their calling as an actor."

"And you, ma'am, either missed your calling in the military or as a police interrogator because you surely know how to torture a man."

She blinked as the humor drained from her face.

Xavier was immediately concerned. "What? Did I say something wrong?"

"No. Um." She tried to laugh off his comment. "Just got sidetracked. That's all."

He nodded. "So. Do you want me to go out there and talk to your sister or do you want me to escape out the window before you get grounded?"

"Very funny, but that's not necessary. This is both our places. It's just that…we don't bring a lot of guys around. We try to be really selective about who we introduce Thaddeus to. You know."

"Don't want to have him calling every boyfriend Uncle So-and-So?" he offered.

"See. You do understand."

He nodded. "I guess so."

"So you won't mind going out the window?"

He jerked, his smile disappearing.

"Just joking." Cheryl winked. "I'll be right back."

"Very funny," he said, grabbing a pillow and tossing it to her.

She just barely dodged the pillow, but giggled like a schoolgirl all the way to the door. However, once she bolted out of the room and closed the door, Larissa was on her like white on rice.

"Who on earth is that?"

Cheryl drew a deep breath and settled her hands on her sister's shoulders. "Look. I know that you're probably upset—"

"Upset?" Larissa's voice rose.

"Shh." Cheryl slapped a hand over her sister's mouth. "Keep it down. He might hear you."

Larissa reached up and pulled her sister's hand down. "Upset? Are you kidding me? I'm jealous as hell. Where did you find him and does he have any brothers?"

Cheryl's eyes bulged with shock. "What?"

"I mean, damn. I just saw his chest and arms and...grrrr." Larissa curled her arms and struck a Mr. Universe pose.

"Okay. Now you're just being silly."

Larissa struck another pose. "Grrrr."

Clearly not wanting to be left out, Thaddeus rushed down the hall and started striking poses next to his mother.

Laughing, Cheryl rolled her eyes. "All right, you two. Cut it out."

Larissa joined her sister in laughing, mainly because Cheryl's face was darkening with embarrassment. A second later, she covered Thaddeus's ears and sung in a near whisper, "Cheryl has a boyfriend. Cheryl has a boyfriend."

"What are we, in junior high?"

"I'm just saying." Larissa giggled.

"Damn. You'd think that he was *your* boyfriend."

"Aha!" Larissa pointed at her. "He is your boyfriend. Oh, my God. How long has it been since you had one of those?" She knocked the top of her head as if she was trying to process the information in her head. "Date, yes." Larissa covered her son's ears again. "An occasional one-night stand, yes. But I would have to go all the way back to college since you called someone your boyfriend."

"That's only because relationships are messy and complicated and I'm a very busy woman."

"Yeah," Thaddeus agreed, and held up his hands like he was ready to karate chop someone. "She fights crime and kicks major butt."

"Oooh. About that..." Cheryl smiled awkwardly. "Thaddeus, I'm going to need you and your mother to do me a big favor...."

Xavier had never felt more uncomfortable in all his life. Until that moment, he thought that he could handle almost anything in almost any situation. Nope. Turned out an overprotective six-year-old was not unlike being interrogated as a suspected terrorist. There was a lot of squirming and sweating going on.

"So how come you don't wear clothes during your sleepovers?" Thaddeus asked before shoving a forkful of pancakes into his mouth.

Xavier, Cheryl and Larissa all spit out their coffee at the same time.

Thaddeus's eyes grew wide before he erupted into a fit of giggles. "My turn." He went for his orange juice, but his mother quickly moved it out of reach.

"No, Thaddeus," she said sternly, and then glanced at Cheryl and Xavier. "That was just an accident. We didn't mean to do that."

Cheryl hopped up from the table to grab a roll of paper towels and proceeded to pass sheets around so that they could all clean themselves up.

The little boy looked disappointed, but then turned his curiosity back to Xavier. "I went to a sleepover one time. My friend Scotty lives up the street and sometimes I stay over there when Mama and Aunt Cheryl have to work late—but we have to wear pajamas, and we sleep in different beds. Is it a lot more fun when you share the same bed?"

All the adults' gazes shifted around the table.

"No," Cheryl answered, and then cleared her throat when Xavier's head whipped in her direction. "It's really hot and uncomfortable. It's probably better how you and Scotty do it—in separate beds."

"Oh. It was hot? That's why you took your clothes off?"

Larissa set her elbow on the table and then hid her head in the palm of her hand.

"It was something like that," Cheryl said. "Now eat your breakfast."

Thaddeus nodded and then shoved another small bite of pancakes into his mouth.

Xavier started cramming food into his mouth, as well.

The sooner he finished, the sooner he could escape the boy with a million questions. But so far that appeared to be just wishful thinking on his part.

"Xa-Xavier, do you, um, live around here?" Thaddeus asked, locking his big brown eyes on him.

"No. I actually live in Buckhead." When his answer didn't compute, he added. "Have you ever heard of Phipps Plaza?"

"You mean like the mall?"

Xavier nodded. "Yeah, I live over there in this really tall building."

"Mama, you go to that mall sometimes, right?"

Larissa smiled awkwardly. "Yes, baby. Sometimes we go to the mall over there."

"Can we go and visit Xa-Xavier's house next time we go? He's my new friend." He glanced sheepishly at Xavier as if it was a statement and a question at the same time.

"Um, I'm sure that Xavier is a very busy man—" Larissa started.

"No. I would love to have you come over," Xavier interrupted.

It was Cheryl's turn to whip her head around toward Xavier. Under the table, she placed her hand on his thigh as extra reassurance. "Xavier, you don't have to—"

"Don't be silly. I think it's a great idea for you guys to come over. Who knows, maybe it could be a weekend when my brothers are in town."

"You have brothers?"

Larissa's brows sprung up, as well. "There are more like you?"

Xavier's smile doubled in size. "I have two brothers. One just recently got married."

Larissa quickly did the math. "That still leaves one available."

Cheryl sent her foot flying against her sister's shin.

"Ow!" Larissa jumped up in her seat like a toasted Pop-Tart.

Xavier snickered. "Yes. That still leaves one. Though I have to tell you that of all the King brothers, Jeremy is the least likely one to settle down."

Larissa shrugged her shoulders. "I don't know. Maybe it's just the romantic in me, but I think that all men have the capacity to settle down. It just takes finding the right woman." She turned her head toward Cheryl. "Don't you think so, Cheryl?"

Cheryl's eyes narrowed on her sister. "I don't have an opinion on the matter."

Xavier looked over at her. "Really?"

She shrugged, unable to see what was wrong with her answer. "Really."

"You'll have to forgive my sister," Larissa said. "She's not much of a romantic."

"I do get the sense that she's a hard cookie to crack," Xavier said. "Maybe that's what fascinates me."

"Oh. So you like a challenge?"

"Who doesn't?"

Cheryl shook her head. "Typical."

Larissa frowned while Xavier continued to look intrigued, "And what is that supposed to mean?"

"It means that men always want something that they can't have. Because God forbid the minute they have what they *think* they want, then they no longer want it."

Xavier's frown matched Larissa's. "How come that sounds like something you got out of one of those glossy women's magazines? Self-psychoanalyze for $5.99."

Larissa snickered.

"That's not true," Cheryl defended.

"No? That wasn't your stack of *Essence* and *O* magazines I saw in your room? You're not trying to learn the '10 Ways to Keep Your Man Satisfied'? Or 'Learn the Signs of When Your Man Is Creeping'?"

"There are some good articles in those magazines."

"Puh-lease." Xavier rolled his eyes. "You want to know the number-one problem women have?"

"From you? No," Cheryl snapped defensively.

"I do," Larissa butted in, and received a sharp look from her sister. "What? I could use all the tips I can get."

"All right." Xavier set his fork down. "The number-one problem that the *majority* of your fair sex has is…*listening* to other women."

"Oooh," Larissa said, bobbing her head as if Xavier had just come down from Mount Sinai with that ridiculous statement chiseled on a stone tablet.

"Give me a break," Cheryl said, rolling her eyes.

"It's true," Xavier insisted, smiling. "It's not men criticizing whether you're wearing last year's fashions or unstylish shoes. They don't tell you how to look, dress, and give you tips about what to do to us in…" He glanced at Thaddeus. "Forget that last part. But yes, men like a challenge. Last time I checked, so do women. But more than that, men are attracted to *confidence.* I've met and dated women of all colors, sizes and incomes—and so have my brothers—so I know what I'm talking about." His gaze centered on Cheryl. "I'll admit that the moment I met you I was attracted to you. But you may have noticed that I work with a lot of attractive women. It was the way you carried yourself—your swagger. It's in everything you do. The way you work the bar, the way you walk and even how you always look like you're two seconds from cussing me out—like you do right now."

Cheryl tried to fight it, but a smile curled the corners of her lips.

Larissa broke her own table rules and planted both elbows on the hard top and cradled her chin in the palms of her hands. "And what did you say was the name of your single brother?"

Xavier's laughter exploded just as the front doorbell rang.

Larissa sighed. "I'll get it." She stood and patted the back of Thaddeus's head. "Hurry up and finish your breakfast."

"Yes, ma'am."

After Larissa walked past the table, Xavier leaned over toward Cheryl. "I think your sister likes me. If I get her stamp of approval, will you finally go out with me on an official date?"

Cheryl's brows dipped together.

"I'm talking the whole nine. Dancing, dinner—" His gaze skittered across the table toward a smiling Thaddeus so he leaned closer to her and whispered, "Perhaps another sleepover at my place?"

"Xavier!" She slapped him on his muscular arm.

"What?" He chuckled.

Larissa's voice floated back toward the kitchen table after she opened the door. "Oh, hello, Johnnie. What are you doing here?"

Cheryl jumped up, sending her chair screeching backward.

"Whoa." Xavier stood, as well. "What's up?"

"Yes. She's here. She's in the kitchen," Larissa said, and then closed the door.

Cheryl panicked. "Excuse me. I need to—"

"Cheryl," Johnnie barked, once seeing her in the kitchen. "Why haven't you answered your cell? I got that information that you..." Xavier stepped into Johnnie's view and she froze, leaving her mouth wide open.

"Hello," Xavier greeted with a smile, and then his eyes floated down to the weapon on Johnnie's hip. "Oh, I didn't know that you were a cop."

# *Chapter 18*

"Mr. King," Johnnie said, flustered before shifting her gaze to her partner.

Cheryl quickly moved from the table. "Johnnie, you're here. I totally forgot that, um, we were going to do that… *thing* we had planned." She tried her best to telepathically communicate to her partner to just roll with her on this one. She hoped that Johnnie wouldn't suddenly start drooling like the last time she met Xavier.

"Huh?"

Or plan B—close her eyes and mentally scream.

"Oh, right." Johnnie finally jumped on board. "That *thing*. Yeah. We better get going 'cause I really don't have a lot of time. I need to get back to the station."

Cheryl turned toward Xavier with her best apologetic smile. "I'm sorry. Do you mind if we cut breakfast short? We really need to take care of this."

"Oh, no problem," Xavier said, looking uncomfortable. "I really don't want to be the one to keep you away from your...*thing.*" His gaze swung between the two women. "But I'll catch up with you later?"

"At the very least you'll see me tonight at work," she countered, careful not to commit to anything.

"All right...I guess." Xavier glanced over at Thaddeus. "It was nice to meet you, li'l man. Remember, that invitation is always open."

Thaddeus beamed up at Xavier like he was his favorite new superhero. "Did you hear that, Mom? We can go visit Xa-Xavier at his place."

Larissa moved from beside Johnnie to rejoin her son at the kitchen table. "Yes. I heard him. Now sit down and finish your breakfast."

"But I want to walk Xa-Xavier to the door," he whined.

"That's all right, li'l man. You do what your mama says. We'll catch up another time." He winked, turned and planted a kiss on the side of Cheryl's temple.

Johnnie stood still, though her eyes continued to widen in size.

"See you tonight," he mumbled, and then strolled out of the kitchen.

"Cheryl," Larissa hissed. "Go walk him to the door."

Cheryl frowned, but her sister rushed over and shoved her behind him. "Xavier, wait up. I'll walk you to the door."

"I swear. No home training," Larissa mumbled behind Cheryl's back.

When Xavier reached Johnnie, he gave her a departing smile and a quick wink. "Nice to see you again, Officer."

Following behind him, Cheryl gave Johnnie an I-know-that-you're-going-to-kill-me grimace before saying, "I'll be right back."

Johnnie folded her arms. "I'll be waiting on pins and needles."

Once outside, Xavier turned toward Cheryl with a pensive expression. "Is there something you want to tell me?"

Cheryl blinked and then pulled the front door closed behind her. "What do you mean?"

"Just that." His gaze intensified. "You were acting pretty strange in there."

"No. It's just that—"

"Look. I don't make it a habit of trying to force myself on someone. I have to tell you, you're making me feel like *that dude.* You know, the kind that just doesn't take the hint?"

*This is your opportunity. Just tell him that it's not going to work.* "No. It's not that. It's just…complicated."

"It shouldn't be this complicated."

He trapped her gaze for a brief moment. But because there was a growing lump in the center of her throat, she didn't try to speak.

"Right." He nodded and then looked around for a brief second. "So why don't I just uncomplicate things for us and we can just take this back to an employer-employee relationship?"

The question hit her like a wrecking ball. This is what she should want…so why was there fresh tears burning the backs of her eyes?

"Nothing?" he asked with his gaze narrowing. "You don't have anything to say to that?"

"I—I…don't want to hurt you."

Xavier nodded as he tried to process the information. "It might be a little too late for that." He started walking backward. "But don't worry about me. I'm going to be all right." He turned and walked to his SUV.

Cheryl remained rooted in the front doorway while she watched him climb behind the wheel. The debate raged in her head whether leaving things this way was for the best while her heart felt like she had just made the biggest mistake of her life. When her heart started gaining ground, those damn tears broke through the barrier and streamed down her face. Xavier shifted the car in Reverse and when his vehicle began to back up, she finally got her legs to move. "Wait!" She rushed toward the SUV, wiping away her tears.

Xavier hit the brakes and rolled his window down halfway. "Yes?"

"I don't…want us going back to how it was… I want to see you."

"You do?" Xavier said, hiking up his brows. "You kind of have a funny way of showing it."

"I know. It's just… Look, I've never really been any good in relationships. And I've made a few bad choices in the past and…I don't know what I'm doing. But I don't want us to be just employer and employee. That'll be too hard."

"So you're saying…?"

Cheryl cracked a smile. "You're not going to make this easy on me, are you?"

A smile returned to his lips. "Nope."

She rolled her eyes. "All right. I'm saying that…I want… you to be my boyfriend."

Xavier shifted the SUV into Park and then rolled the window the rest of the way down. "Now. Was that so hard?"

"It was like eating glass," she admitted while her lips spread wider.

"You better get used to the taste." He winked. "Now lean over here and give your boyfriend a kiss."

Cheryl stepped closer to the vehicle and then leaned in through the window where Xavier held a finger under her chin. "You certainly know how to keep a man on his toes." His gaze lowered to her lips before tenderly brushing his mouth across hers. But that was just a teaser. He delved deeper for another kiss. And then another. Each one was deeper and sweeter than the last until at last their lips were locked and their tongues caressed each other.

By the time he released her, she was breathless and damn near tempted to launch herself inside the SUV and really give her neighbors something to talk about. At that moment she stopped herself and just rested her forehead against his.

"I think it's time we actually go out on a date."

"Nothing like putting the cart before the horse," she joked.

"All that matters is that we have a cart and a horse. Who gives a damn what order we put them?"

"Hmm. I kind of like the way you think, X-Man." She stole another quick kiss.

"Really?" He stole one for himself. "I have it on special authority that my thinking isn't the only thing you like about me."

She grinned wickedly. "Is that right?"

"Mmm-hmm." Another kiss. "But that's all right. I have a little list of my own on the things I like about you. Why don't we get together, say, Friday night and you can review it?"

"That sounds like fun. But I'll have to see if I can get that night off. It's one of our busiest nights and I work for this really…this—" she reached down and squeezed his cock through his jeans "—really hard-ass boss who might not let me have the night off."

Xavier laughed as he nibbled on the bottom of her lip. "I wouldn't worry about that. Something tells me that you have your boss in the palm of your hand."

They laughed at the corny exchange, and then shared one last, deep kiss.

When Cheryl pulled back, something caught her attention to the left. She turned just as a man pulled his head back into a silver SUV and rolled up the window.

*Hodges?*

"Is something wrong?" Xavier turned his head just as the silver SUV pulled away from the curb and drove off.

Cheryl quickly scanned the license plate and committed it to memory. "Well…you better get going," she said, all business again. "I shouldn't keep Johnnie waiting all day."

Xavier nodded.

When his gaze tried to read her again, she flashed a smile and tried to distract him with another quick kiss. "See you later." She tapped his door and then stepped back from the vehicle.

Xavier tossed her a wink and then shifted his SUV in Reverse again.

Cheryl kept smiling as he rolled back, and when he pulled out onto the street, she stood there and waved goodbye to him. But the minute he was out of view, she turned and raced back into the house. As soon as she was back inside, everyone was still scurrying back to the kitchen table.

She let that go. "Quick. I need a pen."

Johnnie took one look at her partner's face and knew something was wrong. "What is it?" She reached in her breast pocket and produced a pen.

Cheryl grabbed the pen and jotted down the license-plate number. When she looked up to blurt out who she'd just seen, her gaze cut away to her sister and nephew. The last thing she wanted was to get them all worked up about seeing a dangerous criminal lurking outside the house. "Give me a minute, I need to change clothes. Mind driving me down to the station with you?"

"Of course not. What happened to your car?"

"Dead at The Dollhouse," she said, grabbing clothes out of her dresser.

"What in the hell happened in here?" Johnnie asked, looking around.

"Give you one guess," Larissa said, pulling up the rear and shutting the door behind her.

"Now really isn't a good time," Cheryl said.

"Oh, no, you don't," Johnnie shot back, folding her arms. "I think now is the perfect time for you to tell me why you're sleeping with the man who we're supposed to be investigating."

"What?" Larissa's gaze swung back to her older sister. "Is that true? Is he some kind of criminal?"

"No. He's not a criminal," Cheryl said.

Johnnie shifted her weight from one leg to another. "Really? You know that for a fact?"

"Yes, I know." At Johnnie's glare, she had to backtrack a bit. "At least, I don't *believe* that he's a criminal—and so far, we haven't been able to prove otherwise."

"You don't think that your BS detector is a little off because you're still sleeping with the guy?"

"No! If anything, it's more in tune. There's not a criminal bone in that man's body. He's too honest…and trusting."

"And handsome and fine," Larissa tossed in.

Johnnie shook her head. "Look. I'm not going to disagree with any of that. But I thought that you slept with him one time and it was over with? You're not going to be able to hide a full-blown relationship from Mackey. He's already convinced that something is going on with you two, after Royo and Gilliam's report indicated you disappeared with him after Mad Monez's bachelor party."

"Mackey is working my nerves—and he's the last person to preach about morality or behavior unbefitting an officer."

"True. But he still is our boss and as much as I'm jealous of you right now, you need to put all this on pause, at least until the investigation is over with."

"What is it that he has supposedly done?" Larissa asked. "Thaddeus is already crazy about him and I don't want him getting attached to someone who—"

"He's innocent," Cheryl insisted.

But Larissa gave her a look that said she needed more than just Cheryl's gut feeling on this one.

"We're just investigating whether drugs are being trafficked through his club, and if so, who is involved."

Johnnie jumped in. "So far we haven't been able to substantiate any of the allegations. The teams working the other clubs in the area have waaay more to go on. The Dollhouse looks pretty clean, but Cheryl's credibility will come into question if she's sleeping with the boss."

"Well, it may not be completely clean," Cheryl admitted. She went over to a pile of clothes and searched her jeans pockets. When she stood, she handed Johnnie the small Ziploc bag of drugs.

"Jackpot!"

"Did you run the nickname *Dog Pound* through the system?"

"I did," Johnnie said, unfolding her arms but settling her hands on her hips. "You'd be amazed how many perps are nicknamed Dog Pound in the Atlanta area. I'm giving the brother a minus ten points for originality."

"So that puts us back at square one?"

"Not exactly." Johnnie now smiled and puffed out her chest. "I did a little hocus pocus and cross-referencing on the computer and guess who happens to have a cousin named Dog Pound?"

There was only one name that leaped to the front of Cheryl's mind. "Kendrick Hodges?"

Johnnie frowned. "How did you know that?"

*The Devil You Don't Know*

# *Chapter 19*

Quentin stood up from the long leather chaise and started to walk around Dr. Turner's office.

"Do you want to take a break?" the doctor asked, looking up from her notepad. "You've been talking for a while now. I understand if you want to take a break."

Q ignored the question and walked over to the floor-to-ceiling window, and stared out at the skyline. He allowed a few minutes of silence to pass between them.

"You don't want to tell me about what's on your mind?" she asked. "Something is clearly bothering you."

He allowed the needle to pinch him for a little while longer before confessing. "Have you ever heard the saying, 'The devil you know is better than the devil you don't know'?"

"Yes. It's a fairly common adage."

He turned and looked at her. "It's basically about fear, don't you think?"

"In my opinion, yes. I've always thought it meant that it's

easier to settle for what you know than to risk the unknown. Why do you ask?"

"It was something you said earlier." He leveled his gaze on her. "You said that I was a creature of habit—always seeking the familiar."

Dr. Turner nodded. "What made you think of that now?"

"I'm wondering what made Eamon and Xavier take a leap of faith—decide to step out on that ledge all of a sudden. I mean, I wasn't all that close to Eamon until I spent time with him in Las Vegas. But I sure knew Xavier very well. He wasn't a man who was attracted to a lot of drama. Sure, he's a man of strength and character, I'll give him that. When the chips are down, you couldn't have a better ally than Xavier. So I'm just wondering, when things started falling apart and weren't what they seemed to be, why didn't he just walk away?"

"Is that what you would have done?"

"Never saw anything wrong with taking the path of least resistance."

"I think you just answered your own question," Dr. Turner said, smiling.

Q frowned as if he'd missed the point.

"By your own admission, Xavier loved a challenge, which was probably what attracted him to boxing. He could have been a contender, as Brando would say. I imagine that he loved getting into the ring, and duking it out in a title fight. Why would he be any different when it came to love?"

He fell silent.

"Did you ever fight for her?" Dr. Turner asked softly.

Quentin glanced around the room, relieved that his mirage of Alyssa was nowhere to be found. "I wouldn't have won," he said with tears burning the backs of his eyes.

"That's the problem with never getting into the ring. You never know."

Before a tear could fall, Quentin turned away from

her. "You know what? I think I'd like to take a break for a minute." He didn't wait for her to agree or give him permission. He was out the door and out of her office in less than a minute. However, the elevator was taking its sweet time no matter how many jabs he gave the button. Finally, he gave up and raced to find the staircase. Once he was in the spacious echo chamber, he tackled the stairs three at a time. He didn't know what was happening to him, but if he had to guess he would say that he was experiencing something close to a panic attack.

Even racing down the stairs as fast as he could, it was going to take some time to run down thirty-three flights. He managed about fifteen before he stopped and plopped down on one of the stairs. As he inhaled deep gulps of air, his head filled with thoughts of *what if.*

To his surprise, they weren't all about Alyssa. Mostly, they were about his life in general. What if he'd been a hard worker like his brothers and Eamon? What if he had been more serious? What if he had been more of a fighter? More humble? More honest?

"What if I was just a better man?"

His question echoed up and down the stairwell. He only wished that an answer would follow.

"How was your break?" Dr. Turner asked when Quentin strolled back into her office twenty minutes later.

Quentin took a deep breath and smiled. "Good. I, uh, just needed to stretch, I guess."

She nodded, but her eyes carefully studied him. "Do you want to continue or call it a day?"

"I'm probably eating up a lot of your time. I'm sure that you have other clients."

"I've learned to block out my schedule on the afternoons

that I see you. But don't worry about me. I'm billing you by the hour."

Quentin laughed and then returned to the chaise. "Soooo…where were we?"

## *Chapter 20*

For the next week, Xavier and Cheryl tried to keep their relationship on the down low. But with all the smiles, laughs and lingering looks, they weren't fooling anyone. They even thought they were being slick when Xavier kept coming up with various excuses to see Cheryl in his office. Of course, the minute Xavier closed the door, he would pin her up against it and literally devour her whole. One reason everyone knew what was going on was the way the door bumped and bounced when Xavier really got going hammering his hips.

Cheryl also got quite a few withering looks from dancers and waitresses. The only person who was openly giving her props for pulling off the impossible was Lexus.

"I ain't mad at you," Lexus said, leaning against the bar while she waited for Cheryl to make her four Long Island Iced Teas for her customers. "You do you, girl. That's my motto."

"I'm sure that I don't know what you're talking about."

"Uh-huh." Lexus tossed her a wink as she set her drinks on her tray. "Keep playing crazy if you want to. But on your next break, make sure that you wipe your lipstick off Xavier's mouth: Q is just letting him walk around looking like he's in drag."

Cheryl laughed and then moved down to the end of the bar to a customer hollering for a beer. "Here you go, sir." She set the bottle down without looking up. But the dude wrapped his hand around hers before she was able to release the bottle. "How much do I owe you, *Officer?*"

Cheryl's gaze jumped up to see Kendrick Hodges's humorless smile. "I told you before that you have the wrong girl." She tried to snatch her hand away, but Kendrick refused to let her go.

"Are we really still playing that game, Detective Grier?"

Cheryl clamped her jaw tight and glared at him. "Let go of my hand."

"Why? I just want to talk to you." He shrugged his shoulders. "What? You too good to have a conversation with me, Officer? Or am I keeping you from doing your job or something?"

"As a matter of fact, yes." She jerked her hand as hard as she could. "I have drinks to make."

Someone yelled out for a few White Russians and she quickly turned away to make them.

Kendrick's sinister laugh followed her. If she was hoping for him to take a hint and leave the bar, she was sadly mistaken. For the next hour, Kendrick remained rooted on the bar stool, watching her every move. When he finally ordered another beer, she approached him with more caution.

"It's okay, Officer. I'm not going to bite."

"Is there a problem here?" Xavier asked, materializing behind Kendrick suddenly.

"No problem," Kendrick said, angling his lips to the side.

*Oh, God. He's about to blow my cover.*

"I was just talking to…your lovely bartender here," Kendrick said. "I wanted to apologize for my rude behavior at that bachelor party a while back. Ain't that right… *Cheryl?*"

Her eyes narrowed. "Right."

He smiled. They both knew that her simple answer was all the confirmation he needed. Then again, he didn't need it, since he'd been stalking her outside her home. The license-plate number that she ran at the station was actually registered to a Cadillac owned by a little old lady in Albany, Georgia, so clearly the one Hodges was riding around in wasn't legit.

"Still," Xavier said with a low, simmering anger in his voice. "I don't like you hanging around here. So I'm going to have to ask you to leave."

Kendrick turned to Xavier, his face registering incredulous disbelief. "You kicking me out?"

"Good. You understand English."

Kendrick laughed. "Damn. This *bitch* got you sprung like—"

Xavier's punch was lightning fast and so powerful that the cracking sound that reached Cheryl's ear actually made her own jaw hurt.

As for Kendrick, his entire body was lifted off the stool, airborne for about three seconds before he crashed into a few bystanders and onto the floor. But the fight was over with that one punch. Kendrick was knocked out cold.

To add insult to injury, Xavier ordered Dog Pound, Kendrick's own cousin, to toss him out back.

Cheryl stood there with her mouth open, mainly because she wasn't sure that what just happened was reality or fantasy since she had wanted to throw a punch herself. When she realized that the whole scene was real, she rushed around the bar—to check on Xavier's hand. "Oh, my God. Are you all right?"

"Yeah. I'm fine. What about you?" He moved his hand so that she couldn't look at it.

"Let me see," she insisted.

"It's fine." He laughed, letting her take his hand.

He was right. There wasn't a scratch or a bruise to be seen. "That was…impressive," she said in awe.

"All right! Nothing to see here!" Quentin shouted, threading his way through the crowd. "Let's keep the party rollin'!"

Immediately, the Dolls went back to shaking their moneymakers and their devoted fans went back to appreciating their services and raining money on them.

"Are you finished playing Rocky in this joint?" Q asked Xavier.

"Since when have you had an issue with a little bar fight?"

"Since the last time I got stuck with the tab for remodeling," Q shot back. "Now, what was all of that about?"

"Nothing," Xavier said, shaking his head.

"Nothing?" Q asked incredulously. "You better come up with a better answer than that. If that dude comes to he's likely to sue for that broken jaw a few hundred people just witnessed you giving him."

"Trust me. The last place Kendrick wants to go is a courtroom," Xavier said, and then turned his attention back toward Cheryl. "What did he say to you?"

Cheryl blinked. "What do you mean?"

"You don't think that I believe he just came here to apologize, do you?" He gave a half laugh. "One thing I do know about Kendrick is that he never apologizes for anything. So what did he want?"

Cheryl's mouth flapped, but she couldn't think of anything to say. "Nothing much. He was just…saying that he wanted to talk."

"About what?"

"I don't know," she shot back defensively. "I wasn't all that interested in what he had to say."

"It's okay." Xavier pulled her to him. "Calm down. He's not going to bother you as long as I'm around. Okay?"

Cheryl exhaled.

"Okay?" he asked again, cupping her chin and lifting it up so that she would meet his gaze. "I promise."

"You don't have to do that. I'm more than capable of taking care of myself."

"So you keep saying." He chuckled.

Quentin tapped Xavier on the shoulder. "I hate to interrupt this beautiful scene, but do you mind if I holler at you for a few minutes?"

Xavier rolled his eyes and loosened his grip. "I'll be right back." He kissed the tip of her nose and then released her.

Cheryl went back behind the bar to a slew of new drinks being yelled at her.

Quentin shook his head as he led the way to the back of the club. Once he entered Xavier's office, he took it upon himself to take the big leather chair behind the desk. "Come in and sit down."

Xavier's brows shot up, but he did as his cousin asked and took the empty chair in front of the desk. "Yeah. What's up, cuz?"

"I was hoping that you could tell me that. What's going on with you and Cheryl out there?"

Xavier opened his mouth, but Q cut him off.

"The truth."

"When have I ever lied to you?"

"Well, I didn't want you to start any new bad habits."

"Ha. Ha." Xavier eased back in his chair. "There's nothing really to tell. I'm really feeling her right now. She's cool."

"Feeling her how? I mean, I know that you two have been, you know..."

"It's more than that, man. I can't explain it, but there's something more there, something deeper."

"I think I'm going to be sick," Q said, opening Xavier's top drawer. "You have some Rolaids or some Pepto-Bismol around here? You got my stomach upset."

"Why? Because I've fallen in love?"

"Oh, God. Not the L-word. I can handle anything but the L-word."

Xavier laughed. "It was bound to happen sooner or later."

"Okay." Q shot up his hand. "I vote for later."

"C'mon, man. Be serious."

"I *am* being serious." Quentin leaned back in the chair. "What the hell am I going to do if *you* fall in love? I mean. What's going to be left between us?"

Xavier's eyes narrowed. "Uh, you do know that I'm completely straight, right? I don't feel that way about you. I mean. You're cool and all."

"Will you get serious," Q retaliated. "And for the record, if we were gay, you'd be damn lucky to have me. Believe that."

"Yeah. It would be a lot of fun, watching you flirt and sleep around with other dudes. No, thank you."

The absurdity of their conversation hit them at the same time and they busted out laughing. After a minute, Q exhaled and shook his head. "So you really think that you're in love?"

"I think so. I've never been in love before, so it's all pretty new to me."

Quentin held his gaze for a long time before he nodded. "Then, I guess congratulations are in order. Any idea whether she feels the same about you?"

"Honestly? I have no clue. She's a complicated woman."

"All the good ones are," Quentin said, but he still didn't look too happy about it. "You know, I was thinking about heading out to Los Angeles."

Xavier frowned. "What? Why?"

"Well, I've been here for a little while and—" he heaved a long sigh "—you know I get a little antsy when I've been in one place for too long."

"I don't believe it," Xavier said, shaking his head. "You're leaving just because I've fallen in love? Are you afraid that we won't be able to hang out anymore or something?"

"No. No. C'mon. It's not all about you, you know?" Quentin probably would've been more convincing if he'd at least been able to meet Xavier's gaze.

"You're going to have to stop running one of these days."

"I'm not..."

Xavier held up his hand. "Please. Don't insult my intelligence. I've known you for far too long. Besides, my falling in love doesn't mean that I'm going to run off and get married tomorrow. Love takes time, right?"

Quentin nodded. "Right."

"Sooo...stick around. Who knows? I might miss you."

Q's lips curled. "Really?"

"Don't get a big head about it."

"No. No. Of course not."

Xavier stood up from his chair. "Besides, any woman who marries me is going to have to accept you, as well. We're a package deal."

Quentin stood, too, as his smile stretched across his face. "You mean it?"

"Of course I mean it." Xavier swung his arm around his cousin's neck. "You're my best friend. And whether you know it or not, I love you, too." He pulled Q into a headlock and rubbed the top of his head. "Just don't tell anyone."

# Chapter 21

"I want that bitch dead," Kendrick barked, spitting blood from his busted lip.

"Calm down, Ken man," Dog Pound said, easily toting his cousin from the back door over to his black BMW. "I told you not to come here and just let me handle it."

"You're taking too goddamn long. With that bitch here, we're never going to get more product in other than what you're able to move at the front door. And that ain't much. I got the Gutierrez brothers breathing down my throat. We owe them some serious-ass money and they ain't running the kind of bank where we can renege on the loan. You feel me?"

"I feel you, but damn. Ain't we moving some serious weight through Cougars and the Big Forty Club?"

"It's not enough," Kendrick barked. "We could double, if not triple, our money if we can just infiltrate this place. Look at it. Hell, I didn't know that asshole was going to reopen a Disneyland for adults or I would have taken him up on getting my job back."

"I don't know," Dog Pound said, opening the front door for his cousin. "I feel bad just moving what little I can at the door. I mean, Xavier is cool."

"You're kidding me, right? Look at my damn lip. Not to mention that Mr. Cool damn near choked me to death at that gig I got him."

"Yeah, but you only did it so you could get close to the dancers and find a hookup in the club."

Kendrick popped his cousin on the back of the head. "I know that. But he doesn't know that. And that's not the point. Xavier has been a pain in my ass since I was a kid when he would take up all of Ricky's time. He got him believing that he was actually going to make it all the way to the top and bring Ricky's starry-eyed ass with him. And what did he do? Just dump Ricky without any explanation so he could go back to running that raggedy gym that's draining his bank account dry. Meanwhile, he's living high off the hog in his second career."

Dog Pound glanced back at the club while he processed his cousin's words.

"But you want to side against family for Mr. Cool. Do I have that right?"

"I didn't say all of that," Dog Pound said guiltily. "It's just that, it doesn't seem like Ricky is holding any grudges."

"That's because he's too damn soft. Besides, what is he going to say? Anyone can just look at him and see that he's a broken man. Xavier used him and he doesn't show the slightest remorse for having done so."

Dog Pound nodded. "So what do you want me to do?"

"Do what you promised—and get rid of Detective Grier."

An hour after closing, Xavier rushed to check that everyone had left the club. Lexus lingered by the front door, suddenly wanting to turn small talk into a full-blown conversation. If he didn't know any better, he would've thought that she was delaying him on purpose.

"Is something wrong? I'm not keeping you from anything, am I?" she asked, her lips splitting into a wide smile.

Xavier's eyes narrowed. "I do have something…that needs my attention," he admitted.

"Ah." Her eyes lit up. "That's an interesting way of putting it."

"Good night, Lexus." He held open the front door.

"Night. Tell Cheryl I'll see her tomorrow." She winked.

"I'll make sure to do that."

Laughing, Lexus strolled out of the club. Since she'd parked up front, Xavier stood there and watched until she'd safely made it to her car and pulled off. After that, he turned all the locks and then raced back through the club.

"Looking for me?"

Cheryl's voice floated out to him and his legs stopped so fast that it was a wonder they didn't just lock up on him. Pivoting around, his eyes bulged when he saw Cheryl behind the bar with no shirt, but just a pair of black suspenders positioned over her breasts and hooked to an itty-bitty red miniskirt.

"Wow."

Cheryl smiled. "So what's your pleasure, X-Man?"

His brows bounced up. "I'll take whatever it is you're serving, Ms. Shepherd."

Her smile faded a bit, but then she curled her finger at him and he strolled over to the bar like a good little boy. "Yes, ma'am?"

"Have you ever had Sex with a Bartender?" she asked, arching an eyebrow.

"Are you kidding me? I try to every chance I get." He reached across the counter to pull her close.

She sidestepped him and reached for the coconut rum and triple sec. "You know what I mean."

"A drink?" He laughed. "Please. The last thing I want right now is a drink. I want to have the real thing." Xavier's gaze roamed over her body. "I think that is officially my favorite outfit."

Cheryl stood back and worked her hips. "Really? You like this?" She turned and hiked her butt up just enough for him to see her black lace thong peeking from under the hem of her skirt.

Xavier reached into his back pocket and pulled out his wallet. "That deserves a tip," he said. This time when he reached over she leaned forward and allowed him to slip a hundred-dollar bill into one of her suspenders—right next to her puckered nipple. Liking the way that looked, he waved her over again and slid another hundred-dollar bill into the other suspender and broke the house rules by pinching her hard, puckered nipple.

Cheryl jumped back and then waved her finger at him. "Ah. Ah. Ah. You know the rules."

"I guess that means you'll have to report me to your boss."

Her lips slid wider. "Funny."

"But I got to tell you. Me and your boss are like this." Xavier held up his two fingers pressed together.

Cheryl set his drink down in front of him. "Well, I hate to tell you, but me and my boss are pretty close, too." She hopped up on the counter, kept her knees together as she struck a pose.

Xavier's eyes darkened as they raced over her dangerous curves. "Is that right?"

"Uh-huh." She reached over and stroked his face. "And he's a little possessive when it comes to me."

"Really?"

"Uh-huh. Like tonight, you should have seen him

coldcock this one guy that was giving me a little trouble at the bar."

"Well..." Xavier brought his gaze back up so that it would rest on her face. "Seeing what I see and knowing what I know, I can't say that I can blame him. You look like the kind of woman that brings out the protective side in a man."

Gently, Cheryl allowed her finger to drift across the lining of his bottom lip. "What if I don't need protecting?"

"I'd want to protect you, anyway," he said honestly.

Her eyes softened. "You're...amazing," she said. "I don't think that I've ever met anyone quite like you."

He leaned forward and brushed a kiss against her soft lips. "I can say the same about you and these naughty suspenders." He pulled on one of them and then quickly released it so that it would snap back.

Cheryl gasped at the pleasant sting against her nipple, and before she could catch her breath, he pulled on the other one and let it go, as well.

The absolute pleasure that washed over her face made Xavier hard as a rock. He took the sweet drink that she'd made for him and, instead of tossing it back, held it over her and slowly drizzled it over her body.

After a quick gasp, Cheryl laughed. "What are you doing?"

"What does it look like? I'm going to drink you." With his free hand, he jerked up her short skirt and soaked her black thong through and through. Once that was done, he tossed the glass aside and didn't even flinch when it exploded against the floor.

Their gazes locked as he planted his hands on the counter and, with one mighty jump, leaped up onto the counter and over to the other side.

"Let's see what else we have over here." He went to the minifridge and started pulling out a few items. "We have maraschino cherries, pineapple wedges—ooh, my favorite… chocolate syrup—and even some whipped cream."

"Are you making a drink or a sundae?" she joked.

"Don't tempt me, woman. We have bananas."

"You really are a freak."

"You have no idea." He winked. "But let's get this party started with a little chocolate?"

He reached for her suspenders and unhooked them. At the first sight of her marble-size nipples, he emitted a groan and then lowered his head for a quick taste.

Cheryl sucked in a long breath while dropping her head back and closing her eyes. But when he scraped his teeth along the tender flesh, she hissed while her clit started swelling with need and pulsing as hard as her heartbeat.

But Xavier didn't spend a whole lot of time there. He started lapping up the coconut rum that ran down her body with his tongue. He took his time licking the small pool of rum that had collected in her belly button.

Toes curling, Cheryl reached out and ran her hand around his head and then down his smooth back. She could even make out the tiny scratches she had made the last time, which were still healing. As usual when their clothes were in the way, they went flying over Xavier's shoulder and landing God knows where. Next thing she knew he was opening her up.

Everything that she was doing was wrong, Cheryl knew, but damn if she could stop it. These stolen moments had come to mean the world to her, despite the fact that they could very well cost her her job. In fact, it most likely would. But for now, she was ready for this man to take her to heaven.

Xavier flicked his tongue against her clit and then sucked it in between his teeth, beating it with his tongue until she moaned out his name. Her whining moans filled Xavier's ears and prompted him to slide his tongue toward her pussy. There he licked and caressed her opening.

"Oooh." Cheryl laid all the way back on the bar top and squeezed her breasts together while Xavier continued to feed himself.

She pinched and pulled her nipples just as a spasm jerked her body. She tried to close her legs, but Xavier easily kept them open. The next thing she knew, she was crying out and squirming restlessly. There was no time to rest before the second wave started building. This time, she was so much into the groove that she rotated her hips while his tongue went counterclockwise.

Cheryl was getting so overheated that Xavier reached over to the ice bucket and slid two cubes inside her strawberry-colored pussy. Her hips came straight up into the air and Xavier laughed.

"Hold tight, baby. Let me get that for you." His lips latched onto her clit again, and then slid downward so that he could suck on the honey-coated ice cube.

The sounds Cheryl made didn't even resemble the English language, but it certainly sounded like she was having a damn good time. When the second orgasmic wave hit, her cries were accompanied with fat tears leaking from the corners of her eyes.

"Hmm." Xavier peppered kisses across her firm thighs. "I didn't even get a chance to use the chocolate."

Panting, Cheryl smiled. "Then maybe I should use it." She climbed off the counter with Xavier's help and took the bottle of Hershey's chocolate and simply said, "Strip."

Xavier not only had a quick right hook, but he could get undressed like a rock star in between sets. Boy, did she have fun drizzling chocolate all over his rock-hard cock, even topping it with whipped cream.

He snickered.

"You think this is funny?" she asked, glancing up at him.

"From this angle, I have a cock with a hat on it."

"Mmm. I think it looks sexy." She rolled out her tongue and then slowly slid it underneath his cock for one long lick.

He shuddered.

"It tastes nice, too." She slid her tongue up one side and then down the other.

Xavier sucked in a breath and shuddered. The vision of her tongue licking and then wrapping around his thick mushroom head had him leaning back and bracing his weight with his powerful arms.

"Mmm," Cheryl kept moaning as her mouth bobbed up and down, occasionally squeezing him with the back of her throat. He could feel a few drops of pre-cum mix with the whipped cream, but she gobbled that up before it could fall. Cheryl was determined to put in work.

His eyes rolled to the top of his head while her hard suction took him to places in his mind that he'd never been before. His knees began to shake. "Damn, baby." He moved one hand, supporting himself on one arm. He used his free hand to comb through her hair so that he could have a different view of how she looked servicing him. But soon his hand stopped and instead gripped the back of her head to hold her in place. In his mind, he could see himself just splashing hot cum over her face. He even envisioned her lapping up every drop. But he wasn't ready for this to end just yet, so when the temptation started to overwhelm him, he reached down and jacked her up so high that she easily wrapped her legs around his waist so that he could slide straight into her warm heat.

But if Cheryl thought that it was just going to be an easy ride, he had something for her. He bounced her luscious ass up and down for a few strokes, but he also reached over and opened the ice bucket for a couple of cubes. She didn't see it coming, mainly because her head was lolled back while she babbled incoherently. Xavier plopped the ice into his mouth and then tilted his head forward so that he could then latch his mouth to her right nipple.

She gasped the moment the ice cube touched her nipple. It was so cold that it was a little painful. The sort of pain she liked.

His strokes quickened as he delivered hard slaps against the side of her ass cheek. While she moaned and he groaned, their bodies were having their own conversation—one that was even louder than they were. With one strangled cry, Cheryl's honey cream overflowed around his hammering cock; a second later Xavier exploded and filled the walls of her pussy. It was all he could do not to drop her. Somehow he managed to hold on.

"God. I love you so much," he moaned, peppering kisses along her neck.

His words stung her, but not as much as the tears flooding her eyes. *How can you love me? You don't even know me.*

# Chapter 22

"I want off the case," Cheryl said the minute her butt touched the seat of the chair in Lieutenant Mackey's office.

Mackey's head spun around while his brows dipped together. "Come again?"

Tugging in a deep breath, Cheryl prepared herself for an explosion that she knew was sure to come. "I've thought about it and I think that it's the best thing to do…given the circumstances."

Mackey allowed a long silence to stretch between them while he eased back in his chair. "And what circumstances would that be exactly?"

*He's not going to make this easy.* "I've engaged in some inappropriate behavior while on this case."

"Such as?"

"Jason." She gave him a measured look.

Ignoring the look, he braided his hands together and waited her out.

"All right," she said, drawing in a deep breath. "I've

been…engaged in an intimate relationship with Xavier King."

Another wave of silence crashed between them.

"I see." He nodded. "An intimate relationship. Sounds a bit sterile to me," he said. "I would have said something like, you've been fucking his brains out, but then that's just me. I'm glad that you've finally admitted it, though I'm sure you've noticed that I'm not surprised."

"Don't act like I do this all the time. I don't. Other than one lapse of judgment when I slept with you, I'd say I had a pretty good record."

"You want off the case, fine. But I also want your badge."

"What?" She jumped up out of her chair.

"I'm suspending you, for behavior unfitting an officer."

"Please say that you're kidding."

"No. And that's for starters. I intend to comb through the books and see whatever else I can slap you with."

"You can't do that."

"I can't?" He leaned back in the chair and grinned up at her. "Did you forget exactly who I am—or did you think that just because you've slept with me, too, that I would be more lenient?" His eyes narrowed as he nodded. "Yeah. I bet that is exactly what you thought. No dice."

Cheryl shook her head. "We're never going to get past this, are we?"

"I'm sure that I don't know what you mean."

"Don't you? You're not writing me up because I slept with Xavier King. This is still about me *not* sleeping with you."

"Or, and you're going to love this one, this is about your inability to do your job."

"I was investigating whether there were drugs being trafficked at The Dollhouse. It was a claim that couldn't be substantiated. Royo and Gilliam have been working the floor as well and they haven't come up with anything, either, other than that one bag outside, which could've belonged to anyone."

"I wouldn't say that entirely."

"What do you mean? Why haven't I heard anything about it?"

"Maybe there's been some concern over whether or not you've been compromised."

"Concern by whom?"

Mackey fell silent while he twirled his thumbs.

"You?"

He shrugged. "It looked like I was right. You've been *screwing* our target."

"Xavier King is not a criminal."

"You were sent in to investigate. Not become the judge and jury and then render your own verdict. Once upon a time, you used to know that."

She clamped her jaws together.

"As a matter of fact, how do I know that you haven't being helping Don Juan out and undermining this whole investigation?"

"I would never do that and you know it."

"Oh, I do, do I?" He laughed. "And how in the hell would I know that? Because you believe in following the rules? Because you would never *use* someone to just get what you want?"

Cheryl laughed. "This is about you again." She tossed up her hands. "Will you get over yourself already? This case has nothing to do with you. I'm still committed to doing my job."

"Is that right?"

"Yes. That's right! Damn it! I can't do this anymore. You want to suspend me, fine. I'll do you better," she said, reaching for her badge and her weapon. "I quit."

Mackey laughed. "Well, I'll be damned. Are you that

sprung that you're willing to throw away your career? The brother got it like that?"

Cheryl walked up to his desk and sat her badge and gun on his desk. "As a matter of fact, he does." She gave him a smile and then turned and walked out of the office. As she strolled through the squad room, her smile slid wilder. A part of her couldn't believe that she was quitting, while the other part was giving herself high fives.

"Detective Grier," Mackey barked.

Cheryl kept walking.

"Detective Grier!"

Johnnie looked up from her desk and covered her hand across her phone. "What's going on?" she whispered.

"Detective Grier, if you walk out of here don't you even *think* about coming back!"

"It's been great working with you. I'll call you later." She tossed her buddy a wink.

"Detective Grier!"

Cheryl held up her hand and flashed him the middle finger.

Xavier strolled into the gym and looked around to see if Cheryl was there. Because of her weird schedule, she only made it into the gym twice a week where as now he came in every day. Not always at the same time, but he did make it in. In hindsight, he couldn't believe that he had stayed away as long as he had. There was just something about the energy of the place that he didn't get anywhere else, not even at The Dollhouse.

When he pushed through the door of the locker room, he was surprised to see My'kael sitting on the bench, hunched over and…crying?

"Yo, man. Is everything all right?"

My'kael lifted his head and swiped at his tears, but those were quickly replaced. "Nah, man. Everything ain't all right.

I let y'all fill my head with all this bullshit, all this believing in your dreams and making it to the top." He shook his head. "I should've known better. A brother like me ain't never gonna be more than I am right now—just a hustler always chasing paper. Nah-what-I-mean?"

Xavier walked over to the bench and sat down. "What's going on? Talk to me."

My'kael gave him a disbelieving laugh. "You don't know?"

Xavier's brows dipped together.

"Man, Ricky's closing the gym. He's not going to be able to train me no more."

"What? When the hell did this happen?"

"He just told me, man. I mean, I got my girl's hopes up. My family. I've been talking all this smack, and now I got to tell them…what? That they were right?"

"Is Ricky still here?"

"Yeah, that old liar is in his office."

Xavier popped him on the shoulder. "Hey. Cut it out. You got problems, we got problems. I'm going to go see what this is all about. Get changed and work the bag. I'll be back."

"But—"

"Don't argue and be out there in ten minutes." Xavier stood and then strolled out of the locker room to search for Ricky. Turned out that he was just where My'kael said he was, in his office, hunched over his desk with his head in his hands.

Xavier knocked.

"Go away," Ricky moaned, not bothering to look up and see who was standing on the other side through the square-pane glass window in the door.

Xavier ignored the response and entered the office.

"I said…" Ricky glanced up. "Oh. It's you." He lowered his red, swollen eyes and started moving papers around his desk. "What do you want? I'm busy."

"I see that." Xavier took a seat in the chair in front of Ricky's desk.

Ricky planted his elbows on his desk and started massaging his forehead. "Look, X-Man. This really isn't a good time. Maybe you can—"

"What's this I hear about you closing the gym?"

Ricky grumbled something that he couldn't hear.

"I don't speak mumble. How about speaking up?"

"All right. So what? I'm closing the doors. I can't go on pretending that this money pit isn't doing a number on my bank account. So I figured I'd get out now and toddle on down to Florida and act my age."

"Yeah. I can see you living it up with water aerobics and Jell-O pudding nights," Xavier said, nodding. "Who knows, you might even take up bingo or shuffleboard."

Ricky's face twisted miserably. "God help me."

"Or," Xavier said, easing back into his chair. "You could consider taking on a partner. Get someone to help you out around here."

"Yeah. And who would want to invest in this hole in the wall?"

"Oh, I don't know. I have a couple of dollars in the bank. Maybe if we rubbed them together, they can make some more babies and I could become your partner or something."

Ricky blinked. "You'd want to go into business with me?"

Xavier shrugged. "I don't see why not."

"Because there is a very slim chance that you'll make any money," Ricky answered honesty.

"I have to tell you, you're doing a lousy job of selling me on this."

"I'm not interested in pissing on you and telling you that it's rain. If you're really interested in doing this, then I want to make sure that you know exactly what you're getting into."

"Then consider me duly warned." He smiled. "And I want to add one more thing."

"Okay, here it comes." Ricky rolled his eyes. "When something sounds too good to be true, then it usually is."

"Please cut the soliloquy short, Hamlet. I don't have all day."

Ricky smiled. "All right. Lay it on me."

"I want to help you train My'kael," he said.

Ricky lit up. "He's a star, isn't he?"

Xavier nodded. "Yeah. I think so."

"Anything else?" Ricky asked.

"Nope. I think that's it."

"Then welcome aboard, partner." Ricky jutted his hand across the desk and Xavier wasted no time in shaking it.

Now in a jubilant mood, Ricky popped up out of his chair, laughing. "Me and the X-Man, together again. Who would have ever thought it, huh?" He slapped Xavier on the back.

"I guess that life has a funny way of working itself out."

When they returned to the gym floor, a suspicious My'kael stopped punching the heavy bag and bounced his gaze between the two men. "So what's up? You still closing the gym?"

"Closing the gym?" Ricky asked with his brows jumping up. "Where on earth did you get such a ridiculous idea like that?"

"But you said—"

"And why aren't you working out? You think that you're going to get a championship belt wasting time and throwing punches only when you feel like it?" Ricky barked.

My'kael looked to Xavier.

"Well, you heard the man. What are you waiting for?"

"Something is wrong with you two." He threw one punch against the bag. "Seriously wrong." But as he added the tag, a smile slowly hooked the corners of his mouth.

Smiling, Xavier glanced over at his new partner and made another major life decision.

# *Chapter 23*

Johnnie and Larissa sat quietly on the edge of Cheryl's bed for about fifteen seconds after Cheryl revealed her plan before turning to look at each other and bursting out laughing. It wasn't the polite kind of laughing, but full-blown belly laughs.

"Are you two finished now?"

"Oh. Oh." Johnnie wiped her eyes. "You have got to be joking. *That's* your plan? You're going to sit down to dinner and just announce, 'Guess what, I'm a cop and I've spent the past two months investigating you for drug trafficking'?"

"'But good news,'" Larissa added. "'You've been cleared and I quit my job because I'm in love with you.'"

"Well, I'm not going to say it like that." Cheryl shrugged. "I'll leave the sarcasm at home."

Johnnie shook her head like she couldn't believe her friend was so naive. "And what exactly is the plan when he jumps up from the table and runs off screaming like his head is on fire?"

Larissa nodded. "Yeah, because you're definitely going to need a plan B."

"C'mon," Cheryl whined. "I'm already nervous as it is and you two aren't helping."

Larissa stood and then wrapped her arms around her sister's neck. "I'm sorry. You're right. We should be more supportive." She glanced over at Johnnie and motioned for her to get up.

Johnnie was much slower in getting up from the bed. "Even though I think it's much too soon to ignore the I-told-you-so part of this conversation, I genuinely wish you good luck. You're certainly giving up a whole lot for a chance to make this relationship work. You're a hell of a lot braver than I am…but then again, we always knew that, didn't we?"

Cheryl smiled, but in the next moment, her nerves got the best of her and she bolted toward the bed and then dived straight in. She had made a mistake. What was she thinking when she gave up her job to take a chance on love. *Love.* When on earth did she start believing in something as crazy and unreliable as that?

Hell, she'd never made time for it. She was never interested in being someone's Boo. She was a kick-ass-and-take-names kind of chick who was the one who *made* the booty calls—not waited for them. That is, until she entered Xavier King's world, and she was reduced to behaving like a rookie cop, making one mistake after another.

"He's not going to understand," she groaned into her pillow.

"Aw." Larissa followed her over to the bed. "Of course he will. I've seen the way he looks at you. He's crazy about you."

Johnnie sat on the other side of the bed and tossed in her two cents. "Yeah. After he processes it for a minute, he's going to understand that you were just doing your job."

"Yeah?" She lifted her head from the pillow. "You really think so?"

"Of course I do." She brushed Cheryl's hair back away from her tearstained face. "I've seen how he looks at you, too. Trust me. You have nothing to worry about."

"You want to do what?" Jeremy asked, his incredulous face filling the flat-screen television in Xavier's living room.

Across the room at the bar, Quentin made himself a whiskey sour and shouted, "It's an abomination."

"C'mon, guys. Please try to understand," Xavier said. "This is something that I really want to do."

Jeremy shook his head as if trying to get something unhinged. "Give me a minute. There's gotta be something wrong with my hearing."

"Nothing's wrong with your hearing," Xavier droned, shaking his head. He knew this was going to be hard, and so far he had been proven right. His stomach was twisting in knots and he couldn't stop rubbing his hands together.

"You want to give up your shares in The Dollhouse in order to go run a hole-in-the-wall gym with your old trainer?"

"Yeah, I do," he said, nodding. "I didn't *know* that I wanted to do it until the opportunity was right there in front me. Then it was all so...crystal clear."

"Uh-huh," Q said, unimpressed, before tipping his drink.

"Now, what is that supposed to mean?" As soon as he asked the question, he immediately wanted to take it back. It was like serving a tennis ball right into Quentin's sweet spot.

"I mean...this sudden decision sure does come at a convenient time. It kind of lines right up with you falling in love with our bartender."

"What?" Jeremy asked, scooting closer to the screen. "What bartender?"

"You know which bartender." Q set his glass down so that his hands could outline the shape of an hourglass.

"Ooooooh," Jeremy said, smacking his head. "I should have known. First Eamon and now you. When is the big day?"

"Stop it. Nobody has proposed yet. This is something that *I* want to do."

"Fine." Quentin tossed up his hands. "Why can't you do both? You can still run the club, she can run the bar and occasionally you can run around your gym. Problem solved."

Jeremy nodded. "Sounds like a plan to me. All in favor say 'aye.'"

"Aye," shouted Quentin.

"Well, it looks like the 'ayes' have it." Jeremy beamed. "Case closed."

Xavier shook his head. "Nice try, guys. I'm serious. I want to run the gym—turn it into something big. I even want to get into training some potential fighters. I think I'd be good at it."

Jeremy cocked his head. "You want to get back into the ring?"

Q just blinked at him. "Color me shocked. Hell, I never knew why you stopped boxing in the first place."

"Guys, guys. Pay attention. I didn't say anything about me climbing back into the ring. I said I wanted to *train*. And hell, I think that I have a lot to bring to the table." He glanced around, looking for his amen chorus. Instead, he got a couple of head nods.

"Thanks for the vote of confidence, guys." That just earned him some low grumbling. "Please. Please. Don't extend yourself."

Jeremy tossed up his hands. "You couldn't have thought that we were going to be happy about this?"

"I knew that you would initially take it hard, but I thought for my sake you would at least put your personal feelings aside and just be happy for me." He suffered through another round of grumbling. "Or not." He shrugged.

"All right. All right. Go and run your gym. Follow your bliss. Find your pot of gold at the end of the rainbow."

Quentin snickered and poured himself another drink while Xavier rolled his eyes. "Are you finished?"

"I had a few more, but I can stop now if you want." Jeremy shrugged. His disappointment was evident.

"Please don't guilt-trip me. I really want to do this."

Jeremy and Quentin sighed at the same time, but Xavier could tell that he was making headway when his baby brother changed the subject. "Sooo…you said that you haven't proposed *yet*. Does that mean that you're going to?"

Xavier smiled. "You caught that, huh?"

Quentin groaned.

"All right," Jeremy said, wrapping up. "We'll get the paperwork drawn up." He turned to look toward Q. "I guess this means it's just me and you, old man."

"All right, junior. Enough with that old-man crap. And while we're drawing up new partnership papers, we might have to add another clause."

"And what is that?"

"A no-marriage clause."

Jeremy smiled slyly. "You got yourself a deal."

# *Let's Make a Deal*

# *Chapter 24*

"You were making marriage deals?" Dr. Turner piped up.

Quentin smiled. "Sounded perfectly reasonable to me—especially since this whole *love* thing was slowly causing my one successful enterprise to fall like a house of cards. I think that I had a legitimate reason *and* a financial one to put in some added insurance."

"With Eamon and Xavier leaving your boys' club, did that end up financially compromising your business?"

Quentin coughed.

"Tell her the truth," Alyssa said, suddenly appearing in the large window.

Quentin frowned. "I thought that you were gone?"

"Seems like I don't have any real control over when I leave. That's up to you," Alyssa said evenly as she glanced over at Dr. Turner. "Your doctor is looking at you strangely."

Quentin jerked his head around to face Dr. Turner, only to find that she was indeed looking at him as if he'd just sprouted a second head.

"And just where did you think I had gone?" Dr. Turner asked.

"I wasn't referring to you," Q said, and then touched his left temple. "I was talking about a particular headache that I can't seem to get rid of."

"Oh. I see." Dr. Turner eased back in her chair, but her scrutiny only intensified.

"Not bad," Alyssa said. "But I don't think that she bought it."

Quentin drew in a deep breath. "Maybe these sessions aren't working," he said. "If anything, I think I'm getting closer to being locked up in a psychiatric ward than I am figuring anything out about love."

Dr. Turner snickered. "Please. You are a long way from that."

He smiled and relaxed. "Wait. Far from which one?"

Dr. Turner changed the subject. "So you struck this deal with Jeremy King, but what happened with Xavier and Cheryl? How did it all work out?"

"It's love." He shrugged. "It tends to work out…for everyone but me…."

# Chapter 25

Everything was lining up just as Xavier had planned. He had a new career, one that, in hindsight, seemed so obvious that he didn't know why he'd never thought of it before. And tonight, he and Cheryl were going to have their first official date. It seemed odd, given the amount of time they'd actually spent together between work and their secret rendezvous. But with any luck, this brand-new business venture would give them a whole lot more free time.

Of course, she still had the crazy medical school schedule during the day and working the club at night, but they could work through all of that later. He hummed to himself in the shower. He added lyrics while he got dressed and when he headed out to his SUV to go pick up Cheryl for their big date, he damn near broke out into a dance.

He felt good. Damn good.

Then again, that might have more to do with the diamond ring he also had in his pocket. Did it matter that he had only known Cheryl for a little over two months? No. In fact, it was one of the facts that he marveled over—that he could be this crazy in love and totally convinced she was the one that he wanted to spend the rest of his life with had to be a great sign.

Xavier climbed into his SUV and started up the engine. To make sure that she was ready when he showed up, he pulled out his cell phone and typed a quick text message that he was on his way. Before he slid the phone back into his chest pocket, he noticed that his battery was low and then reached over to hook the phone up into the charger. Then he noticed something on the floorboard.

Curious, Xavier leaned over and picked up a small white packet. "What the hell is this?" He knew what it *looked* like, but there was no reason in hell why there would be drugs in his vehicle. But as he turned the small bag over in his hands, he knew that that was exactly what it was.

"Who on earth…?" His mind quickly scrambled over who had been in his car recently. And he could only come up with one name. *Oh, God.*

Cheryl had never in her life taken three hours to get dressed. Being a jock for most of her life, she considered herself low maintenance. Give her a couple of daubs of cocoa butter and a once-over with lip gloss and she was good to go. But tonight, she fussed about everything. Her hair, her makeup and most certainly which dress to wear. Somehow she had convinced herself that the better she looked, the easier and more forgiving Xavier would be when she told him that she'd been lying about who she was for the past couple of months.

*Ding dong.*

"Oh, God. This is it." She glanced at herself in the mirror and loved the way the short red dress hugged her curves. *I just hope that he likes it.*

*Ding dong.*

Now she regretted asking her sister and nephew not to be

there when Xavier arrived. She could've used some moral support right about now. Breathing in a deep breath, she rushed to go open the door.

Every time Cheryl saw Xavier, he seemed more handsome than the time before. Tonight was no different. Dressed to kill in simple black, he walked through the door, looking like he was about to walk the runway of a Milan fashion show. Cheryl's smile was instant and easy as it slid across her face.

"Hello."

His smile was nice, but not quite so wide.

"Is something wrong?" she asked. If he wasn't in a good mood, then maybe tonight was not the time to spring her news on him. At that realization, she started to relax a bit. Of course, she would've taken any excuse to put off telling him the truth.

"No. Everything is fine," he said, though it was an obvious lie.

That surprised her. She had always known Xavier to be an open book.

"Are you ready to go?"

Her frown deepened. He hadn't said anything about her dress. Maybe she needed to go and make a quick change.

His brows dipped when she hadn't answered him. "Cheryl?"

"Oh, huh. Yes. I'm ready."

He nodded. "Then we better get going if we're going to keep our reservation."

"All right. Let me just get a jacket."

At least he walked over and helped her slide into it, and when they started out the door, he finally said, "You look beautiful, by the way."

"Thank you." She smiled and glanced back over her shoulder at him. Seeing his genuine smile and the familiar softness return to his eyes, the knots in her belly relaxed again. *Maybe he'd just been distracted.*

However, after he opened his passenger door and helped her climb inside, she felt that shift again. On the drive to Le Roi, a small French restaurant in a corner of Buckhead, it was as quiet as a tomb. *This was going to be a long night.*

Xavier wrestled with how he was going to handle this sudden realization. How did one handle finding out that someone you loved had a drug problem? He snuck a few glances in her direction and he still couldn't believe that Cheryl did drugs. It just didn't make sense with what he knew about her.

*And what was that exactly?*

The rogue question caught him off guard, but he was determined to answer it. He knew what he needed to know—that Cheryl Shepherd was a warm, kind person, but also a spitfire, a strong, no-nonsense, fiercely independent woman. Clearly, she loved family—though hers was considerably smaller than his own. Still, he believed that she would fit in nicely with the Kings.

His smile widened. *Okay. So she has a little problem.* Was it enough for him to just toss up his hands and walk away? When you love someone you don't just walk away at the first sign of trouble. He could help her with this. Atlanta had some good drug rehabilitation facilities. He could help her beat this problem.

Xavier straightened in his seat and glanced over at Cheryl again. At her timid smile, he slid his arm over and reached around the back of her headrest. She relaxed and leaned against his arm. Yeah. He could do this…if she would be willing to let him help her.

At Le Roi, they were quickly led to a small table in the back of the restaurant as he had requested. It was perfect. The table was adorned with rose petals, and the minute they sat down, a chilled bottle of champagne was produced.

"Wow. This is nice," Cheryl said, and heard her own voice quiver. She cleared her throat and tried again. "You really didn't have to go to so much trouble."

"It was no trouble at all. Besides, I like doing nice things for you. I hope to be doing a lot more in the future."

She sighed and relaxed with his talk of the future. "I hope that we will be able to do a lot of nice things for each other in the future."

The waiter popped the cork of their champagne and she jumped in her seat.

Xavier laughed. "Are you all right?"

"Yeah." She covered a hand over her heart. Hell, she couldn't remember if she had *ever* been this jittery—not even when she'd had to make her first arrest. "I guess I'm just a little nervous."

He laughed. "It is a little odd. A first date, after all we've, uh, shared."

"We've shared a lot in some ways."

His gaze locked on to her as she bobbed her head. "Some ways."

Cheryl reached over for her champagne and inhaled the whole glass in one sip.

Xavier's brows rose in surprise. "A little thirsty?"

"Something like that." She flashed him a nervous smile.

Then, in sync, they blurted out, "We need to talk." They jumped and blinked at each other. Once again, they said at the same time, "You go first." Smiling. "No. You go first."

Cheryl held up her hands. "Okay. We're not getting anywhere like this. Why don't you go first?"

"Are you sure?"

"Please. I insist."

"All righty." But before he could get started, their waiter appeared and asked whether they were ready to order.

"Just give us a few more minutes," Xavier told him. When they were alone again, he drew a deep breath and reached across the table for her hand. "I know that we've only known each other for a short time." He started rubbing the backs of her fingers. "But I have to tell you that, in some ways, it feels like I've known you my entire life. I don't know why, but I just do. And I don't want you to think that it's just sex because it's not. What I feel when I'm around you…is much deeper and more complicated than that. I felt it the first time I turned and saw you standing in the club with that crazy Got Milk T-shirt. There's a connection here. And I'm convinced that you feel it, too."

Cheryl bobbed her head while her eyes filled with tears.

"But I also know that there…are a few things that we haven't talked about—a few secrets."

*Oh, my God. He knows.*

His grip on her hand tightened. "I want you to know that you can tell me anything. I'm not going anywhere. I care and love you too much…to just walk away."

Cheryl blinked.

He reached for her other hand. "I'm not one of those guys that just takes off the minute things get rough. No one is perfect. Lord knows I'm not."

She didn't think that being a cop was some kind of fatal flaw, especially since running a strip club was hardly something that made one a pillar of the community. Her smile fluttered weakly on her lips. "I agree. Neither one of us is perfect."

The waiter returned and refilled Cheryl's empty glass. "Have you two decided?"

"A couple more minutes," Xavier said.

Cheryl slid her hands from Xavier's grasp so that she could take another shot of bubbly courage.

Xavier noted her nervousness and took heart in the fact that he was getting to her. He didn't know much about addiction, but he did know that the first step was getting the addict to acknowledge that they had a problem. If this relationship was going to move forward, then he needed for Cheryl to come clean with him, and maybe in order for her to do that, he needed to do the same.

He waited for her to finish draining her second glass of champagne before reaching over and reclaiming her hand. "I want to share something with you," he said solemnly.

*Okay. This sounds serious.* Cheryl swallowed a huge boulder that was suddenly clogging her throat. "What is it?" He paused for so long that Cheryl wondered whether he'd changed his mind.

"I miss boxing," he said softly, but earnestly. "All my life I knew what I wanted, I knew how to go about getting it. And that's exactly what I did. I was lucky enough to have a family that not only loved me, but encouraged me to follow my heart. As long as I put in the hard work and dedicated myself to the sport…and my schoolwork, the sky was the limit."

He fell silent again and it was Cheryl who switched their hands around so that she was comforting and supporting him. Clearly, there was something heavy on his mind. For now, she would have to put her own bombshell on the back burner.

Suddenly a low rumble of laughter shook Xavier's large frame while his expression grew distant. "I wanted to be the best. I wanted Muhammad Ali to wag a finger at the world and say, 'Now, Xavier King is truly the greatest.'"

Cheryl laughed, but started to feel and even bask in the incredible warmth emanating from their connected hands.

"All right. So I was a bit of a goofy kid."

"You just sound like you were ambitious. There's nothing wrong with that. In fact, I think it's adorable."

His grin stretched wider, turning him into an adorable man, as well. *Why couldn't she have met him under better circumstances?*

"Anyway," he continued. "My obsession with boxing

meant that I put in very little time doing teenage things. Like dating and hanging out with the boys."

"Please. You're not going to try and sell me the line that you were unpopular in school or something, are you?"

"No. Actually, I excelled in sports and academics. But I considered myself a late bloomer as far as the opposite sex. I mean, I've done my fair share of dating and, uh—"

"Sowing wild oats?"

His face actually darkened with embarrassment. "Yeah. Let's roll with that. Anyway, my whole point is that it was really hard for me to walk away from all of that, especially when it seemed like I was well on my way. I had one hell of a support team. My trainer, Ricky..." He shook his head. "That man sacrificed a lot for me and my dream. He believed in me from the beginning. We worked tirelessly around the clock. If we weren't training, we were reviewing boxing matches—mine or upcoming opponents'. It was draining and exhilarating all at the same time."

As Cheryl watched his face, one nagging question kept circling in her mind. "Then why did you give it all up?"

Xavier's reminiscent smile faded. "I guess you can say that I did it...for love."

Cheryl cocked her head in confusion.

Xavier lowered his gaze. "Love for a man who is like my second father."

Their eyes connected and suddenly she knew. "You threw a fight?"

His eyes dropped again. "See. Mr. Honesty has a big dent in his record."

Shock colored her entire face as her grip tightened and she leaned halfway over the table. "But why?"

Xavier sucked in a long, deep breath. "It was spring of '04, Las Vegas...."

*Xavier listened to the thunderous chants, cheers and jeers that easily permeated the walls of his designated locker room. His fight with Tyrone Forster wasn't the main headline for the night. In fact, the boxing world was abuzz about this fighter Manny Pacquiao. That was all right with him because a year from now Xavier was convinced that his name would be the one on everyone's lips. At least, that was what Ricky was pumping into his head while he wrapped his hands and wrists in preparation for the fight.*

*"How are you feeling, X-Man?" Ricky asked, bright-eyed and just as pumped as his fighter.*

*"I feel like kicking some ass, old man," Xavier answered, stretching his neck from side to side.*

*"You're going to get your chance in just a few minutes. Remember, the best way to take Forster down is to keep going through his gloves and landing those upper cuts. I ain't saying it's gonna be easy, but on the tapes, clearly the man has a problem with moving that right side."*

*Xavier nodded as Ricky reminded him of everything they'd learned about his opponent.*

*There was a rap on the door, and when they looked up, most of the King clan flowed like a steady stream into the small locker room.*

*"There's the man of the hour," Eamon announced, and was the first to reach him for a high five and a shoulder bump. Jeremy was next and then his father, Jorell.*

*"Son, I'm soooo proud of you."*

*Their hands clasped, but the bear hug they exchanged warmed Xavier to his core. Jorell was still beaming with pride when he turned toward Ricky and gave him the same greeting. "There aren't enough words to express my gratitude for the work and dedication that you've put in with my boy."*

*Ricky's face flushed. It was probably the first time that Xavier had seen him do so. "Trust me, Mr. King. It's been a pleasure working with your son."*

*The door was thrown open again and Quentin strolled*

*in with two women draped under his arms. "Party is not a party until Q rolls through!"*

*Jeremy and Xavier laughed while Eamon and his father rolled their eyes.*

*"C'mon now," Ricky barked. "You know the rules. No women allowed back here."*

*Quentin looked at him, horror-stricken. "Who in their right mind would make up such a ridiculous rule?"*

*"I did. Now out!" Ricky said, meaning business. He rushed to the door, shooing Quentin and his female fans back out the door.*

*"Fine. Fine," Q said, backing up. "I'll see you from the front row," he yelled out to Xavier.*

*"Thanks, man. I appreciate you coming." That was all he was able to get out before Ricky shut the door in his face. "I swear, I don't know what you see in that big kid."*

*"Amen," Eamon agreed. "Talk about being spoiled. Isn't he supposed to be married?"*

*"Annulled," Jeremy said, and then added, "I'll tell you about it later."*

*Xavier laughed. "Hey, he's my best friend—plus he's family."*

*"Don't remind me," both Eamon and his father said, and then grinned at each other.*

*Xavier stood up from the bench and started bouncing in his new black boxing boots and jabbed a few air punches. While his family started pumping him up, there was another knock on the door, but this time it was Kendrick Hodges who poked his head in.*

*Ricky was just as surprised as Xavier.*

*"Ken."*

*"Hey, Pop," he said, flashing a nervous smile to the people assembled in the room. "Mind if I talk to you for a minute?"*

*Xavier got a weird sensation in the back of his head. He*

*didn't like Ricky's son Kendrick, though he would never admit that to Ricky himself. It just seemed like either the kid loved trouble or trouble loved him.*

*Ricky glanced back at Xavier with an almost apologetic look. "Be right back."*

*Xavier nodded and his gaze tracked his trainer as he headed toward the door. When he pulled it open a little wider to walk out, Xavier spotted two huge men in black lingering behind a nervous Kendrick.*

*He didn't like the look of that.*

*Eamon and his father were still trying to hype him up, but his air punches lost both strength and velocity. He pretended to listen to what was being said around him for a few minutes, but he couldn't get the troubling image he'd just seen out of his mind.*

*"Hey, you guys, can you just give me a few minutes?" he asked. Xavier really didn't wait for an answer. He went straight to the door, but didn't see Ricky or Kendrick anywhere around. The hallway was crowded, and the music pulsing from the arena was deafening. But he pushed all that to the side and started combing through the crowd. A few sports reporters spotted him and wanted a quick interview, but he shook his head and kept it moving until the crowd thinned and he heard some angry voices coming from the last rooms.*

*"Have we made ourselves clear, old man?" one ominous baritone growled. "Your man goes down in the third round or you and your boy here will be buried out in the desert by Monday morning."*

*Ricky's voice trembled with a fear Xavier had never heard. "I c-can't ask Xavier to do something like that. Just tell me how much Kendrick owes you. I'm sure that we can work something out."*

*There was a rumble of laughter. "Xavier King is an overwhelming favorite to win this. The point spread is bananas. Unless you got about two point three million in cash, I don't think that there's much room to negotiate."*

*Xavier's brows jumped.*

*"I can't come up with that kind of money," Ricky gasped, and then clearly turned his attention to his son. "How in the hell could you get involved in something like this?"*

*"Pop, I never intended to get you involved. I thought I could handle this situation myself, but—"*

*"Enough with the family hour. We have a deal or not?"*

*"Not," Ricky barked. "This has nothing to do with me. Ken—Kendrick is his own man. And he's responsible for his own problems."*

*"Pop!" Kendrick yelled. "Maybe you're not understanding the situation here. These men will kill me if you don't come through for me on this."*

*"No. No. This time you're asking for too much! I can't tell that boy to take a dive. So, what? So you can run back out here and get yourself in trouble again—which we both know that you will do. And then you'll ask me to do it again, and again. No. It ends tonight. Whatever happens happens."*

*"I don't think that you understand, old man," the voice said. "It ain't just your kid's neck that is on the line. The kid has already guaranteed the big man that you were on board. So your ass is on the hook, as well."*

*"Like I said." Ricky injected more courage into his voice. "Whatever happens happens."*

*"I don't believe this," Kendrick sniped. "You're going to choose Xavier over me?"*

*Silence.*

*Kendrick roared, "I'm your fucking flesh and blood!"*

*"Yeah...don't remind me. Are we finished here?" Ricky said.*

*"Sure," the voice said. "It's your funeral."*

*Xavier turned and walked back to his locker room. His*

*family was still in there, still excited and bragging about how badly he was going to take Forster down.*

*"Is everything all right?" his father asked, his face blanketed with concern.*

*Xavier quickly smiled. "Yeah. Everything's cool."*

*Behind him the door opened and Ricky came in without a hint on his face of what had gone on in the other room. "Are you ready to go out there and give Forster hell?" he asked.*

*"You know it," Xavier answered, faking enthusiasm.*

*Eamon glanced at his watch. "Well, we better get to our seats. Your fight will be starting soon."*

*"Yo, man. I really appreciate you all for coming out," Xavier said. "It means a lot that you guys always show up."*

*"Of course we show up," Jeremy said. "Front-row seats to watch someone pound on that ugly mug of yours? It's like Christmas morning every time."*

*They all cracked up and then gave him a hug on their way out of the locker room.*

*"Well, let's get you suited up," Ricky said.*

*Xavier nodded, and as he started to get ready he waited for Ricky to approach him about taking a dive in the third round...but he never did. Even when he had donned his silk robe with the name* X-Man *stitched on the back, Ricky kept smiling and reminding him of the boxing tips they had learned through watching Forster's old fight. It wasn't until he'd stepped into the ring that he made his own decision.*

"You threw the fight for Ricky?" Cheryl asked, stunned. "Did he know?"

Xavier shifted in his chair and eased his hands back. "No. I certainly didn't tell him."

"But—"

"I wasn't going to risk killing someone I really cared about by winning that fight. But then throwing that fight made me feel like a fraud, regardless of the reasons. I stopped boxing because of the guilt I felt about what I'd done. And Ricky was right. Kendrick didn't shape up after that near-death scrape. He's been in and out of trouble ever since. He just couldn't use me or his father to bail him out anymore."

"Still, it was such a high price to pay," she said, reaching for his hands again.

He allowed her to hold them again. "Yes. It was. And to be honest, there are plenty of days where I play the game of what-if."

Cheryl shook her head while she let Xavier's story sink in.

"I've never told anyone that story." His eyes lifted. "You're the first."

"Because you trust me?" she asked softly.

Xavier nodded while he flipped their hands around so that he held her hands. "And I want you to feel as if you can trust me, as well. You can tell me anything."

"Anything?"

He nodded. "Anything."

There was a sharp stinging in her eyes and his handsome face was blurred behind her tears.

For perhaps the twentieth time their waiter appeared, wanting to know whether they were *finally* ready to order.

"Um. I need to just run to the ladies' room real quick," Cheryl said, getting up from her chair. "I'll be right back." She took off before her tears ruined her hour-long makeup job and to gather her courage before she told the man she was falling in love with that she was a complete fraud.

*Didn't he just say that he felt like a fraud, too? Great! We can compare notes about which one of us is the bigger fraud.*

Cheryl glanced at herself in the mirror the moment she

walked into the bathroom. "Stop kidding yourself. You'd win that contest hands down."

Waiting at their table, Xavier drew in a deep breath and marveled at how much it felt like a weight had been lifted from his shoulders, just sharing that story with Cheryl. He felt completely liberated. *Now I just hope I can help her feel the same way.*

Just as he was reminding himself to be patient and a good listener when she returned, a tall gentleman settled into Cheryl's empty chair and smiled at him.

Xavier was taken aback for just a second. "May I help you?"

"No. Actually, I came over to see if I could help you."

"Come again?"

"Oh, I'm sorry. I didn't introduce myself." The man stretched out a hand. "The name is Jason Mackey. Lieutenant Jason Mackey."

# *Chapter 26*

Cheryl continued to take deep breaths as she stared at her reflection in the mirror. Why was this so damn hard? *Because there's a good chance that he will walk out on you.* She rolled her eyes and thanked the needling voice in her head for such a comforting and reassuring answer. One thing for sure, she couldn't just hang out in the bathroom indefinitely.

"You can do this. You're strong, tough—get it together." Still, she didn't move away from the mirror. What if she *did* lose him? What if she did lose this…amazing feeling he'd stirred within her? It was crazy, but it was growing increasingly difficult to remember what life was like before that feeling came along. If she had to describe it, she would say that it was nothing and everything at the same time.

So could she risk losing everything?

Hell. Turning in her badge didn't give her this much angst.

"Just go out there, put it on the table and deal with the consequences as they come," she chided herself. She hesitated for an extra second, but then turned on her heels and marched out of the bathroom. But as she neared the table, she noticed that a man was sitting in her chair. She felt a tingling in the back of her head, the sense that something wasn't right about this picture. She noted the angry lines deepening across Xavier's normally smooth forehead.

Then everything seemed to move in slow motion. Xavier's narrowing gaze shifted toward her and the man at the table slowly turned around. *Oh, my God.*

Mackey's full lips split into a wide smile. "Detective Grier, fancy seeing you here." He stood and towered over her.

She froze. Her mind was a complete blank.

"I hope you don't mind my coming over and introducing myself to Mr. King. I wanted to congratulate him for stealing one of my best police officers on the force. A good man can admit when he's been beaten." He turned back toward Xavier. "But I think that it's only fair to warn him to stay on his toes." He faced her again. "We both know that you have a nasty habit of sleeping with people you work for."

Cheryl attempted to find her tongue. "Xavier—"

"Personally, I'm convinced that once you satisfy this itch that you'll move along again." He took one step and then stopped to lean and whisper into her ear. "And when you do, your badge and I will be waiting for you."

Cheryl closed her eyes while he patted her on the shoulder.

"By the way, you look stunning this evening." Mackey made one final glance over his shoulder at Xavier. "It was a pleasure to meet you. I'd wish you luck, but we both know I wouldn't mean it." With that, he walked away.

The silence that landed between Cheryl and Xavier hit with the force of a nuclear bomb. The emotions that played across Xavier's face ranged from disbelief to pure rage. The need to say something—anything—overwhelmed Cheryl. But the fear of saying the wrong thing paralyzed her.

Their waiter picked that perfect moment to reappear. "Okay, have we made our decisions yet?"

"Yes," Xavier said coolly. "I would like to have the check."

The waiter sputtered. "Y-yes, sir."

Once he rushed off, Cheryl finally got her legs to work and she quickly returned to her chair. "Xavier, please. I was going to tell you."

"You've been investigating me?"

"I was investigating the club," she corrected.

"*And* me," he corrected her.

Realizing that she wasn't going to win any points by nitpicking, she decided to let those go. "All right, yes. I went undercover at The Dollhouse to investigate suspicion and charges of drug trafficking. That was my job. Yes."

"And fucking me was also part of the job description? Damn. I didn't fully understand what all my taxpaying dollars were going for in the war on drugs."

"Xavier—"

"Then again, one could argue that I was actually paying you to sleep with me." He cocked his head. "There's another name for that, isn't there?"

She blinked at the cutting remark.

The waiter set their bill down.

"Hold up," Xavier said, retrieving his wallet and slipping a Benjamin into the leather holder. "Keep the change."

The waiter beamed. "Thank you, sir!"

"Well, thank you for a very…eye-opening evening." Xavier stood.

Cheryl reached out and grabbed his hand. "Xavier, please. Let me explain."

He pulled his hand free. "What's there to explain? Our whole relationship is a lie. I got it," he said with a humorless smile.

"It's not a lie," she insisted. "I love you."

His jawline hardened as acid dripped from his voice. "Is that right?"

"Yes," she said. "That's why I pulled myself from the case. It certainly wasn't part of my job to sleep with you and it certainly wasn't to fall in love with you, either."

"And I'm supposed to believe you because…you've been so honest with me, right?"

She closed her eyes. "Look. I know that you're hurt. I understand that. I do. And I wish that there was something that I could say that could convince you that I never intended to hurt you because I didn't."

He bobbed his head but it was clear that her words were not penetrating. When there was a pause in her minispeech, he asked, "Are you finished, *Detective Grier?*"

Her shoulders collapsed as she saw the hard wall that he'd erected. "Only that I'm sorry…and I hope that you can find it in your heart to forgive me."

Eyes shimmering with unshed tears, Xavier gave her a short nod before turning and strolling confidently out of the restaurant.

Cheryl could only sit there and watch, her heart broken.

"Wow," Mackey said, returning to the table, but this time taking Xavier's vacant chair. "I don't think he handled that too well."

She ignored him while her gaze remained glued to the front of the restaurant. Maybe, just maybe, Xavier wouldn't really be able to leave. Maybe he would get into his SUV, sit behind the wheel and not be able to start the car. She hoped, she had to hope, that had he known her true name he might have known her heart, had felt her heart all along.

"Oh, don't look so upset," Mackey said, grabbing the champagne bottle and tipping it back for a long gulp. "You'll bounce back. You always do."

*Xavier, please come back.*

"But I don't see why we should let a perfectly good

evening go to waste," he continued, oblivious or ignoring the fact that she wasn't paying him any attention. "There's certainly no reason to let a fabulous dress like that go to waste."

She closed her eyes. *Please give me another chance.*

"You know what they say, 'To get over a man, you need to get under one.'"

Cheryl's head whipped around. "Will you shut up, you… pompous ass!" She picked up her champagne glass and tossed the rest of her drink in his face. "It's over! And if you ever come near me again, I'll cut off that two-inch dick of yours that you're so damn proud of and feed it to a tank of piranhas. Do I make myself clear? It's over!"

Every head in the restaurant whipped around to their table. And Mackey's dark and wet complexion turned into the color of eggplant.

Turning, Cheryl stormed out of the restaurant, hoping to find Xavier sitting in his SUV unable to drive off. Instead, when she pushed out of the front door, all she saw was a glimpse of his taillights as he drove off into the night.

*The Queen of Lies*

# *Chapter 27*

"Lies, lies, lies," Quentin said, shaking his head. "They'll get you every time."

"It does sound like a complicated web of deception," Dr. Turner agreed.

"That it was. For the next couple of weeks, my man was walking around with his bottom lip hanging down about as long as mine usually was. I think that's about the same time I realized how pathetic I'd been. Nothing like facing a mirror to put your life into perspective."

Dr. Turner chuckled.

"What?" Quentin sat up and looked at her. "Is something funny? Are you guys allowed to laugh at your clients like that?"

"You're overly sensitive today."

Q stiffened. "No. I mean, I'm curious as to what you found so funny."

"I don't know if it's funny so much as...how striking it is when you see yourself through everyone else's eyes. I mean, on the surface, you wouldn't think that would be the case. You're Mr. Party All the Time. You certainly don't believe in being alone, and you're very hands-off even when it comes to your successful business."

"I don't know if I follow you."

Dr. Turner folded her hands while she tried to approach her analysis another way. "You work very hard to give the impression that you're a man marching to the beat of his own drum. You live life in style and carefree, but I find it…"

"Striking," he supplied the word for her.

"Yes…*striking* that you constantly compare yourself and your mental state to your brothers and your cousins."

"No. That's not true." He shook his head.

"You just compared Xavier's heartbreak to your own. And not really in terms of the depths of what he was going through, but how it looked. It even sounds like there was a bit of resentment that his emotional break somehow detracted from the sympathy that you've come to depend on from him."

Quentin didn't like the way that sounded.

"Face it, Mr. Hinton. You're an emotional vampire. And it sounds to me like you feed off the ones that you claim to care for the most."

Her words hung in the air as he mulled over whether to argue or take her ridiculous theory seriously.

"Let me ask you something," Dr. Turner said. "How much support did you give Xavier after this major blow? Did you give him as much attention and sympathy as he'd given you when you were in a similar situation?"

"Well, yeah," Quentin answered much too quickly.

Turner kept her gaze leveled on him.

"I mean, as much as I could."

Turner picked up her pen and started scribbling again.

"Wait. Wait. I'm not liking what you're insinuating.

Xavier is my friend. And I'm a damn good friend to him. I listened and I tried my best to help him get over his undercover lover the best and only way I knew how...."

# *Chapter 28*

"Welcome to The Dollhouse Atlanta," Quentin boasted at the top of his lungs as he led a throng of brothers into their private oasis for the night. Tonight, he was playing host until he and his sole partner, Jeremy, could put their heads together and decide on an Atlanta manager for the club. Occasionally, he could talk Xavier into filling in, but that was getting harder and harder to pull off.

After hearing that Atlanta's finest had recently been investigating the club for drug trafficking, the first thing the cousins initiated was installing an additional level of security at all three club locations. In no time at all, they were able to catch Dog Pound's drug dealing at the door.

Given how close Xavier was to Dog Pound's uncle, Q took matters into his own hands and simply fired him and threatened that if he or anyone on his staff saw him hanging around the club again, he would press charges. That seemed to be enough to spook the man, but Quentin hadn't expected the dude to burst out crying. Seemed he was more fearful of his uncle Ricky finding out and being disappointed in him than he was at the possibility of going to jail.

Once that situation was settled, things around The Dollhouse were back to normal. The place stayed packed and Quentin promoted Lexus to head their Bachelors Adventures services. So far, it was looking like it was going to be an easy transition from being a silent partner to a hands-on partner.

And he was loving it.

"I hope that you all came prepared to have a good time!"

The cluster of forty men sent up a loud cheer and Quentin quickly waved in the waitresses and Dolls for the evening. He brought the groom up to the stage and sat him down in front of a golden pole and introduced him to Cinnamon Brown, who would perform his first lap dance of the evening.

Having a new dancer at the club, Quentin stuck around to see how the Meagan Good lookalike dipped it down low and mopped the floor with all the junk that she was packing. It was a hard job, but somebody had to do these employee evaluations. Unfortunately, before he could appreciate Ms. Brown's Brazilian wax, there was a tap on his shoulder. He turned and Lexus leaned over, "Your cousin is on the phone."

He frowned. "Which one?"

"Jeremy."

Quentin nodded and stole one last peek at Cinnamon's hypnotic curves before sighing in regret and then making his way to the office. "Yo, partner. What's up?"

"Sorry to pull you from the floor. I tried to get you on your cell."

Q scooped his phone out of his pocket and saw that he had six missed calls. "Sorry about that, cuz. What can I do for you?"

"Have you talked to Xavier lately?"

"As a matter of fact, I talked to him this morning. He was heading out to the gym. I don't know what he's been doing there, but in the past month the man has packed on at least ten pounds of muscle."

"I think he's working something—or someone—out of his system."

"The cop."

"Exactly," Jeremy agreed. "I have to admit I'm starting to get a little worried about him. The few times either Eamon or I could get him on the phone, he just doesn't sound right. You gotta do something to get this chick off his mind. I can't get out there for at least another week, but—"

"Say no more. I got this." Q disconnected the call and immediately hit Xavier up on his home phone. Instinctively knowing that he was there, he didn't leave a message the first time his call went to the answering machine. He just hung up and kept calling until Xavier finally picked up.

"Yeah. What is it?"

"Rise and shine, X-Man. Guess who's coming over to rescue you from the four walls closing in on you."

Xavier sighed. "Man, I'm beat. I've been putting in some serious hours working with My'kael. A couple more months, and I'm going to see about getting him his first professional fight."

"So soon?"

"Ricky had been working with him long before I came into the picture and, frankly, I think he's ready."

Quentin nodded, but suspected that Xavier was really lining up the fight as a way to keep himself busy and focused on anything other than the woman who'd broken his heart. "Look, man, I'm not going to take no for an answer. I'm getting you out of the house. It's been a long time since we've hung out together and tonight is the night."

There was a long pause over the line.

"You know, I can hear those rusty cogs in that big head of yours slowly churning, trying to come up with an excuse as to why you can't hang with your boy, but I'm not taking no for an answer."

"Q—"

"It's time, Xavier. And I know just the string of beauties to call to make sure that we get the lady cop off your mind." He slammed his eyes shut. "Sorry."

"It's all right. Thanks, but no, thanks. I'm already in bed and—"

"What's that?" Quentin asked, straining to hear on the other line. "Are you listening to Al Green?"

"Uh, no."

It was an obvious lie, especially since Q was able to make out the chorus, "How can you mend a broken heart?"

"Oh, hell. I didn't know that it was that serious. I'm on my way." Before Xavier had a chance to object, Q hung up the phone and asked Lexus to take over the night's bachelor party.

Twenty minutes later, he was at Xavier's condominium, banging on the front door and threatening to have it kicked in. "I'm going to count to ten," he threatened.

Xavier jerked opened the door and leveled a look at Quentin that clearly said that if it wasn't for the fact that they were cousins, he would be getting white-chalked right about now.

"Don't give me that look," Q said, pushing both Xavier and the door back. "Fear not. I've come to save the day."

"For some reason, that doesn't make me feel better."

Q chuckled as he strolled into the living room as Anthony Hamilton's "Can't Let Go" floated through the entire condo. He stopped and looked over his shoulder at his cousin. "Damn."

Tightening the belt on his black silk robe, Xavier shuffled into the living room, looking like a Mack truck had run over him two or three times. "What? You think that you have the market on heartbreak cornered?"

Quentin shook his head solemnly. "No. I guess I didn't really know that… I'm sorry."

"For what?" Xavier asked, making his way over to the leather sofa, plopping down and stretching out as Hamilton's song started having the same effect on Quentin as his cousin, realizing how impossible it was to let go of someone you love.

"For not being here, especially after all that you've done for me these past two years." He eased into the chair kitty-corner from the sofa. "What's on your mind, man?"

"You mean other than me feeling like a complete fool? Nothing much."

Maxwell's "Pretty Wings" played next and Quentin was back on his feet. "I need a drink. You need one?"

"Man, just bring the bottle of whatever you're having."

That was saying something since Xavier wasn't exactly what one would call a heavy drinker. Q ignored the bottle request but made two whiskey sours before rejoining his cousin for what was clearly shaping up to be a pity party.

"I didn't even know her real name, man. She wasn't a medical student. Hell, I don't even know if that was her real family I met. Is there a place I never heard of where you can rent families?"

"Don't know. Course I got you and your brothers on a bottom basement deal."

Xavier shook his head, but also managed to smile.

"Aw—a smile. There's still hope," Q joked. "All is not lost."

Xavier doubted that. "Keep your apology," he said. "If anything, I owe you one. Until this…fiasco, I don't think I truly comprehended just how painful love can be. It feels like…"

"Someone ripped your heart out of your chest—without anesthesia?"

Xavier thought about it. "Exactly."

"That's just the first stage."

"Great." Xavier tilted back his glass and downed its contents in one long gulp.

Quentin shook his head. "This is going to be an interesting evening."

"The Black Chippendales?" Cheryl said, turning toward Johnnie. "Are you serious?"

Johnnie hopped out of her car and rushed over to wrap her arm around Cheryl's waist. "This is just the kind of thing you need to try and cheer you up. You've been tripping on that bottom lip now for weeks. It's time to get the old Cheryl back."

"Hell, I don't even remember that girl." Cheryl dug her heels in and turned to her well-intentioned friend and shook her head. "I really don't feel like going in there."

"No. You want to go on ten-mile runs and pound punching bags until you drop. It's not healthy."

"And watching men gyrate in front of a bunch of screaming women is going to make me feel better?"

"C'mon. This used to make you feel better and it's gotta be better than having to watch a bunch of women do it for the past couple of months…unless there's something that you want to tell me."

Cheryl rolled her eyes.

"Joking. Ha. Ha." Johnnie poked out her bottom lip. "C'mon. Cheer up. I'm running out of tricks here."

"I'm not interested in tricks. This is just something that I'm going to have to work through. The one man that I've finally fallen in love with can't stand my guts. What is it that you don't understand about that?"

Johnnie tossed up her hands. "I guess everything. How could you have fallen in love with someone you hardly know? At most, you two were just lovers. You went on one date and he dumped you." As soon as the words were out of her mouth, a blanket of regret covered her face.

Cheryl pulled away.

"That didn't come out right."

"Yes, it did." Cheryl shook her head at her friend. "Look. I wish that I could explain this to you. Really I do, but that would require me understanding it myself. And I don't. I don't understand why I feel the way I do. I just do. It's like my mother once said about love. When it comes, you know it. And no one—*no one*—could have screwed up something so perfect more than I have."

Johnnie stepped forward. "Stop beating yourself up. You were just doing your job."

"My job wasn't to sleep with him."

Her ex-partner clammed up on that one.

"Maybe if…after the investigation was over and I told him before something went down between us…"

"You don't know that."

"Yes. I do."

Someone opened the front door to the club and the whoops and hollers of the women flowed out of the club.

Cheryl shook her head. "I think I better go home."

Johnnie's lips twitched in disappointment, but she understood. "Come on, girl. Maybe we should stop and pick up a couple of gallons of ice cream while we're at it. It looks like it's going to be one of those evenings."

Laughing uncontrollably, Quentin waved his hands. "Wait a minute. Let me get this straight. You were all set to forgive Cheryl if she had a drug problem, but when you found out she was a cop, it was a deal breaker? Do I have that right?"

"Well, it was a little more complicated than that." Xavier snickered and slurred. "I wanted to show her that I wasn't the type to just abandon someone because they had a problem or an addiction. I was willing to stick it out and help her through it."

"That's mighty big of you." Q nodded. "Commendable."

Xavier puffed up his chest. "Thank you."

"It still don't change the fact that you'd rather date a drug addict than a cop. In that sense, it's a little fucked up."

Xavier frowned. "What? No. Wait. You're comparing apples to oranges."

"What difference does that make? They're both fruit."

In his inebriated state, that remark tripped Xavier up to the point that he had to really think about that. But then Teddy Pendergrass's "Love TKO" floated out of the speakers and the two men rocked their heads.

"Awww. Man. That's my jam," Xavier said, snapping his fingers and getting his groove going.

"Teddy P., Teddy P., Teddy P." Quentin got his own groove going. "'I try to hold on, my faith is gone. Whooo.'"

Xavier laughed and then Quentin quickly joined in.

"We're a hot mess. You know that, right?" Q said.

"Yeah. But misery loves company." He held up his glass for another toast. "Thanks for being here, man. I appreciate it."

Quentin tapped their glasses together. "Any time."

"It could all be so simple," Lauryn Hill crooned from the speakers as Cheryl shoveled another heaping tablespoon of rocky-road ice cream into her mouth. "Mmm. Now, this is the kind of therapy I can get with."

With Thaddeus long gone to bed, Larissa had joined her sister and Johnnie in the living room, spoons in hand, for their blues party. "'Tell me who I have to beeee.'"

Larissa winced at the missed note her heartbroken sister hit and then shook her head. "I think you should just wait a little while for him to calm down and then go over and talk to him again," she said, cramming in a good helping of butter pecan in her mouth.

"Why? So he can just humiliate me again?" Cheryl said, shaking her head, realizing that she was starting to crest on a sugar high. "Please. I had to sign up with another gym just because I'm afraid of running into him."

"What do you have to lose?" Johnnie asked.

"Other than all these calories I'm gorging on?"

Larissa rolled her eyes. "Please. Not as much as you work out. Your metabolism is so high that those suckers are probably disappearing the moment you swallow."

"Are you eating ice cream or Haterade?" Cheryl snickered.

"I don't know. I might have a little bit of both mixed in here."

Johnnie peeked into her double chocolate chunk. "That makes two of us."

Cheryl laughed. "C'mon, guys."

"Hey. She's laughing," Johnnie said.

"Yeah. That means that there's still hope for her."

"I don't know," Cheryl said, jamming her spoon back into the carton. "It feels like I'm trying to breathe at the bottom of the ocean."

"Been there, bought the T-shirt," Larissa said. "When I broke up with Thaddeus's dad, I thought I'd die. The way it felt was like someone had cracked open my chest and ripped my heart out."

"Without anesthesia," Johnnie said, bobbing her head and reflecting. "I have drawers and drawers of T-shirts. Breakups are never easy."

"Great." Cheryl plopped her carton onto the coffee table and leaned back on the floor against the sofa.

"Just go talk to him," Larissa insisted. "You never know. He might've had time to calm down enough for him to hear you this time. He was hurt and it couldn't have been easy to get that information from another man."

"True. Of course, Mackey is roaming around the office still tripping over his bottom lip."

Cheryl shook her head. "I don't know. If he felt half as bad as I do right now when I broke up with him, then maybe I'm just getting back what I put out there. Karma."

"I wouldn't go that far," Johnnie said. "The man has tried blackmailing, stalking and bullying. Keep that brother in your rearview and keep it stepping."

Cheryl deliberated about that while Teddy Pendergrass's smooth "Love TKO" filled the living room.

The three women rocked their heads back and forth.

"Awww. Man. That's my jam," Cheryl said, snapping her fingers and getting her groove going.

"Teddy P., Teddy P., Teddy P.," said Johnnie as she got her own groove going. "'I try to hold on, my faith is gone. Whooo.'"

Larissa got up from the floor and started dancing with an imaginary partner.

Not to be outdone, Cheryl and Johnnie climbed to their feet and started rocking their hips, as well.

Cheryl didn't know who the other women were grooving with, but in her mind Xavier was rocking a mean two-step with his hands locked around her hips and his head pressed against the side of hers. With her eyes closed, she was sure she could hear him singing along, "Takin' the bumps and the bruises of all the things of a two-time loser."

Her heart squeezed. It was just too much. By the time the song ended and they all collapsed onto the floor, she had discovered another level of depression.

"We're a hot mess. You know that, right?" Johnnie said.

"Yeah. But misery loves company." Cheryl held up her spoon. "Thanks for being here, ladies. I appreciate it."

Johnnie and Larissa tapped their spoons against hers. "Any time."

# *Chapter 29*

"You went into business with the man?" Kendrick thundered at his father in the back office of Ripped Gym. "What about me? Did you think that maybe I might want to go into business with my old man?" His face twisted in pain from what he thought was a serious offense.

Ricky pulled in a deep breath and shook his gray head. "No offense, son, but it's not like you have a head for business."

"How in the hell would you know? You're too busy out here wishing that Xavier King was your son. Newsflash, I'm your son. I'm your flesh and blood. Not him! That asshole has a daddy."

"Not this crap again." Ricky sprung up from his chair. "I'm not in the mood to hear this today. I have things to do. I run a *legit* business."

"Oh. So that's it? You're ashamed of me, Pop? Is that it?"

Ricky glanced away.

"Yeah. That's it. I've made some mistakes in the past

and you can't get over it? You're going to stand there and tell me that you're perfect? How many families have you abandoned?"

"Look, Ken. I'm not proud of some of the things I've done or how many people I've disappointed—you included. But I don't intend to spend the rest of my life—how much or little there is left of it—always apologizing for whatever grievances are riding your back for the day. The past is the past. It's over with. I've apologized and now it's up to you to accept it or toss it in the trash. I'm way past giving a damn anymore."

Kendrick shook his head while staring at his father. "I don't know how to reach you anymore."

"Oh. If only that was true, my life would be so much simpler. My heart wouldn't stop beating in the middle of the night when the phone rings because I'm scared that when I pick it up it's either going to be some drug thug or gangster telling me how much you owe him and what they're going to do to you if I don't mortgage everything I own to save your precious limbs or your damn life.

"And I don't want to hear another word about Xavier coming from you. That man has done a lot for me *and* you over the years. He deserves your appreciation, not your scorn."

"The hell he does."

"What?" Ricky's eyes narrowed. "You really think he lost that fight to Forster back in '04? Are you really that stupid?"

Kendrick's eyes narrowed. "You said that you didn't ask him to throw the fight."

"And I didn't. He found out about it somehow. He had to. I know that man just like I know you. And the only reason that he would have thrown that fight was because he thought he was saving me—which in turn saved your ungrateful butt. Why else do you think that he just up and walked away from his career? He couldn't bear the thought of getting back in the ring after having thrown that damn fight. He gave up his dream—*my* dream—because *you* have daddy issues."

Kendrick's jaw hardened.

"I worry about you," Ricky said. "I do, but I can no longer let you worry me to death. You are responsible for your life, your happiness. Stop looking to me for the love and approval that you already have—have always had. I have to let you live. I have to let you fall. That's the only way that I'll ever get the chance to see you pick yourself up again. Can you even understand that?"

"How can I ever prove myself when you're always shutting me out? My getting involved here in the gym would have been the perfect opportunity for me to go *legit* if that's what you're concerned about. As it is, I made money the only way I know how—on the streets. The same streets that you left me and Mom to survive on, the same streets I got my education on. And now you want to stand there and act like you're so ashamed of me."

"I got to get out of here. We're just going around in circles." Ricky tossed up his hands and stormed out of the office.

"That's right. Leave," Kendrick yelled after him. "Just like you always do."

Despite nursing one hell of a hangover, Xavier hit the gym at 5:00 a.m. that morning where he worked on his speed and threw punches. This was his element. This was where he thrived. His agility, footwork and coordination was still tight and he would be lying if he denied having the desire to test his mettle against the current heavyweight champion. He wondered whether he still had what it took to get in the ring again.

He continued shadowboxing around the ring while

imagining the roar and cheering of a packed house at the MGM Grand. Wouldn't it be nice?

"So you're just walking away from me? Is that it?"

Xavier dropped his arms at the sound of Kendrick's angry voice slicing through the gym. It was still twenty minutes before opening, so at least it was just him and maybe My'kael in the locker room who would hear the father and son going at it…again.

Xavier shook his head the moment the men came into view. He wanted to like Kendrick, but the brother made that pretty damn hard to do.

"Fine. Walk away. I'm sick and tired of dealing with you, anyway," Kendrick continued.

*He's sick of Ricky? Isn't that rich?*

Ricky marched, shaking his head and looking like he wished his son would get off his back.

"Is everything all right?" Xavier asked.

"Damn," Kendrick barked. "Can't I have a private conversation with my father without your ass jumping into the mix?"

Xavier's gaze narrowed. "Maybe. If you knew how to talk in a reasonable and respectable voice."

"Ain't this about a bitch?" Kendrick redirected his anger back to his father. "You see what I mean? You see how you let your *fake* son talk to me?"

*Not this crap again.* Xavier rolled his eyes and turned his back to the enraged man. One of these days he was going to give himself a stroke, blowing up all the time.

"A'ight. I'm going to squash this," Kendrick declared. "I hope Sanford and Son enjoy this crappy hole in the wall. You, him, this place—ain't never gonna be about nothing. Believe that!" Kendrick turned and marched off.

Ricky didn't even bother to watch him leave. He just shook his head and sighed as if the weight on his shoulders was just seconds from crushing him.

Xavier walked over to the thick ropes around the ring and climbed out. "Don't worry about it. He's just blowing off steam. He'll get over it."

"Maybe. Maybe not." Ricky shook his head. "The longer I live the more I'm convinced that loving is easy and forgiving is damn near impossible. Kendrick doesn't have it in him to forgive me and I can't convince him that I love him." He shrugged.

Xavier felt for his old friend and reached out and patted him on the back with his gloved hand.

My'kael walked out of the locker room, bouncing and stretching his neck muscles.

Xavier and Ricky broke apart and flashed their potential star a smile.

"I hope that you're ready to put in some serious work today," Xavier said.

My'kael cocked a smile. "I can handle anything you toss my way, old man."

Xavier blinked. "Old man?" He looked over at Ricky. "Did you just hear him?"

"Welcome to the Geriatric Club." He winked.

"Boy, I ain't that much older than you. Get warmed up. It's me and you today."

Both My'kael and Ricky arched their brows in surprise.

"We'll see just who the old man is after you get this little ass-whooping I'm about to dish out."

"Ooooh." My'kael faked a tremor. "I guess I better get scared." In the middle of laughing at his own joke, there was a knock on the front glass door. He turned and blinked. "Yo, man. Your girl is here."

Xavier turned his head to see Cheryl in a formfitting gray workout suit.

"Want me to let her in?" My'kael asked.

When Xavier didn't readily answer, Ricky spoke up. "Go ahead."

Xavier's gaze cut toward his old friend like Caesar toward Brutus.

Ricky shrugged his shoulders feebly. "She can see all of us. No point in being rude."

My'kael opened the door and smiled. "Hey."

Cheryl flashed the boxer a quick smile, but her gaze remained locked on Xavier by the boxing ring. Now that she had managed to get herself to drive back to her old gym, she could hardly remember the rehearsed soliloquy she'd come up with during the middle of her sugar high last night. That probably had a lot to do with Xavier standing there looking like a chiseled black god with sweat pouring down his body.

Just looking at him made her knees weak.

"Good luck," My'kael whispered.

She glanced back over at him and he flashed her a sympathetic smile.

Cheryl finally forced one foot in front of the other and walked up to Xavier. As she drew near, she noted how a hard mask of indifference fell over his face while his jawline hardened and his eyes narrowed.

"Hey," she said when she stopped in front of him.

Silence.

Cheryl swallowed, but somehow that just made the lump in her throat bigger. She cut her gaze toward Ricky and he quickly caught the hint.

"C'mon, My'kael. Let's get you warmed up," he said, strolling over to the young boxer near the speed bag.

Alone, Xavier and Cheryl looked at each other.

"So," she started. "How have you been?"

Xavier shook his head. "C'mon, Cheryl. Let's not do this."

His words crushed her. "So. That's it? You're not even going to consider my side in this situation? You can't even try to forgive me?"

He shook his head while his jaw worked silently.

"Then maybe I was wrong about you, too. The Xavier I've come to know wasn't this hard, unforgiving man in front of me now. He was a man who loved hard and realized that people make mistakes. That people aren't perfect. I'm sorry about how you found out, but I had every intention of telling you the truth that night. I have no proof other than my word. Take it—for whatever it's worth." She stepped closer to him. "When you told me why you'd walked away from your promising career just so you could protect someone you loved, it connected and resonated with me because…I had walked away from my career in order to be with you. That's the part my *ex*-lieutenant didn't tell you. I had turned in my badge because I couldn't continue to deceive you."

He closed his eyes. "It still doesn't change the fact that the woman I thought I fell in love with doesn't exist. If we took away what I thought I knew, you have to ask, What is left? Sex?"

"No. Love. Love is still there. Love is not facts on a piece of paper. It's a feeling—a connection. And if you're honest, then you have to admit that it was something that has always existed between me and you. The minute our eyes connected, I felt as if someone had punched me in the gut. Don't tell me that you didn't feel it, too."

Xavier dropped his head. No way was he going to get that lie across his lips.

"I miss you," she said earnestly. "I miss us. Don't you?"

"Of course I miss you," he said.

Hope finally penetrated her heart, but then it quickly disappeared.

"But I just don't know how to go about trusting you. And what is a relationship without the foundation of trust?" He pressed his lips together while his eyes glistened with tears. "I'm sorry."

Sucking in a deep breath while batting back her own tears, Cheryl nodded as she stepped back. "I understand."

Silence.

"Well. At least I tried. I wish you luck." Her voice cracked and she spun around and rushed toward the door.

A battle raged within Xavier as he watched her go.

"Remind me never to take advice from you," Ricky said, walking up behind him.

"You don't understand," he said, turning away just before Cheryl walked out of the door.

"*I* don't understand?" Ricky laughed. "I don't understand what it feels like when someone doesn't want to forgive me for mistakes and bad decisions? Is that what you're saying? What the hell were we just talking about ten minutes ago?"

Xavier's resolve softened.

"I tell you what," Ricky continued. "I admire that woman. It took a lot of guts to come in here and just put her heart on the line like that. To stand in front of a man like you emotionally naked like that. That's something else I know about real well."

"But I didn't lie to her. How do I go about learning to trust her again?"

"One damn day at a time, kid," Ricky said simply. "One day at a time."

"So what did he say?" Dog Pound asked from the passenger side of Kendrick's latest stolen vehicle.

"Exactly what I expected him to say—nothing." Kendrick sat behind the wheel trying to cool off before starting the car and pulling out of the gym's parking lot. But the argument between him and his father continued to loop over and over in his mind. "That damn Xavier King."

"C'mon, man. Don't start that again."

"Why?" Kendrick whipped his head around to his cousin. "Are you still worshipping at the altar of His Majesty, too?"

"Man, I'm just saying that it's not that serious."

Kendrick's jaw tightened while he shook his head. "What the hell do you know?"

"Damn, cuz. You act like you're the only man out here that didn't have a father coming up. My daddy was M.I.A., too."

"That's because he got locked up."

"Same difference. He would be around if he didn't do what he did, right?"

"Whatever." He shook his head and caught sight of Detective Cheryl Grier exiting the gym. Kendrick continued to watch her as she rushed past his vehicle. "Humph." A smile curled his lips.

"What?"

"Since Xavier took someone from me, maybe it's time I took someone from him so he can see what it feels like." He opened his car door.

# Chapter 30

My'kael kept his eyes on his steady jabs against the speed bag, but that focus was broken suddenly when a scuffle outside of the gym caught the corner of his eye. "Yo, somebody is trying to grab your girl!" He raced toward the door.

Xavier's breath caught as he dropped the gloves Ricky had just taken off of him and ran toward the door, too. Time seemed to stand still while the pounding in his chest was more painful than any punch that he had ever taken. His legs moved faster than they ever had and his brain churned with thoughts of what-ifs at an astounding clip.

What if he was too late?

What if she's hurt?

What if she's killed?

That last question came just as he burst through the door and tried to make sense of what his eyes were seeing. Kendrick had his arm wrapped tight around Cheryl's neck as he tried to drag her toward a car.

"What the hell are you doing, Kendrick?" Xavier barked, finally slowing down when he spotted the gun pressed against Cheryl's temple. He didn't look too good himself. Clearly, Cheryl had gotten in a few punches and scratches because Kendrick was bleeding profusely from his face and lip.

"I'm paying you back, man. What does it look like?"

Dog Pound climbed out of the passenger side of the car, raising his hands up in the air. "I ain't got nothin' to do with this," he shouted.

"Kenny! What the hell?" Ricky shouted, finally making it outside into the light of early dawn. "Put that gun down. Are you crazy?"

"What the hell do you care? Huh? You got your favorite son there. He's the one you love, right? He's the one that you prefer over me. Mr. Gallant. Mr. Noble. Mr. Perfect."

"Kendrick, that's not true."

"Shut up," Kendrick yelled so loud that Cheryl winced and tried to jerk her head away. "What? How in the hell am I'm supposed to compete with you? Huh? You fell on your heroic sword and threw that damn fight. You walked away from a golden career to save my old man. Now you're forever the hero and I'm the villain," he roared.

To Cheryl's credit, she looked absolutely calm as Kendrick kept trying to move her toward the car door.

"Oh, God, Kenny," Ricky moaned, every ounce of his heartache echoed in his voice. "Don't you see what you're doing, son? This is no way to handle this. It's between me and you."

Kendrick shook his head. "It stopped being about me and you a long time ago, Pop. That's what you don't get. That's what you refuse to understand."

Ricky groaned. "What I don't understand is what you want from me *now?* What am I supposed to be doing for you *now?*"

"You're supposed to love me—*more* than him!"

Ricky moved up next to Xavier. "I do. And I even love you more than you love yourself. You just won't allow yourself to see it."

Xavier's gaze remained locked on the gun at Cheryl's temple while he kept taking slow, measured steps forward as the father and son continued their argument. But Kendrick remained suspiciously alert as his gaze darted from Ricky to Xavier and back again.

"The way I see it," Kendrick said. "You took someone from me and now I'm going to take someone from you," he said ominously.

The pain in Xavier's chest increased tenfold. At the same time, his and Cheryl's eyes connected. Instantly, he felt that punch to his gut that Cheryl had referred to earlier, that singular, powerful connection that stole his breath and reaffirmed the love that existed between them.

Kendrick's brows dipped. "What? You think that you're going to get close enough to knock this gun out of my hand, X-Man? Seriously, is that what you think is going to go down out here? Huh?"

Xavier stopped moving.

A sinister smile crept across Kendrick's face.

However, to his right, My'kael kept inching his way toward the distracted gunman.

"Yeah, that's what you thought. You think I'm stupid?" He shook his head. "Nah. I'm going to enjoy this. You've never lost anything in your life. Have you? You have two parents, two brothers—probably a boatload of cousins. I'm even guessing your grandparents are still living."

Xavier didn't answer.

"I'm right, ain't I? You have all of that and still…" He shook his head. "You know what? I'm going to have fun watching the light drain out of your little girlfriend's eyes.

Maybe that way you'll finally get a little taste of what I've been feeling all of this time." Kendrick sniffed.

"You don't want to do that," Xavier said with a measure of calm that he didn't feel.

"You have no idea how much I want to do exactly that."

"No. You want me," Xavier countered. "I'm the one that you hate—because you know that no matter what you do, you'll never measure up. Shooting her will just land you jail. I'll still be out here, working with your dad—hanging out with him." He shrugged. "You would've changed nothing—except your address. But if you take me out, you would rob your father of the son he really wants, the one that he really loves. Now that's revenge."

Kendrick sniffed again.

Xavier sensed that he'd piqued Kendrick's interest. "C'mon. Admit it. You'd like nothing more than to put a bullet in the center of my forehead. You've dreamed about it."

Both he and My'kael inched closer.

"Well, here I am." Xavier swung out his arms wide in surrender. "Take your best shot."

"Now how could I resist an offer like that?" Kendrick asked. Once again, everything moved in slow motion.

The gun swung away from Cheryl's temple to take aim at Xavier.

With a sudden burst of agility, Ricky jumped in front of Xavier.

*Pop! Pop!*

Cheryl's elbow came up and slammed into Kendrick's neck just as My'kael closed the distance to knock the gun out of Kendrick's hand and tackle both him and Cheryl to the ground.

Xavier's ability to move forward was blocked when Ricky slammed backward into him. "Ricky!"

Hearing his father's name, Kendrick looked up and saw his bloody father collapse into Xavier's arms. "Nooooo!"

# *Chapter 31*

For two hours Xavier paced the floors of Grady Hospital, waiting to hear word from the doctor about Ricky's condition. Cheryl had her few bruises looked at and was now more concerned about Xavier and the worry lines deepening his forehead. She knew what he was going through. Not so long ago it was her and her sister walking the floor, waiting to hear whether her mother would pull through. And this time, just like the one before, there was no real way to dodge the guilt that continued to tap her on the shoulder.

What if she hadn't been there?

What if she had been able to break away sooner?

What if he had shot Xavier?

Her gaze skittered up Xavier while he continued to pace back and forth. He'd been willing to die for her. He nearly begged for the bullet. What did that mean? And why wouldn't he now look at her?

They both glanced toward their left when it sounded like a stampede of feet was headed in their direction. A second later, Quentin rounded the corner with an older couple. The woman was a tall, willowy, silver-haired beauty while the man next to her was clearly what Xavier was going to look like in about thirty years. Handsome, fit and he had the same worry lines stretched across his forehead.

"Oh, thank God," the woman who Cheryl assumed was Xavier's mother said, rushing toward her son's open arms. "What happened? Are you okay?"

Xavier cocked his first smile since they'd walked into the hospital. "Yes, Mama. I'm fine." He pressed a kiss on the top of her head.

"You had us worried there for a second, son." His father's long arms enfolded both of them.

Quentin stood off to the sidelines for a moment, but then coughed.

The Kings glanced up and then opened their arms to allow more room for him, as well.

To Xavier's right, the doctor walked through a pair of double doors. "Are you with Mr. Miller?"

"Yes," Xavier said eagerly. "How is he?"

The doctor smiled. "He's going to be just fine. You got yourself a major fighter on your hands."

"You have no idea." He shook the doctor's hand and then turned back toward his family with an overwhelming sense of relief. After a number of hugs and well wishes, Xavier realized something was missing. "Dad and Mom, there's someone I'd like for you both to meet." He flashed them a smile and then turned toward Cheryl—but her chair was now empty. "Where did she go?"

His mother frowned. "Where did who go, sweetheart?"

Xavier glanced around and then up and down the hallway. "Wait right here." He rushed around his parents and then jogged down the hall until he spotted Cheryl walking out of the hospital doors. "Cheryl!"

Heads popped up and swiveled in his direction as he took

off after her. When he pushed through the door, she was nearing her car. "Cheryl!"

She looked up. Their eyes locked and delivered that familiar punch to the gut.

Xavier swallowed, gathered his courage and then rushed across the parking lot toward her. When he stopped before her, he suddenly realized that he didn't know or have anything prepared to say so he settled on, "Where are you going?"

"Well…your family came…and I didn't really want to get in the way, so I just thought…"

"You weren't in the way," he said, shaking his head. "In fact, I really appreciate your being here."

A smile flickered on her lips. "While we're talking, I want to thank you. That was really brave what you did back there."

"I…I…" He exhaled a shaky breath. "I don't know what I would have done if something happened to you."

Cheryl felt a new wave of hope wash over her, but this time she was too afraid to trust it.

"You were so cool and calm," he said, shaking his head.

"Police training," she reminded him.

Xavier nodded while he tried to push up his own nervous smile. When it failed, he had to admit, "I was frightened."

"It didn't show."

Xavier pressed his lips together while the sound of the passing traffic filled the space between them. He wanted to say so much, but didn't know where to begin. It wasn't that he couldn't admit that he'd made a mistake or had been too harsh or too hard, it was because he was weighing whether or not he even deserved *her* forgiveness for those wrongs.

"I guess I better get going," Cheryl said, gesturing over her shoulder.

"What if I said that I didn't want you to go?"

"I'd ask you why."

"Then I would say because I want and need the people I love around me right now."

Her gaze probed his. "You still love me?"

"I've never stopped. And I can't explain it. Clearly, when it comes to love it…"

"…it just happens," they said in unison.

Cheryl loved how her mother's words floated back to her. "So what do we do now?"

"How about we start by forgiving each other…and then start loving each other…while we get to know each other?"

"That sounds like a great plan." Cheryl's lips split into a wide smile as she rushed into his open arms.

*Then There Were Two*

# *Chapter 32*

"And six months later, Xavier made an honest woman out of her. I'm sure I don't have to tell you about the bachelor party," Q concluded.

"A love story about forgiveness," Dr. Turner said. "Very touching. Perhaps not so much for Mr. Miller's son."

Quentin shrugged. "One could see it that way."

"Oh? And how do you see it?" she inquired, easing farther back into her seat.

"Another one bites the dust?" Q laughed, but the joke fell flat. "Tough crowd."

Dr. Turner's pen started flying back across the page. "Do you ever get tired of deflecting serious questions with jokes?" At his hesitation, she continued. "Clearly, you think that you're a funny guy."

"Actually, I was aiming for charming," he said, sounding wounded.

"Still. It has to be tiresome to always be 'on.' You're Mr.

Party. Mr. Playboy. When are you ever just Quentin—or Q, as you like to be called?"

Quentin frowned. "I'm not sure that I follow you."

She laughed. "And how did I forget about Mr. Playful?" She shook her head. "Let's leave that alone for now and let me ask you another question. How was it that Xavier's story did not inspire you to pick up the phone and call Sterling? Do you ever want to mend this fence with your brother?"

Q hesitated.

"Don't you miss him?"

"Of course I miss him. What kind of question is that?"

"A genuine one," she countered. "Look, I have to tell you, Quentin. I think that you're playing a dangerous game with time. You're taking for granted that you'll be able to handle or solve this rift between you and your brother on your terms and when you're ready. Life doesn't always work out like that. If you knew the number of patients I have walk through that door who tell me how much they regret not having told someone how they felt about them before some illness or death made it an afterthought, you'd be astounded. You won't be talking about how you can't bring yourself to forgive him, but rather how you can't forgive yourself for wasting so much time."

"Is that your professional opinion?"

Dr. Turner nodded. "That is my professional opinion."

Quentin nodded and then glanced at his watch. "Wow. Would you look at that? Our time is up."

She stared at him and then shrugged. "So it is." She stood and then placed her pad and pen on the desk before leading him to the door. "Same time next week?"

Q hesitated.

"C'mon. I'm sure that you have plenty more stories to tell me. And who knows, maybe in between we can even discuss you a little more."

Dr. Turner flashed him a schoolmarm-sexy smile.

*It's been a while since I've kissed a girl with glasses.*

"All right. Next week."

"I'll be here." She winked and opened the door.

Her next patient was already sitting in the waiting room. Q tossed a smile to the patient and the receptionist on his way out. While he rode the elevator down, he turned over the doctor's words in his mind. Why couldn't he just put everything on the table now and not deal with it piecemeal? Wasn't he just wasting both their time with therapy?

Climbing behind the wheel of his black Mercedes, Quentin didn't immediately start the car. Instead, he scooped out his cell phone and then stared at Sterling's name in his address book for at least a full minute. Drawing in a deep breath, he pressed the call button and put the phone to his ear.

When the line started ringing, his heart pounded harder in his chest. Just when he thought the line was going to voice mail, he started to disconnect the call.

"Hello."

Quentin placed the phone back to his ear. "Hello, Alyssa?"

There was a short pause. "Q?"

"Yeah, it's me. Is, um, is Sterling in?"

There was another long pause. "Hold on."

He started to hang up, but instead tightened his grip on the phone and waited. Two minutes later, Alyssa returned to the phone.

"I'm sorry, Quentin. But he…"

"He won't take my call," he answered for her.

"I'm sorry. Maybe—"

"That's all right. Thanks, anyway." Quentin disconnected the call and then stared at his phone as tears burned the backs of his eyes.

His imaginary Alyssa appeared in the passenger seat. "Maybe he'll come to the phone next time," she said.

"Yeah, maybe." He put the key in the ignition and started the car. "Or maybe there just won't be a next time."

* * * * *

# *HOPEWELL GENERAL*
## *A PRESCRIPTION FOR PASSION*

**Book #1**
by *New York Times* and *USA TODAY* bestselling author
**BRENDA JACKSON**
*IN THE DOCTOR'S BED*
August 2011

**Book #2**
by
**ANN CHRISTOPHER**
*THE SURGEON'S SECRET BABY*
September 2011

**Book #3**
by
**MAUREEN SMITH**
*ROMANCING THE M.D.*
October 2011

**Book #4**
by *Essence* bestselling author
**JACQUELIN THOMAS**
*CASE OF DESIRE*
November 2011

www.kimanipress.com

KPHGSP